# HIS TESORO

Their fiery passion ignited her dark skies

### NUELLA OGWU

# DEDICATION


I dedicate this book to my fellow dreamers who want to forget the harsh reality and dive into my made fictions where a happy ending is guaranteed. I dedicate this book to my younger self who would be so proud of me right now for fulfilling our dreams and most importantly to my family.

# CONTENTS

# Chapter One

14 years ago…


"Mum, you're hurt" my small voice came out barely a whisper, he wasn't supposed to hear us.

"I'm fine muffin" she smiled faintly, through her cut and bruised lips.


I held battered and bruised face in my little hands, her purple swollen eyes, her busted lip, her bruised cheekbones. Through all this she still looked beautiful as she had always been. The beautiful smile that held a lot of pain behind it. Her smile never faltered, maybe it did but she never showed it. She smiled through it, through everything. She smiled.
She held onto my little wrists, pulling my palms to her lips. She placed kisses on both of them.

"I said I'm fine muffin, I promise. Don't worry about your mother, I'm a tough cookie" she tried to crack a smile but it came out as more of a grimace displaying her bleeding gums.


Shutting my eyes tight I wrapped my hands around her neck, burying my face into her long brown hair. It always smelt like jasmine and roses. it was my safe haven; she was my safe haven. Her trembling arms wrapped around my small frame as she nuzzled her face into the crook of my neck. I could have sworn I heard a whimper escape her lips, but it was gone as soon as it came. I don't know why but I held onto that moment, it was engraved in my memory, etched in my subconscious mind. That little moment of peace before everything changed and all hell broke loose. I cherished that hug unbeknownst to me it was going to be the last time I ever felt her warmth again...


Here I was, sitting on the same couch I did 14 years ago, every single night nursing his punching bag back to health. The memories hit like nostalgia- It killed me every single day to see the woman i loved, the woman that raised me,
The woman that gave me everything was beaten and violated like some piece of crap. Her screams would echo throughout the house, her agonizing and heart wrenching cries gave me constant


recurring nightmares. When it was all over I tried the best I could. The best a 7-year-old child could do.
But it wasn't enough. Nothing I did was enough and at the end it was off no use, she was taken away from me. She had suffered enough.

Everyday I ask myself the same question- why?
Why didn't she just leave?
She could have run away from his abuses but she didn't. She stayed and why?
And then I look at the reason every single day in the mirror. I hate the reason, this one, worthless reason took my mother away from me forever. I wasn't worth it. I never was, I was never worth all the hours of suffering she would go through but yet she endured them with a smile on her face.

Her smile haunted me, sometimes it kept me going and other times it brought tears to my eyes and broke me down all over again. She would always be my source of strength but what she stood for wasn't worth any of it. In the end kit killed her. It was my fault. My therapist said i only blamed myself because i needed someone to blame, self-loathing and self-hatred were my coping mechanisms, she said it wasn't my fault but the pit in my chest says otherwise. I was a burden to her but she never casted me aside. In the end she was too good, too good for the asshole she married, too good for the life she was sold and subjected to, too good for any of this.

Sometimes I wondered if she found her freedom in death. If her demons went quiet and finally couldn't reach her where she went. Was it cruel of me to wish I had followed her, to let all she suffered go to waste. Yes, I was ungrateful but in the end my life is meaningless without her.

# CHAPTER TWO

## Jasmine

"I'm sorry Jasmine, but we're going to have to let you go," my boss's deep voice echoed through his office. The 57-year-old American turned around slowly revealing the black and white suit he normally wore as the restaurant's owner. He was probably expecting something other than my tear stained cheeks, considering the way his eyes widened once they settled on my glassy ones.
What was I supposed to do really?

He just fired me from a job I'd been working for 7 months now. Yes, being a waitress at a 5-star restaurant won't be the ideal job but I loved it.

I loved the quiet and peaceful nature of serving top class customers, although I preferred not having to deal with bitchy ladies that behaved like they owned the restaurant. My fake smile only boosted their enormous egos.
This job did have its ups and downs but I didn't hate it enough to want to lose it!
"I'm really sorry Jasmine" he apologized with a pained face, he came up to me and held onto my shoulders avoiding any form of eye contact with me. I stared at his face through my teary eyes. "We are trying to cut costs, the neighboring hotels are demanding we pay for the space and we just don't have enough.

I sighed once I felt the warmth of his hands engulfing me in a hug. I tried my best not to melt into his fatherly embrace.

"It's okay Mr. Kelly" I gave him a sweet smile that was still pretty far from genuine, but hey who was checking?
I didn't want to question Mr. Kelly's reason, being he has been here for me when I needed moral support, he understood my current situation more than anyone so I trusted he was doing this because he had no other option and I wasn't about to make it harder than his face already showed it was.

"Of course I will pay you for this month, anything I could do to help I would"
I pulled away from the hug with the same fake smile plastered on my face. The rough pad of his thumb came in contact with my plum olive cheeks as he wiped away my tears. I held onto his wrists but I wasn't ready to have his warmth leave me just yet so I didn't pull his hand away.

"Go serve your last customer" his smile lines became more prominent as a sympathetic smile played on his face. His concern and affection made me sick, he showed more concern to me than I had received in a long time. So he understood when I backed away and walked out of his office, without another word said on my part. Mr. Kelly cared more than my sperm donor ever did, he was exactly what I called him. A sperm donor and nothing else, nothing but a beast, and he deserved whatever punishment he was receiving right now.

I walked up to a random table that seemed to have a neatly dressed young man in a black Armani suit.
Guess I'm going to be serving yet another rich asshole.

Forgive me for the stereotype!

"Good evening sir, can I take your ord-"

The air hitched in my throat as his head rose and my eyes found a pair of mesmerizing hazel ones staring back into my dark orbs.

I could feel his eyes on me as I set down his plate, not once meeting his gaze. It wasn't the first time I was going to have to pretend like I was a clueless and tender girl. It was what men like him needed, behaving the way I did made sure men like him kept coming back to eat here.

I finally met his gaze, sending him a small smile before walking away with an added sway in my hips.

————————————

I walked down the dark and lonely alley with my duffle bag hanging loosely behind me. I had shed some more tears walking down memory lane, from the first day I started working here till now, my experience would have been more cherished if I had made some friends. But I wasn't exactly the social butterfly, I only spoke to people I needed to and no one else.

I sighed as reality came tumbling down like a pile of bricks.
I needed to find a new job. It was going to be very hard to find a job in this overpopulated city, especially one that pays well enough to help with my bills. I kept my eyes trained on the path ahead as I held tightly to the hand of my bag and I proceeded to turn by the sharp corner.

I jerked when I felt a hand on my shoulder.
"Hey"
I stared wide eyed at the man with hazel eyes. My hands clenched tightly to my chest as it rose and fell.

"Sorry if I frightened you, miss......?"
He trailed off waiting for my response.

"Jasmine, but you can call me Jess" I tried to hide the discomfort that was painted all over my face. Did this guy follow me?
Was he a kidnapper!
I probably shouldn't have told him my name. I mentally face palmed, if he was indeed a kidnapper he was a good looking one at that. I wouldn't mind being kidnapped by him tho...

"Okay Jess... " he trailed off as his eyes fell on my duffle bag and a pinch formed between his eyebrows. "What's in the bag?"
I adjusted my bag to sit further behind me, away from his line of sight.

"Oh... Uh nothing much, just a few stuff from my old job"

Why was I telling him this!

"Old job?" He asked with an amused look on his face.

"Yeah, old. I got fired today"
I avoided his gaze, uncomfortably tapping my ballet flats on the hard tailed sidewalk.

"That's great" he said with a small smile on his face that immediately faded once he saw my facial expression.
"No I meant, I wanted to offer you a job, now that I heard you've been fired it's just the right timing" he blurted out quickly and nervously, playing with the end of his blazer, boring holes into the sidewalk. His hand went into his blazer and he pulled out a white card, handing it over to me and I hesitantly took it.


My eyes fell on the words "BLACK EMPIRE" written boldly in gold cursive.
I looked just below the words to see an address.
"What-" I trailed off looking up to see the empty alley that I had just come from. He was gone, without another word.
I started from the business card in my hand to the empty ally where he stood a few minutes ago.

# Chapter Three

Jasmine

I paid the taxi driver and stepped out, coming face to face with a tall skyscraper that looked like it had 100 floors within it.

I gulped down hard remembering I forgot to be nervous this morning when I was getting ready. Against my better judgement I had decided to come to the address that was under the card handed to me by the man with hazel eyes.

I didn't even know his name!
Was this a bad idea?
I really needed the money after all and what could possibly go wrong?

I pushed away all the negative and possibly logical thoughts about this away as I clasped my hands tightly on the hand of my bag and walked in through the revolving doors of the skyscraper.
Immediately I stepped inside I was hit with a cool and subtle aura

"Good morning miss, I was given this card?"
I approached the woman I had spotted behind a table. She looked neat with her white, wrinkle free shirt and her black pencil skirt, she had her hair packed in a tight bun. When she finally looked up from her computer I immediately felt myself shrink under her gaze. She was as beautiful as a model, I suddenly felt so out of place

"Okay let me have a look-"
She took the card from my hand and examined it turning it around
to reveal a name I hadn't seen earlier on Raymond
" Oh yes, you are expected on the 81st floor. There your interview
will commence. Here".  She handed me back two cards. The second
one was harder and seemed to be made of some kind of metal.  It had
a QR code on it.

"Use this card to access the elevators and when you're done please
return it" she gave me a straight smile and I said my thanks before
walking to the elevator.

The doors were slowly closing and I was thankful I was alone in
here, at least I would be able to calm my nerves. I had just realized
my palms were sweaty and my heart was beating more furiously. My
body was reacting like I was taking a ride to my doom, stupid
nerves!
Why was I even here again?

"Wait!" I heard someone yell from the other side of the elevator
door before it closed. I panicked, pushing the stop button way more
times than I needed to. The doors finally opened to reveal a brunette
dude with tons of bags and papers in his hands, looking a mess. His
round glasses sagged at the tip of his nose as his curls framed his
forehead, he rushed inside and I pushed in my floor button when I
was certain he had gotten properly situated beside me.

"Thank you" I heard his raspy voice from just a few inches beside
me

"Your welcome" I sent him the sweetest smile I could fake and
turned back to face the doors. I nibbled on my lower lip and fiddled
with my hands, trying my best to control my nerves.
They were going through the roof right now.

"The name's Sebastian, I don't think I've seen such beau-
I mean you around here"
There went my little hope that this would be a quiet elevator ride.
I turned to him, letting my smile fall.

"Hi Seb, I'm Jasmine and no it's my first day here. Actually here for an interview, not going to stick around"
I turned back to the doors as I watched the number switch from 75 to 76.
Can't this fucking elevator go any faster!

I groaned, was this elevator trying to kill me!

I always got annoyed and easily irritated when I was nervous. I never knew how to deal with them.

"Here"
I turned to my side to see the brunette guy now Sebastian holding out to me a bottle of water. I started from the bottle to his face with a confused look.
What did he want me to do with-

"For your nerves, trust me cold water helps" he gave me an encouraging smile as I accepted it and downed half the bottle in less than a minute.
"Hope your interview goes well, see you around" he said with a smile as a ding sounded in the background, followed by the elevator doors slowly opening and Sebastian walking out not before throwing me a wink.

I walked into a lobby to see a woman around the corner seated behind a table, dressed the same way as the lady from downstairs.

"I'm here for the-"

"Yes the interview, the room is just around the corner to your left, you can't miss it"
She spoke without looking away from the computer screen in front of her.

Okay....
I took a deep breath and approached the see-through door that was different from all others.
I gulped down hard as I pushed open the door.

# Damon

"I'm really sure about this one Damon, she's a striking beauty, unlike any other you'd ever see, she's really sexy too. There's just something about her that you won't be able to resist I'm sure"

I stared at her file and the picture of the girl in here was definitely beautiful, gorgeous even.
I read her name out loud, "Jasmine Scott"

Age: 21
Height: 5'4
"You can't expect me to give a girl, I know nothing about a job just because you find her sexy and attractive Raymond"

This was definitely not the first time he had done this. The last few girls he brought were all sluts, they were so unbearable and irritating. I couldn't even stand them for 2 seconds let alone making them my personal assistant.

"She's already on her way sir and I know I haven't been the best at judgement prior to this moment but she's different, trust me. I want this one, she's the one for me sir"

Is he serious right now?

I am not going to waste my time entertaining a slut when I have better things to do.
Where did he even find her?

He is over selling this, yes I fuck with some off them but that's it. One night and that's all, but I didn't want to entertain this idea any more. "No, call her off!" I commanded.

I'm going to kill him


"Hello, a-am I in the right place?"

An angelic voice cut me off and I stared at the girl with milky brown hair walking discreetly into my office, her light footsteps putting me into a trance.

"Sir, sir?". I put down the phone refusing to let my gaze leave this girl, afraid I would just wake up from a dream.


Her brown milky curls were pulled up into a loose bun as some strands framed her perfect youthful olive face. Her big dark eyes stared back at me and I could feel a knot forming in my chest. It was like she was seeing right into me; her gaze was penetrating into mine.

She was perfect, everything about her was perfect. Raymond's words and her picture did absolutely no justice to her beauty. Her face was rosy red as she stared down at her two feet, she nervously played with her fingers and nibbled on her lower lip. An action that didn't go unnoticed by me, I watched her lips shamelessly as she pursed them, momentarily sucking on them.

She stared at me, definitely intimidated as I got onto my feet.
I came face to face with her, towering over her petite figure, careful I wasn't completely overshadowing her.

"Ms Scott, it's not very polite to walk into someone's office without knocking" I spoke in a calm and subtle tone, my voice coming out deeper than intended as I stared down at her.

"M-my apologies s-sir"
Her angelic voice came through in barely a whisper as the word
rolled off her lips so naturally. I don't think anyone has ever called
me sir that way before, it was like she gave it a new meaning.

She was perfect, everything I wanted and didn't even know I did

Sorry Raymond, but Ms. Scott is mine.

# CHAPTER FOUR

## Jasmine

The interior of this office was so posh and clean. The white tiled walls, the black marble floors and the windows that held the view of the whole city were breathtaking. I didn't have enough time to admire the view as this drop dead gorgeous man towered over me, he was like a head taller than me. His eyes roamed my body from head to toe and I just stood there, staring awkwardly at his dark leathered shoes.

I took a quick glance at him. Drop dead gorgeous would be an understatement, his emerald green eyes were a vibrant color, jet black tendrils styled to the back with few strands framing his perfectly sculpted face. The thin fabric of his white T-shirt showed the definition of his masculine build, his muscular chest, his broad shoulders, big biceps and small torso. He looked like a Greek god to be completely honest, no he could make even Hercules jealous.

It should be illegal to look this nerve wrecking

The first three buttons of his shirt were undone, revealing a patch of clear slightly tanned skin. The sleeves of his shirt were rolled up to his elbows, showing off the prominent veins that ran up his arms. It felt like every part of him was intended on teasing and prodding at my self-control. I felt the breath hitch in my wind pipes as our eyes met, his mesmerizing green stare made my cheeks flush and my knees go weak, it was like I was paralyzed as I stood there while his eyes still roamed me.

"I don't think I've introduced myself. Damon Blackwood" his husky voice made my heart rate pick up. A smirk crawled into his features as he stretched out a hand for me and I just stared in awe, his words sinking in.

Damon Blackwood, as in Black Empire Blackwood. The self-made billionaire, that's impossible-

I quickly slid my hand into his, realizing I had left him hanging.
Bad first impression Jasmine!
You idiot!!

I mentally scolded myself, I needed this job. Don't fuck it up! Don't fuck it up!
I played those words in my head like a song on repeat. Calm deep breaths were in order, breathe Jasmine. It was just our first meeting and I was already drooling all over him like a thirsty cow.

# Damon

Her skin felt like velvet against mine. I had to resist the urge to take her hands to my lips to kiss them and appreciate her effortless beauty. The young lass wears a red blouse which doesn't leave much to the imagination. It cuts down low revealing her cleavage for all prying eyes to see.

Suddenly I felt a wave of anger come over me. No one else is allowed to lay their eyes on her, not unless it's me. She isn't allowed to wear such clothes, unless it's for my eyes only of course. Same goes for her skirt. It's like she was trying to mess with my head. Her long, beautiful legs are clean shaven and a slight tone of olive.
Every inch of her is a work of art, a true masterpiece.

"Shall we continue Ms. Scott" I give her a small smile, trying to relieve the tension and the awkwardness seeping through her fake smile.
"Please come in Ms. Scott, I don't have much time"

I'm afraid if she stays any longer, I won't be able to restrain myself any further than I already am.
What had come over me?

I am the sole owner of the Black Empire and the richest man in the whole of New York City and yet I am going weak-kneed at the sight of a girl.

I had seen a lot of models, top actresses but none of their beauty can match or even be compared to that of Jasmine's.

I turned away from her, heading to my desk.

Her quiet footsteps echoed through the pin drop silent office and I know she has gone for the window. After all, it has the best view of the city.

I turned back to see her looking over the view, her silhouette like an angel's.
I needed to wrap this up quickly, before my body took over.

"Raymond tells me you are looking for a job"
She turns to me, nodding softly, nibbling nervously on her lower lip in the process.

There is no fucking way she is unaware of what she is doing to me! This is bloody torture! I want her now, but I have to wait. I don't want to scare her off, she isn't even working for me yet. I can't risk losing her. I had only just met her but it didn't stop me from wanting her under me. Nothing ever stopped me from getting what I wanted and I knew for sure I wanted Jasmine.

Control Damon.

"Yes, I lost it on the night I met Raymond." her gaze finally met mine and I inhaled sharply. Her dark orbs were making me feel like I couldn't breathe, I tore my gaze away to stare at her file, the intensity getting to me. The air was thick with tension, so thick I could probably cut it with a knife.

I look down at my watch, 15 minutes have already gone by, this is taking longer than it needs to. I grab her file and get to my feet.

"So you're 21? " I want to make sure the information Raymond got on her was accurate.

She nodded, refusing to meet my gaze. She was visibly uncomfortable and it made a smug smile thug at the corner of my lips. So my presence affects her.

"Yes" she gave a short answer, looking at me momentarily before her gaze fell once again. As much as her gaze was nerve wrecking, I wanted her to look at me.
I walked closer, squaring up to her, invading her personal space. Taking in her scent, she smelled like sweet flowers and vanilla. I watched her take in my scent and her cheeks flushed realising what she had just done.

I smiled down at her. She is perfect.

"You have good work experience". I cut the silence, bringing her attention back to me.
She had three to four years of work experience for top restaurants and top businessmen but none could compare to my empire.

I was so close; her small puffs of breath were pushing against the thin fabric of my white shirt. "But have you worked in such environment before, it may be challenging"

I watched her reaction attentively, "I assure you sir, I am up for the challenge" she proudly said without breaking eye contact.

We will see Ms. Scott, we'll see.

"I wish I had more time to discuss this, but Raymond didn't exactly inform me of your coming, otherwise I would have made out proper time for this. I am impressed with you actually, so you can consider the job yours"

I pull out some documents for her to read over and sign
"Read this over and when you sign, feel comfortable to bring up any questions you may have on anything with me. We will discuss this over dinner, drop your cell with the secretary, she will organize it. It was a pleasure Ms. Scott"
I stretch out my hand, offering a handshake

"Thank you for taking out time to speak with me, Mr. Black" a small smile covered her features as she slid her hand into mine. I could wake up to that face every morning for the rest of my life.

"Please call me Damon, I have a feeling we will be well acquainted from here on out"

"Okay". She sucked on her lower lip hesitantly, "Damon". She spoke my name like a song of praise, it sounded so good coming from her.

I looked down at our hands, they were molded together like two puzzle pieces. I didn't hesitate before bringing her hand to my lips and placing soft kisses on each of her knuckles. An action that made her flustered and more uncomfortable

"I'll be seeing you Ms Scott". I led her to the door of my office, stopping at the doorway as I watched her walk tentatively down the hallway, her hips swaying as she did, causing my arousal. "Your mine"
I spoke under my breath, my voice dialing down by an octave, too quiet for anyone to hear.

"Ms Scott"
I pulled the side of my bottom lip between my teeth, biting down hard to control the undying urge to go up to her and capture her plum lips in a kiss and claim her right in that elevator.
I couldn't help the grin that crawled onto my face when our eyes met across the hallway and she didn't look away until the doors of the elevator closed.

Patience Damon
She's already yours. She's fallen into the trap.
My sweet prey.

# CHAPTER FIVE

## Jasmine

So that interview was an absolute train wreck.

I was practically melting into Mr Black's embrace. I'm so pathetic. I groaned having flashbacks of the interview, most of my reactions making me cringe.

Was I really that desperate for a job?
Is that seriously the reason why I was practically drooling over Damon Black?
I didn't know how I particularly felt about getting cozy with my boss, something about him just threw me off balance.

Ignoring how horribly the interview went, I was actually looking forward to our dinner. I didn't know why but I felt like I needed to see him again, I must be running crazy or something. His emerald green eyes played in my mind, the idea of seeing him again making goosebumps rise on my olive skin.

Deciding it would be better to just wait for the call from his secretary, I went ahead to read through the documents he gave me. Making sure I read everything over twice to make sure there were no faults of any kind. My eyes darted to a line that made my light brows furrowed in confusion

"In case of any inconvenience on the assistant's part, concerning transportation issues, living arrangements and so on that affects his or her work, or if the boss decides it would be more convenient, he or she is obliged to change living arrangements and be hosted by THE BOSS."

I gulped down harshly, rereading the sentence over and over again, unsure if I had seen well. My eyes darted to another statement saying if The boss aka Damian was to move, I would have to move with him!?

Was this a sick joke or something!!
There is no way Damon expects me to agree to this!
Living with Damon?!
I began to imagine it, but I shook my head, dismissing the idea immediately.

I made sure to leave bookmarks on each page in the document where those statements were, making a mental note to bring them up with him during the dinner.

I hadn't even picked out anything to wear!
I doubt I had anything nice enough.

A familiar ring tone brought me out of my thoughts. My eyes darted to my ringing phone vibrating on my kitchen island.

"Hello?" I held the phone to my ear, leaning down on the island, having my hands to support my weight.

"Jessy". A deep voice called from the other end of the phone. My breath hitched in my windpipe when I realized whose voice that belonged to.
It had been so long...

"Uncle Thomas?" My voice came out in an unsure whisper, scared I would be right with my assumption.

"We need to talk". The seriousness in his tone made my heart palpitate in my chest, goosebumps rising on my olive skin.

He was never this serious
He never called out of the blue
Has something happened?
Was it about.......my sperm donor?

# Jasmine

I straighten out the wrinkles on my baby pink dress.

Inspecting myself one more time in the window of the restaurant, I unconsciously nod, satisfied that I looked a little bit presentable.

I walked over to the entrance, pushing it open. I walked in and stopped dead in my tracks, the familiar scent wafting through the air. The scene of wealthy looking people chatting and enjoying their meals, waiters running around with trays of different elegant dishes, the slow and melodious sound of soft jazz music playing in the background, creating a pleasant aura around the restaurant, the big diamond chandelier hanging in the middle of the restaurant. Everything was still the same.

I closed my eyes taking in his scent.

It's been so long.
He wore a grey Armani suit, with a blue tie and a white undershirt that was tucked properly into his suit trouser. His three-piece suit

looked as sharp as ever. His ginger red hair was styled to frame his forehead, giving him that serious businessman look. He had grown quite a stubble, making him look old and experienced. A small smile played on his face, warming my heart.

I wrapped my hands around his torso, burying my face into his chest. He wrapped his hands around my shoulder, holding me tightly. Taking in the familiar scent of whisky and oak I smiled genuinely for the first time in days.

"It's been so long Jess"
He spoke into my hair; I could tell he had the same smile still sprawled on his face.

"Too long". I sniffled a little, pulling away and I smiled up at my uncle.

"Come on". He placed a hand at the small of my back, leading me to an empty table.
He pulled out a chair for me and I thanked him with a curt nod. After making sure I was properly situated, he propped down on the chair opposite mine.

"How have you been Jess? You have really grown into a beautiful young lass, you look so much like your mother, it's painful". His gaze dropped to the table, his eyes boring holes into the white silk fabric that covered it.

I sighed heavily, knowing full well how it hurt him every single time he saw me. I looked so much like her, if you'd seen her you would guess we were twins. I was like the constant reminder of the mistake he made, and the person he lost because of it.

I tucked a strand of stray hair behind my ear, the silence welcoming us into her awkward embrace.

"It doesn't have to hurt; it wasn't your fault"
I reached out to his hand that sat on the table, giving it a gentle squeeze.

He smiled up at me, uncomfortably pulling his hand away from my grasp.

I let out another sigh, dropping back into my seat.
No one understood his grief more than I did, he still blamed himself, just like I did.
"She deserved better"
He broke the silence, staring blankly into the distance. I couldn't agree more. The memories were still fresh;they became worse every single time I saw him. The same went for him.

"Do you think she will ever forgive me?". He chuckled bitterly
"Who am I kidding, she would never" he gazes up at me with a pained face.

"She already did, she never blamed you for any of it. She was too good"
I spoke the last part under my breath, trying to fight back the tears that started to prick my eyes.
Again an unsettling silence surrounded us, making the situation even worse.

"You need to be careful Jess, he's back"

I felt all the blood and color drain from my face at those two words. *He's back.* My breathing became uneven as the words sunk in, panic rising in me.
He can't be back, there's no way!
Not him,
Please!

"He doesn't know your whereabouts, I promised to keep you safe. I wasn't able to keep her safe, but I promise Jess, you'll never go through that ever again" he sent me a sympathetic smile, squeezing my hands that were digging into my thighs.
I stood up abruptly, hitting the chair behind me. I could see the shocked expression on my uncle's face.

"Excuse me". I walked away, my uncle's eyes lingering on me a little longer, making sure I was going in the right direction.

It has been quite a while since I last came here, but I know this place like the back of my hand. I spent most of my life here, my uncle's restaurant was the main reason I wanted to work at one. I fell in love with life, but now, things are different. The dreams that little girl once had, were snatched away from her.
He still haunted me, wherever I went.

I rushed into the women's washroom. Stopping in front of the wide mirror, I took in my appearance. I looked like a ghost, my face had turned ghostly pale and my breathing erratic. I turned on the tap, throwing water on my face, not minding my makeup. Grabbing a nearby towel, I dabbed away the water and sprawled makeup from my face. I sighed, looking at my clean face in the clear mirror.

I didn't really need the make up anyway.

"He can't possibly be back" I whispered as I watched my hands shake viciously.
Breath Jasmine, breath. I can't have a panic attack here, not now. I calmed my breathing, taking large swoops of air. Running a hand through my sticking hair I stared at myself in the mirror, making sure I was calm to avoid making Uncle Tom worry.

I walked out of the bathroom, coming out into the hallway.
He can't find me. I have to run away, somewhere, anywhere. He just can't find me. He may already know where I am for all I know.

I walked right into a hard wall, stumbling back I lost my balance. I waited for my body to come in contact with the ground but it never came. I opened my tightly shut eyes, all the breath was knocked out of my lungs as I stared into a mesmerizing pair of green eyes.

"Mr. Black?"
His face was barely an inch away from mine, his breath fanned against my face.

His intoxicating scent invaded my nostrils, making my cheeks flush. He held firmly onto my small figure, stopping my collision with the ground. The only thing stopping our bodies touching we're my two hands that rested on his chest

I inhale sharply, coming out of my daze I pull away from his hold on my waist.

"What a pleasant surprise Jasmine"
He purrs down at me, a playful smirk plays on the corner of his lips, making all the blood in me run cold, my inside stir at the manner he spoke my name.

I adjusted my weight from foot to foot, feeling nervous under Damon's intense stare.

"Same Mr. Black"
I broke the silence, trying to add some humor but he doesn't seem phased.
His eyes still raked my body before they came back to meet my dark orbs.

"I didn't think you could afford to dine at such a prestigious restaurant Jasmine"
He spoke, a dominant tone dripping off his words.

I internally scoff.
He doesn't even know me and yet he's already judging me, who does he think he is!

"I'm here with my uncle, it's his restaurant"
I meet his gaze, trying my best not to let his scrutinizing stare phase me, but my weak knees and flushed face betray me.

He scratches his stubble, eyeing me up the more.

Can't this guy stop staring for one second!!
The way he looks at me makes my knees want to give in.

I hadn't even realized how sexy he looked in his all black suit which I knew all too well was Armani and his matching dress shoes. His dark hair was disheveled, giving him that 'bed head' look which I knew was intentional. I wasn't going to admit it but it was the best and sexiest bed head I had laid eyes on. Everything about him was just annoyingly gorgeous.

**Oh jeez
Did I just think that!?**

**"You mean Mr. Scott?"
He asks, squinting his eyes at me slightly, like he was trying to look through me.**

**"Yes, Mr.-"**

**"Mr. Black!"
My uncle's voice boomed from behind me, cutting me off as he approached Damon with open arms.
The two men exchanged a hearty embrace, like two old friends. My eyes widen with shock; how do they know each other?**

**I knew Damon was a billionaire who was well acquainted with a lot of people but I didn't know my uncle was one of them.**

**"How are you Tom?"
They pulled apart and I just stood between them, a puzzled expression covering my face.**

**"I'm good Damon, it's nice to see you again. I believe you've met my niece"
Uncle gestured towards me**

**"Of course, she got a job at my Empire"
A hint of a smile tugged at his lips.**

**"Why don't we go take a seat, we can catch up on lost times"
My uncle placed a hand at the small of my back, steadying me. He could tell how uneasy I was, meaning Damon could too.**

**"Sure thing Tom, let me get my date and we'll join you"**

**Uncle led us through the hallway, not letting go of me. I was thankful he could still read me as well as he used to.
I guess I hadn't really changed in the past 3 years.**

"I'm so proud of you Jess, I see you are building quite a future for yourself"
He smiled as I propped down on my seat.

"Yes uncle, I really don't want to have to drop everything and leave with you"
I dropped my gaze, staring holes into the now interesting white silk cloth.

"Don't worry Jess, you won't have to move or run away. I will find him and take care of it"
He offered a reassuring smile that calmed me down a bit.

I knew my uncle would try his best to protect me, he blamed himself for what mum went through.

He wasn't there to protect his little sister from this cruel world; He left his parents, he couldn't handle their abuses, but he left mum behind, he promised to come back for her but when he came back after so many years he was too late, she was gone, she had been sold to my sperm donor. He hated himself when he found out.
He blamed himself every single day for not taking her with him. But all hell broke loose the night she was killed.

He blamed himself for that too, he never forgave himself. Even though mum never held it against him.
She was really an angel, no matter how many tried to taint her, she was never stained.

I sigh, smiling sadly at my uncle.
He needed to redeem himself, and I was going to let him. Maybe afterwards his consciousness would be at rest.

# Damon

I let my eyes linger on her a little longer.
Her pink dress isn't body con but it shows a little more of her assets than I would prefer others seeing.

The pink color blends perfectly with her olive skin. She looks beautiful with her milky brown hair pulled into a messy bun, few strands framing her perfect natural face. Little diamond stud earrings hang from her ears. She looked simple and beautiful. She wasn't over dressed like other women here. She didn't even have any makeup on, not like she needed any. Her simplicity was mesmerizing.

"My date, Mrs. King "The two turned their heads to me and I noticed the way Jasmine eyed up my associate Mrs. King.

"Nice to meet you, I've heard so much about you Jasmine"

I watched as Jasmine reluctantly accepted Amelia's handshake with flushed cheeks. She is easily flustered, duly noted. We sat down and started chattering away.
I would never have guessed Jasmine's uncle was the owner of this restaurant, I've been coming here for the past year and half and I didn't even know. It makes me wonder how much about Jasmine I am yet to find out.

I watch my prey as she sits there, watching the exchange. She looks rather uncomfortable with her hands folded, resting on her thighs. Her back isn't rested against the chair,she is seated upright with a rather humorous smile plastered on her face. I had to hold back the smile that threatened to play on my face as I watched Amelia try to bring Jasmine into the conversation.

She dismissed Amelia's efforts immediately by answering with either a 'yes' or a 'rather not', much to Amelia's dislike. Amelia was the chatter box type, always wanting to make friends, but she had a bitchy side to her, overbearing was another way to put it. Seems Jasmine's not a big fan of social interactions.
I tilt my head to the side, taking in every inch of her, every blemish on her face, the beauty mark on her right cheek, the different shades of her hair, from the light brown to the chocolate brown tone

Her dark orbs meet mine and as soon as they do she averts her gaze back to her empty glass of wine.

"So Damon, what position will Jasmine be working in? "
Tom's voice brought me out of my daze but I didn't let it show.

"Personal assistant, I've been needing one for quite a while now"

I swirl the red liquor in my glass before downing it in one go, allowing the burning liquid to slide down my dry throat. I watch from the corner of my eye as Jasmine's dove eyes stare at me, her gaze drops and her cheeks flush the moment my eyes meet hers.

I internally smirk, someone likes to stare.

"It was so nice catching up with you Damon, but I have to go. Time is money"
I stand with Tom and we exchange a hearty embrace.

"See you around Thomas"
I purse my lips in a straight line, giving him a curt nod as I watch Jasmine rise from her seat and walk over to me.

"See you at work tomorrow Jasmine"
She slides her hand into mine. I bring her hands to my lips, placing gentle kisses on her knuckles. I maintain eye contact with her as I place her hands back by her side, her cheeks flush a bright pink. A smirk covers my features as I watch her walk away, hand in hand with her uncle, her hips swaying as she did so.

"Your mine"
I didn't mind if anyone heard me, I was going to make it known.

**Jasmine Scott is mine.**

# Chapter Six

## Jasmine

*I yawn, getting up from the bed and walking out of my room.*
*Where's mum?*
*I rub my eyes as I walk down the flight of stairs, my vision a little*
*blurry.*
*I squint my eyes to see the bright light coming from the kitchen.*
*Mum must be making cookies!*
*I smile, eagerly making my way towards the brightly lit kitchen*
*Anticipating mum's famous chocolate chip cookies.*

*I stopped dead in my tracks as all the breath was knocked out of me.*
*All the blood in me ran cold as I saw mum lying on the floor in a pool*
*of her own blood.*
*I felt my knees go weak and I fell to the ground, my eyes not leaving*
*my dear mother's face.*
*"M-m-mum"*
*I whisper her name, not daring to move closer to her.*

*Her face was ghostly pale; her lips were blue. Her blue eyes were*
*lifelessly cold as they stared at the roof, not moving.*
*I felt my world crumble underneath me, all the color had drained from*
*my face as my breathing became erratic.*
*I stared at my mother's lifeless corpse, no tears came, nothing.*
*I just sat there for what felt like forever, waiting for her to get up and*
*tell me "it'll be fine, my booboo will heal"*
*But she wasn't getting up.*

*"Come on mama, get up"*
*I tried the best I could to clean the blood from her face with the cotton*
*wool I held in my shaky hands.*
*I sat beside her, waiting patiently for her to get up but she hadn't*

*"Mother!!!"*

I shot up, my breathing erratic as I looked around the dark room.
I ran a hand through my sticky untamed hair, sighing heavily.

It was just a dream; I haven't had those in months now. It had to be
all the memories that came back after seeing Uncle Tom and hearing
my sperm donor was back. I thought the therapy was working. I run
a hand down my tear stained cheeks, wiping off the layer of sweat
that coated my forehead. I take in deep breaths trying to calm
myself.


I turn to my wall clock to check the time.
It reads; 7:00am
"Shit!!" I curse out loud, throwing my legs off the bed and I run into
the bathroom.

I can't be late for work on my first day!!
God knows what Damon's reaction would be.
Ugh!!!
I hurriedly washed myself, careful not to rush and end up smelling
like old rags.
I quickly lather my hair with shampoo and rinse it out. Hopping out
of the bathroom I throw a towel over myself, wrapping it properly
around my small frame.
I blow dry my hair, a nice change from air drying it on a regular
basis.

Now the real deal, what to wear.
I groan, tossing a bunch of clothes out of my closet.
Best time to have nothing to wear. I glared hard at the pile on my
bed and the clothes hanging in my closet. I stop, my eyes falling on
the perfect outfit.
I waste no time in pulling it on and securing it around my body. I
look myself over in my full frame mirror. Not too revealing, not too
boring. Just my style, I throw my now dry hair into a low ponytail,
leaving some strands to frame my face. Not going to go over the top
and curl my hair or anything like that. I wasn't dressing to impress.

I prop down on my vanity chair, looking myself over in the mirror.
Do I need any makeup?

"Oh what the heck, a little won't hurt."
I apply a layer of pink lip gloss, some eyeliner and mascara before
grabbing my bag and heading out of my apartment.


~~~~


I'm so late!
And now I can't find a taxi!!!!
I groan, trying to call a taxi to pull up on the sidewalk but none seem
to be answering.
Just then a Navy blue Mercedes Benz pulls up in front of me, the
engine roaring.
I stand there, frozen in place staring at the slick looking car.

The driver's window rolls down to reveal Raymond wearing a pair
of black Aviator's classic sun shades. He turns his head to me and I
stare at him in awe. I notice his head dip and come back up, but I
can't say for certain what he was staring at, the glasses were
perfectly tinted, not letting me see his eyes.


"Get in the car Jasmine, you're late! Damon hates tardiness"

I snap out of my daze, rushing to the other side of the car. I pull the
passenger door open and hop in, careful not to shut my leg as I pull
the door closed behind me.

"Thanks". I turn to him, offering a small smile

"Sure thing, trust me you don't want to get yelled at on your first
day"
He chuckles lightly, starting the car the engine roars back to life and
we zoom off.

What does he mean by yell?
I gulp down nervously, playing with the end of my hair to try to
distract myself from the possible scenarios playing in my head.
~~~~

# Jasmine

"It'll be better if he was mute, honestly. It won't hurt just for a day" he threw his head back exasperatedly, his hand on his forehead like he wanted to faint.

I giggled, holding onto my belly. I felt the tears pricking my eyes. It was the first time in a long time I had laughed so hard. "You're serious?". I managed to croak out through my heavy breathing.

"Very serious. You're really going to have your hands full with him"

I stopped walking and just stared at Raymond's back as he proceeded to walk forward. Noticing I had stopped and wasn't following he stopped and turned. Blinked at his face, trying to see the littlest sign of humor, but there was none

"Jess, breath!"

I felt myself being shaken and I was brought out of my daze. Raymond held firmly onto my forearms, shaking me. I turned my gaze to see Raymond's face, worry masking his expression.

"Jess, are you okay? "

I dropped my gaze, blinking severally to come back to reality. I was having a panic attack.

I sighed deeply.

I steadied my breathing and made sure I was okay before raising my gaze to meet Raymond's. "I-I'm fine", I sigh, tucking a strand of stray hair behind my ear

"You sure?" he asks, concern etched on his face.

"I'm sure". I smile forcefully.

I stepped back from him, remembering his hold was still on me. He uncomfortably straightened out his perfectly ironed black suit.

"Come on", he clears his throat, walking away he refuses to meet my gaze.

I sigh following behind him. He led me through the big and spacious hallways that were beautifully illuminated by the ceiling lights. The walls were occupied with what I could only guess were marble tiles.I hadn't taken notice of all the breathtaking interior designs the first time I came here. The whole place was white and gold, a reflection from the lights. The scene looked like something straight out of a movie, depicting a heavenly out of this world scene.

I was in a whole other sector in the building. We walk up to an elevator and for some reason Raymond stops in front of it.He slides in the key card and the two slick doors separate, enough for us both to get in.

..... The doors closed and we were left to swim in a sea of awkwardness. Her piercing fingers made my heart rate speed up.

"Where are we going? "

Did I really need to know this?
No
Was I feeling incredibly awkward?
Yes

I could probably find out later on when I actually got there, so I didn't need the answer. I just didn't want to stay this quiet all through, it seemed he wasn't going to say anything

"We are going to the floor where all the things you'll need are. Your office, the canteen and many others. We'll be meeting Richelle there" he answered without removing his gaze from the small timer above the elevator doors.

"Richelle?" I turned to look at him, a crease forming between my brows in utter confusion.

"Yes, Richelle. She will run you down on everything you need to do for Damon, she will send you his schedule on your laptop, it's left for you to fix the appropriate time for each meeting and where. "

I gulped down nervously. Honestly, this sounded like a lot.

*****

"So nice to meet you, I heard Damon had gotten a new assistant, didn't think she'd be this beautiful". The young dirty blonde spoke, a warm smile plastered across her rosy cheeks. Her sea blue eyes stared into my dark ones.

"Jasmine, this is Richelle. Richelle, Jasmine"
She offers a hand, smiling sweetly at me. I imitated her gesture, mine was obviously fake but I was being as nice as I could get to this awfully enthusiastic female.

"She will run you down on everything, like I said. Good luck ladies, I'll be leaving now.
When you find the canteen Jess, do join me for lunch"

With that Raymond walked out to the elevator, my eyes lingering on where he had disappeared to. Turning my head back to Richelle I could see an unknown look on her face, an almost cheeky one.

"Okay so, Damon is a very busy guy. You know that, he has a pretty tight schedule that needs to be followed to the number, not even 5 minutes' worth of time should be wasted. Everything has been sent to your office upon your arrival. Just go there and go with the flow. Come along". She pushes me forward, keeping a comfortable distance between us.

"Love your outfit by the way". She was backing me, leading the way but I could sense the little smile on her face.

She was about my height, a few inches taller though. Her dirty blonde hair was curled into little waves, stopping at her shoulders. Most parts of her skin was hidden under the blue jumpsuit she had on. The nude heels she had on pulled the whole look together. She was really pretty, I had to admit I felt a little regretful about the way I had chosen to dress today.

We walk into a big, spacious office.
The windows have a full view of the city. I walk up to the window, gazing down and adoring the view that made the city seem under my feet and control. I felt powerful here. The aura around this office was more of a homey one, with brown wood floors, white furniture, a table with a computer and files of paper stacked beside.
A big Flat black screen occupied the wall a few steps away from my glass table.
There was a marble table with an L-shaped couch around it, situated close to the windows. I looked back to the screen, something about it seeming off.

"This is your office; you'll be here when Damon doesn't need you. Come"

She walks out and I follow behind her. We go three floors down. As the door slides open, there are people walking around, some seated at tables with foods and drinks in hand, while others stand chattering along. The smell of freshly brewed coffee and cinnamon wafts through the air, making my mouth water for some.

As if Richelle could read the look on my face... "It smells lovely, I know. This is the canteen "she gestured to the entirety of the large cafe-like establishment. "You'll be coming here every morning to get Damon's coffee. And please don't make a mistake with the order, it has to be precisely, two shots of espresso. Nothing less and nothing more. Damon loves his things how they are, nothing different"

I listened intently for some reason, nodding every once in a while to let her know I was paying attention. She seemed to know him well. I was almost tempted to ask how she did, deciding to keep my question to myself, knowing it would eventually pop up.

**I just hoped I wasn't in for a whirlwind of stress.**

# Third Person

Jasmine stood beside Damon and watched as men and women strolled into the conference room. All the men ogling and gawking over her. Most stopped to stare before walking to their seats behind the large table.

Damon had a hard time controlling the amount of rage that filled his veins.
His jaw tightens as he watches all his shareholders stare shamelessly at Jasmine.
He wanted nothing more than to snap their necks like twigs and stop them from looking at what was his.

"See you got yourself some new arm candy Damon, I have to say your taste this time is so.... Exquisite... ". He watched Jace's eyes hungrily rake Jasmine up and down like she was a piece of cake he wanted to devour right now.

A loud bang echoed through the conference room, causing Jasmine to jump and the rest to snap their heads to the source. She watched wide eyed as Damon had his hands fisted on the table as he stared dangerously at his associates, his eyes in slits and dark. If eyes could kill, then they all would already be 12ft under. The vein on his head was popping with rage as his jaw tightened. The look on everyone's face was that of fear and anguish, all except one, Jace.

He just stared at Damon. He seemed to enjoy his outburst a little too much.

"If you rather spend your time eyeing up my assistant than doing what you came here for, I'll fire all your good for nothing right out

of this company and I'll make sure you don't get a job in this city.Have I made myself clear!!"
His voice was low and full of venom, so much so that the bleeding facade that was his calm tone and toned face was seen through. It sent shivers down Jasmine's spine as everyone looked utterly petrified, all except Jace.

Jace looked like he was enjoying this. Something about Jace made Jasmine uneasy, not only his aura but the look on his face spelt trouble and mischief.

Everyone quieted down as Damon took his seat, watching everyone intently in case they dared to stare at Jasmine.
He wouldn't hesitate before gouging their fucking eyes out...

The rest of the meeting went awkwardly, with everyone at the edge of their seats, trying their best not to anger Damon while Jace kept making remarks to anger him all the more. Something Jasmine found strange.

Did he really like Damon angry?
And why was Damon reacting that way?
She could easily defend herself against these promiscuous men.
Damon didn't need to do well.... anything.

She looked away from her notes and locked eyes with a pair of ocean blue orbs, staring back at her with a level of intensity that made her avert her gaze immediately.
Those eyes held a hint of mischief as she watched him smirk and eye her up.
She felt tense under his gaze and felt the pen in her hands become ever so heavy.
Something about the way he looked at her made her.... Scared.
Jasmine almost lost her balance as Damon got up sharply from his seat, the force at which he stood pushing his seat back. He put his hand on the small of her back, securing her closely beside him. He walked out of the conference room with long strides, making it hard for Jasmine to keep up. She felt the heat creep into her cheeks as everyone stared wide eyed at both of them as they exited the conference room.

Damon walked over to his table and sat down, his head in his hands he ran his hands down his face. Jasmine just stood there in front of his desk, watching him.
She still felt the tingles from where he had held unto her. She stood there for a while, neither of them saying anything, just swimming in the cold embrace of awkward silence.

"Who was that?". Jasmine finally broke the nerve wrecking silence, hoping for Damon to get the idea and continue the conversation.

"Jace", he sighed, understanding what Jasmine meant. "Hopefully you won't be seeing him around"


"He's already left boss, but he promised to drop by"
Raymond walked in with a serious look on his face, which immediately became softer once his eyes landed on Jasmine.

He walks to stand beside Jasmine as he offers a charming smile, which doesn't go unnoticed by Damon.
Jasmine politely smiles back before they return their gaze to Damon.

"Jasmine, you can retire to your office. I will call if I need you" Damon dismissed.

Jasmine nodded and walked away. Her movements earned the attention from both men as she exited.

"Hello, you have reached the phone of the personal assistant to Black empire, Jasmine Scott speaking how may I be of service to you? "

Jasmine had gotten accustomed to the greetings pattern she had as a personal assistant. She is to receive incoming calls for the empire and fix meetings for Damon. And yes it was a lot but Jasmine found a little challenge amusing.

"Hello, Mrs. Jasmine. I am Charles from CB limited. I am calling to book an appointment with Mr. Black?"

"Okay.... " she trails off, opening Damon's schedule in her laptop and starts searching for a place to fix this appointment.

From the looks of it the week was all booked out. It's going to be the busiest one yet, Jasmine thought as she sighed quietly. "...... How does Thursday 3:00 pm sound?"
She asked with the nicest tone she could muster.

"Definitely, I'll tell my boss. Thank you Mrs. Jasmine"

She puts down the phone and sighs, staring one more time at the amount of things that were left for the week. She also had to look for a place to get Damon's dinner. For someone who had a food court and a canteen in his building he sure liked to patronize other restaurants.

"Hello, this is Jasmine Scott of the Black Empire. I want to book an appointment at your restaurant for Mr. Damon Black"

"Sure thing Mrs., what time? ". The female spoke from the other end of the line, a light tone to her voice. The famous restaurant L'Amour is known for their excellent service and food, no wonder it was Damon's favorite, he always loved the best of things.

"In the next 15 minutes, can that be arranged?"

"Definitely Madame, we'll see you by 4:45 then"

She says her thanks to the lady on the other end and hangs up.
Sighing she slumps back into her seat, letting her eyes generously
roam her spacey office. Her office door suddenly swings open and
she snaps her head to the entrance.

"I see you're getting used to this"
Raymond strolled in with a smile covering his features.
The smile that always played on his face whenever he set eyes on her.
She honestly could never understand the reason behind his smile,
but it was nice.

"What's not to love? "She asks, rotating herself in the office chair
with hands spread out like she was flying.

"Come on let's have lunch". He walked over to her table and stood
in front of her, towering over the table.

Oh yes!
They always spent their lunch together, bonding and talking about
whatever came to mind which was surprisingly easy for Raymond.
He was quite the talker. She also found out from him Damon's
favorite restaurants and many other helpful things she's been using.

"Lunch, by 4:33?"Jasmine asks, raising a brow at him.

"Well, it is the second time we are eating today so.... "
He trails off, pursing his lips at her, like he wanted her to see his
point.

"I can't Ray; I have to get Damon to his dinner appointment in the
next... "
She trails off as well, checking her watch.

"12 minutes!"
She unconsciously batters her eyelashes at him, trying to get
sympathy and make him understand.
She knew how sensitive he was.

"Come on...

You can at least spare me 12 minutes, and it's not like you have to be on time"
He reasoned, propping his hands down on her table, staring down at her.

"Fine, but-"
She sighs, getting up. She wasn't able to finish her sentence before Raymond hastily took hold of her hands, pulling her out of her office before she could protest.


"You really need to relax and take a breather"

I roll my eyes, bringing my cup of coffee to my parted lips. Letting the hot liquid slide down my dry throat, the sweetness lingering in my mouth.
The taste of cardamom is unmissable.

"I don't overwork myself, at least not as much as Damon does. He hardly comes out of his office". I thought more to myself.

He actually never did. It was always only two points with Damon- from his office to the conference room and that was it. I was shocked that he wanted to come to a restaurant to have his dinner, most of the time he just ordered and I brought it to his office.

"You're actually right though... ". He sips his latte not letting his eyes leave mine.
"He needs to loosen up a bit, I don't think he would even go for the upcoming party"

Party? "What party?" I inquired.

Ray stares at me, looking lost for a second. "Its-"

A familiar ringing noise came from my purse, waking me from my daze.
My eyes darted to my phone where I saw the familiar contact saved under L'Amour.
My eyes widen and my heart thumps in my chest.
I had totally forgotten.

"Shit!! "I curse out loud, hastily picking up my belongings while avoiding Ray's questioning gaze.

I get up sharply, pushing my seat back with force.

"Where are you going? "
Ray asks, taking hold of my wrist, a hurt expression plastered across his features.

"Damon! His dinner reservation. I'm going to be late"
I barely manage to form words in my rush. I pull my hand back and rush to the elevator, every ounce of carefulness and caution flying out the window.
I impatiently tap the tip of my flats against the cold elevator floor, waiting for this goddamned elevator to reach the right floor already!

The door slides open and without hesitation I run through, only to bump into a wall and fall back. I feel a strong pair of arms wrapped firmly around my body.
A familiar whisky scent wafts through the air, chasing all the oxygen from my lungs. I snap my tightly shut eyes open, only to stare into a pair of captivating emerald green eyes.

A swirl of emotions bloom through these eyes, the vibrant emerald shade standing out as the hallway lights reflect through them, giving them a twinkling look.

"Careful tesoro......". His husky voice comes out a tone deeper, sending shivers down my spine.

Okay so what the actual fuck was that!?

What did he call me?
I take a big step back, steadying myself.
Maybe I didn't hear well.

"Don't we have a dinner reservation to get to?" He asks, an amused look on his face....

# Jasmine

I sit here, awkwardly watching the waitress try her best to make conversations with Damon. She flirtatiously batters her long artificial eye lashes at him as she sets his plate down, totally ignoring my very presence.
"If you need anything else, don't hesitate to ask Mr. Black". The light and quiet voice she uses was definitely not hers.

She was so desperate it was pitiful to say the least. The clothes she wore were less than ideal. The thin fabric of her button down dress displayed her slender figure. Her cleavage was on full display and I could see some other men eyeing her up. She folded her hands to her chest, her cleavage spilling out ever so openly.

It was so cringe I had to look away. But for some reason Damon seemed unfazed by her actions. He just kept staring at his phone which was very odd. I mean she was definitely a beautiful lady, although her desperation could use some fixing.
Her jet black hair fell down her shoulders as curtain bangs framed her face. She had on a lot more makeup than she needed. She was eye-catching and definitely caught the eyes of the majority of men here who were without dates even some that had dates snuck looks at her direction. Damon not being part of the visual scene was shocking.

"Thank you, that will be all". He dismissed her, not looking away from his phone.

I watch her scoff and walk away with the tray she came with. We sit there in silence once more, while I study Damon. He raises his gaze to meet mine and immediately I feel my heart beat increase.

"You're not going to order anything?". He asks, holding my gaze.

"... N-no. I'm fine". I smile awkwardly, dropping my gaze. The intensity of his getting to me.

"Someone seemed to like you" I couldn't help but say, watching to gauge his reaction.

"You sound interested tesoro"


I shot my head up, wide eyed.
Did I just say that out loud? Did it sound like I was interested? A smirk threatening to play on his lips.

"-what me?" I asked with a mocking scoff. "No, I just mean the waitress seemed to be interested in you, that's all sir"

He places a piece of stake in his mouth and I shamelessly watch his lips as he chews. "You can call me Damon out of work"

 I taste his name on my lips, "okay. Damon"

I watch as his eyes study me, a blatant expression on his face.
"That's better.
I am not the least bit interested in her if that's what you're thinking" he clarifies, his eyes never leaving mine. "I have my eyes on someone else. Every other woman is little to nothing compared to her, her beauty, her very essence, it's beautiful"


Did I get that right?
That sounded so beautiful and heartwarming.
But who was she? I raised my gaze only to lock eyes with him. The intensity this time was unmeasurable, he held my gaze there for a

while, neither of us saying nor doing anything, just staring. It was like he was staring into my soul.

"Oh, Damian. What a nice surprise.... "

A voice came from behind me, sending goosebumps all over my body.
That voice…"

# Damon

His voice was like a needle, pricking my peace. My grip tightened around the fork in my hand, the anger in me bubbling over. I tried to take in deep breaths to calm myself.
Across the table I could see Jasmine stiffen as Jace came to stand beside us, closer to her.

"I hope I'm not interrupting... ". He trailed off, a smirk forming on his face.
Making me grimace as I felt my blood boil.

"What. Do. You Want"
I stress each and every word through clenched teeth.

Calm down Damon... I tried to take in deep and calming breaths to calm myself as best I could

"Oh nothing. I just wanted to know if you were coming to the upcoming party, you never attend them and each year I always invite you. I hope this time you can attend and bring your.... " He trails off, his eyes drifting to land on Jasmine as he licks his lips.

"I will attend. Thank you for the invitation" I reply, a blank expression on my face.

I couldn't let him have the satisfaction of getting a reaction out of me.
The blatant expression was quite the opposite of what I felt like doing.
I felt like chopping off his tongue and feeding it to dogs.
Pushing my chair back I abruptly stand, startling Jasmine. I push past Jace and hold out a hand for Jasmine, a questioning look covering her features. I give her a knowing nod and she slides her soft hands into mine. I help her stand and we walk past Jace.

"Look forward to seeing you there! "I tighten my hold on Jasmine as we exit the restaurant, the anger subsiding as Jace was no longer in sight.

"What was that about, and what party? Even Ray was talking about it"
I could hear the curiosity in her soft voice and the questions that danced in the middle of her furrowed eyebrows.
God she looked so cute.

"He throws an annual party, for all the top richest dignitaries in the country and each year he invites me"I stop, watching her puzzled expression and she nips on her lower lip, lost in thought

"And each time you don't go?"

"No"

"Why not?". I turned to face her, my eyes meeting her big brown orbs

"Because I never found a reason to nor the right one to go with". I held her gaze for a while before I returned mine back to my phone, which sat casually in my hand.

"So I'm going with you, Why?"

Curious little kitty ay?

"Why so curious tesoro?"

Silence

"Do I have a choice?". She spoke so quietly I couldn't have heard her if I wasn't right next to her

"No, not really. You're coming with me so I suggest you get yourself ready tesoro"

"Will the paparazzi be there? "She asked, sounding a little scared. Worry swimming in her dark irises.

"No, don't worry. They aren't allowed into parties like these. The last few had no coverage"

She nods and rests back into the seat of the car, facing the window. I let my eyes wander over every curve, dip and crease on her face. Although turned away from me I could see the side of her face, her flawless skin glistening under the dim street lights, giving her a warm glow.

I had never looked forward to anything like I looked forward to taking Jasmine with me as my date. My beautiful tesoro. Any thought Jace had of getting what's mine would be out the window.

I look back at her laid back figure...
My want for her growing with an unimaginable paste, each and every day we are in the same building. I have to restrain myself from claiming her and letting the whole world know she is mine and only mine.

**In due time…**

# CHAPTER SEVEN

## Jasmine

I sigh heavily, rewriting a few documents I had to send to Damon.
It was shocking how many documents needed re-proofing.

Damned people left all the work for me to do...

I groan as I hit the save button, deflating back in my seat. The party
was in the next few days, conveniently on a Saturday. That definitely
helped, the only day out of the freaking hectic week I had to rest and
take a well-deserved rest. I missed my comfortable bed, my soft
pillows and my favorite tub of ice cream. This Saturday was
supposed to be my lazy day but of course I was forced to be social.
Thinking about the amount of rest I could be getting right now made
my already tired limbs even heavier.

I shake my head, getting myself concentrated once more. I pull out
my personal laptop. Yes, I never thought I would be able to say those
words... "My personal laptop". I didn't think it was needed until
now, but being provided with a laptop just because...
Was a good reason. Now it has made everything easier for me.

I type in my password and open my account details.
"Let's see how much I have"

I hadn't paid my electricity bill, water bill, WiFi bill and many
others in months.
They were all well overdue, I just hoped I had enough to pay at least
half of them and still have enough to get myself some well needed

essentials. I felt my eyes pop out of their sockets at the amount I found written in bold words where the amount of money in my account was "supposed to be"-

No freaking way! Six solid digits!
That was the biggest amount of money I had ever seen in my account. Surely I would have gotten much more from my rich Uncle but I always declined his money, I could work for myself and get my own riches

But gosh!
This was the largest amount I had ever earned.

Then suddenly something clicked, there was no freaking way!
I opened my second bank account to see an even more outrageous amount seated there.

"There is no freaking way Damon knew about my second account!!" How did he even-

I was brought out of my ranting by the familiar sound of my ringtone.

"Richelle?"

"Jasmine, there is a big problem!". She exclaims from the other line, her breathing heavy as she speaks hastily.

"What happened?". I ask, automatically sitting straight, my shoulders tensed.

"You know our top client?"

Strange question

"Yes, Mr. Stone, 65 years old, Irish man. Why are you asking!? "
I panic, getting into the situation. Anything that had to do with him was definitely something to panic about.

He was Black Empire's top client. We handled his finances and he brought in the largest numbers that almost broke our scales. He is

even our oldest client, having been closest friends with late Mr.
Andrew Black. God bless his soul. They were really close but since
he died we haven't kept in much contact other than business related
ones of course.
But why Richelle was bringing him up was the real issue.

"Well, he is here! And he wants to see Damon! I need you to get
Damon ready and to the lounge room at 15! I'll stall him as long as I
can, but hurry!"

My heart drops to my ankles

There was a bip and the call cut.
I stare at the screen of my phone for a few seconds, panic rising in
me.
I shoot up, running out of my office straight for Damon's.

Pushing his door open, my eyes meet a pair of emerald green irises
staring at me from across the room. He raises a brow at me as I
stand there, calculating.

"Tesor-"

I cut him short, stalking towards him with hasty steps.
He gets up remotely with a crease between his eyebrows.

I place my notepad and tablet down on his table. Spotting his blazer
hung on the back of his leather seat I reach for it and hastily help
him get into it. He stays quiet but I could feel his questioning gaze on
me as I moved quickly around his office.

I took hold of his loose tie that hung around his neck, undone. "Your
number one client Mr. Stone is on his way in the next 10-8 minutes.
He is a little upset and I don't need to tell you how sensitive he gets.
Don't upset him or make him feel awkward.
For the good of everything try to smile a little"

I fiddle with his tie, my eyes not leaving what I was doing. I knot it
properly, dropping it back onto his shirt. My fingers momentarily
brush his broad chest and I could have sworn I felt a tingle in my
fingertips. I brushed away the feeling and procccdcd to straighten

out his suit, dusting out his broad shoulders. I proceed to pull the rims of his suit jacket together to finish the look.

# Damon

This was the first time I was seeing Jasmine like this. She fiddles with my tie, determination clear on her face as she furrowed her eyebrows, concentrating.
I try my best to hold back the smile that curved at my lips, seeing my tesoro so determined. But why?

"Your number one client Mr. Stone is on his way in the next 10-8 minutes. He is a little upset and I don't need to tell you how sensitive he gets.
Don't upset him or make him feel awkward. For the good of everything try to smile a little", okay that was why.

I had to bite back the amused look on my face from playing. She knew me so well already. She drops my tie and I stare at it, just realising I had been doing it wrong all along. I silently watch her dust off my shoulders, straightening out every wrinkle from my suit.  Her fingers grazed my neck momentarily and swear I felt my skin burn under her touch. She walks behind me, straightening out and properly preparing my collars, proceeding to do the same thing with my shoulders. Her touches made me hard instantly. This girl was going to kill me.

She comes to my front, taking a few steps back, I could finally breathe. She squinted her eyes at me, pursing her lips like she was looking over her work. She smiles, content, a look of approval and satisfaction washing over her features. That smile she wore that seemed to warm my insides in ways I couldn't quite explain was beautiful.

"Let's go over it. Remember to try to smile and make small talk with him. Just show him you are interested and you care". She speaks while scrolling through her tablet.
I watch her admirably as she continues to rant things I should take notice of but I couldn't help stare as I zone out, her voice fading into the background as I could only concentrate on her, she was all I could see. How her milky chocolate curls hang down her bent face, falling on the tablet screen

Something about how bossy she was being turned me on, badly...

Before I could think of anything else I had already started strolling towards her like the predator I was.
Slowly and determined

I stop right in front of her and watch as she slowly raises her head from her screen and stares at me with those dark intoxicating eyes of hers. The eyes that hold a force that pulls me in every single time, the eyes that seem to see right through my soul, the purest wood burning eyes, the eyes that flicker with a hint of curiosity and something I couldn't quite decipher. I use my fingers to tuck a stray curl behind her ear, holding her gaze as I proceed to create feather-like touches along her throat.

I watch as she shivers under my touch and her eyes slowly close.

What was this girl doing to me?

"I-i we should g-get going. We don't want to keep Mr. Stone
waiting"
She stutters, her eyes flying open as her cheeks burn a bright pink,
contrasting with her olive skin.

She takes a large step backwards, away from me still looking
flustered. I bite down on my lip, trying so hard to suppress the urge
to make her show me that face again and some other faces and noises
I was certain I could bring out of her.

I recoil my hand, sliding both into my pants pocket to restrain
myself. A stoic expression covering my face once more. I follow her
quietly through the familiar white, brightly lit hallways, watching
her intentionally keep some distance between us, her actions making
a smirk claim my lips.

# Jasmine

I slump down on my seat, setting my coffee down on the table beside
my laptop. I opened my bank details once more, still dumbfounded
on the amount of money that was there. I made a mental note to ask

Damon how he knew about my secret savings. There is no way I could use such a big amount of money, this was stealing.


If Damon thinks I would accept such a big amount of money, then he's dead wrong.
I'm no gold digger. I stormed out of my office, carrying my laptop with me. My annoyance is increasing. I quietly pushed open Damon's office door, careful not to make too much noise just in case he was having a meeting with someone.
My eyes fall on a familiar figure standing in front of Damon's table, backing me.

Damon stops what he was looking through as our eyes meet. I get lost in the green depths of his eyes for a second before I look away, my cheeks a red tint from realising how much I had been staring. The person who was backing me stops and turns as well. I direct my gaze to his face, the round glasses I could never miss.


A warm smile covers his features as I walk further into the office.

"Sorry for the interruption" I apologize meekly, a little ashamed I didn't announce my arrival beforehand, I certainly won't be able to speak to Damon about this with this oddly familiar guy here.

I squint my eyes at him, trying to remember where I had seen him before.
The chestnut brown curls that fell down his forehead, the round glasses were all familiar.

"It's fine tes- Jasmine"

I cringe at the sound of Damon calling me by my full name.
I had oddly gotten so used to the "tesoro" he always called me, whatever the hell that meant.

"So you stuck around after all"

Then it clicked

"Sebastian?" I ask, a small smile curving at my lips at the memory of my first day here, the first day we met.

"Am I missing something here?". Damon's husky voice draws our attention back to him. He cocks his head to the side, studying our exchange.

"Sorry sir, I'll get on it". Sebastian takes a curt nod before walking past me out of the office, not before giving me a small reassuring smile, which I felt meant "see you around"

"What's wrong tesoro?"
The name brings back all the normality, at least what I referred to as normality.

"I think there has been some kind of mistake" I start, earning a raised brow from Damon. I feel my heart skip a beat at his facial expression. I shake it off and walk beside his table, setting my laptop down in front of him. He adjusts it and just stares at the screen

"What am I supposed to be looking at?". He deadpans.
 "Your account balance?" he asks, unsurprised.

"Yes, the amount there is too outrageous. I haven't worked here long enough to earn such a large amount Damon"

I could see something flicker in his eyes and only at that moment did I realize I had called him by his first name. But fuck it. I didn't care right now.

"So you're saying…? " he draws nonchalantly.

"I'm saying you need to take it back or something.
I'll send the amount back to you, I can't accept this" I sigh frustrated

I watch his face become stoic
"It's not my money Jess, it's yours, you worked for it. I'm not accepting it back"

My face deflates

"What, why!"

"You've been working hard Jess, it's just your reward and I'm not taking it back, end of discussion" he says, waving his hand in my face dismissively, slightly pushing my laptop away and facing the opposite direction.

"B-but". I angrily pout, glaring holes into the side of his head.

"Don't be a baby tesoro. Now go get ready for the party. I'm picking you up by 8pm. Don't keep me waiting". He speaks with finality, not making eye contact with me.

I scoff and snatch my laptop back.

"I'm definitely not using any of his money.
I'll find a way to send it back". I reassure myself as I walk out of his office, feeling a set of lingering eyes on me.

# Damon

I couldn't help the sheepish grin that found its way to my face as I thought back to the look Jasmine had. She never failed to intrigue me. Most women I had ever come across, would literally beg for my money and do anything to get it, but here Jasmine was, complaining about it as it was spoon fed right to her. Saying she wanted to give it back!?

She really is something else.

"Are you sure it's all here?"
I bring myself back to the conversation I was having with my senior computer technician, Sebastian.

"Yes sir, everything"
I had Sebastian get me all the information he could on Jasmine. Way more than I needed to know, and he did the job.

"Although some things are missing, a whole 10 years of her life are unaccounted for. They aren't in any school records in the city nor in any home school programs. For those 10 years it's like she was nonexistent. Her records begin when she was 11 and none before" he informed, a disturbed look on his face, one that mirrored mine.

What the hell?
How the hell is that possible!?
How...

Something is definitely wrong here.

"How is that possible Seb?" I look away from the records that hold every single information Sebastian just told me.

"I have no idea sir. Maybe it's possible she moved here at the age of 11 that's why she only has records from that age"

"Possibly" I respond more to myself as I nod, dismissing every other crazy thought that could have made its way into my head. "You are dismissed Seb, thank you" I nod towards him and he nods back, walking out of my office.

"Hello, I need a favor"

# Jasmine

I sigh for the hundredth time since I decided to attempt doing my
own makeup. I could just go with my signature natural look, but for
a party with the highest dignitaries in the city, I most certainly
would look like a mutt that lost her way and just happened to wind
up beside the richest of the richest and sexiest- I mean most
successful bachelor in the city.

I deflate back into my vanity chair as I look over my disastrous
attempt at make-up.
Sure I could do simple beginners makeup, but this. This! Was too
much! Hell I don't even know what they call that, that damn stuff
that is supposed to be smoothed out on your face!

I'm such a mess... I pick up my phone for the umpteenth time to call
Damon to cancel

There was no way I would make it to this party without making an
absolute fool of myself. Just then the ding dong of my house bell
came interrupting my dialing. I directed my gaze to the top of my
phone screen to see the time was well past 7.

Who the hell could it be by this time? I drop my phone and walk down to the door, my footsteps quiet and subtle. For all I knew it could be a kidnapper.
I fist the kitchen spoon I swiped from the counter in my hands, holding it so tightly that by one swing the poor soul standing behind that door will sleep for a long time.

I tiptoe to the door, fear creeping into my spine at the thought...
Could it be... . Him? My sperm donor.
No, no, no. There's no way he'd find me. Uncle Tom promised to find him before he found me.

No!

I stretch out my shaky hands and settle them down on the handle.
The handle rattled with the vibration my entire body was giving off.

I pull the door open and raise the kitchen spoon above my head, ready to swing when an ear splitting scream makes my eyes snap open.
There Richelle was, curled up in a ball on the floor, her hands up in defence

"It's me! It's me! " she yelled frantically

"Oh my gosh Richelle" I let out a breath of relief, lowering my weapon.
I guess our family reunion would have to happen another day.

"I'm sorry, i-i thought you were a k-kidnapper" I just had to stutter, shitty nerves.

"It's okay. It's good to be alert" she laughed awkwardly.
I help her get to her feet and notice the bags she's carrying in her hands.

"What's all this?"

I ask with furrowed eyebrows as Richelle walks into my apartment with hands filled with.... shopping bags!? In total there were about five bags in each of her hands.

"Come and find out! Don't just stand there with the door open! This time an actual kidnapper could come in" her voice fades as she walks further up.

I smile at her antics as I shut the door and make a beeline up the stairs. I watch in awe as she lays all the bags down on my bed, bringing out designer dresses one after the other, she hangs them on any and everywhere as she eyes them, judgement clear in her scrutinizing gaze.

"What the-"

A hand in my face cuts me off and I watch as she brings a beautiful and very expensive looking white lace silk evening gown to my body. She places it against my body, changing angles every two seconds. I didn't even get enough time to admire the feel of the soft silk material against my skin before she ripped it off me and went for another one.

"Richelle" I hold up a hand, stopping her mid-way from bringing another dress "what's going on? Why are you here and with all this! ". I gesture towards the entirety of my room

"Just come sit here first" she leads me to sit in my vanity chair, facing the illuminated mirror.
I watch through the mirror as she turns away and reaches inside one of the bags labelled Victoria's Secret!

She pulls out a bag and turns, only to lock eyes with me. I glare at her through the mirror and she lets out an exaggerated sigh as her shoulders slump. "Fine fine" she waves me off. "I'm here to get you ready for the party, Damon called in a last minute favour and sent all these" she demonstrates to the designer dresses on my bed "for you" she finished.

I just blinked at her face as she stood in front of me. I definitely didn't hear properly.

"Seriously, Damon sent all these" she says reading my shock stricken features. "He called me to help you get ready, so you'd look your best"

I was still trying to wrap my brain around this.

"There is no way I'm wearing any of these"
I frown deeply, getting off my seat and facing Richelle.

"Look Jasmine" she placed both hands on my shoulders, holding me firm as she said "you have to, don't think of it as anything other than him wanting you to look your best as Black Empire's Personal Assistant. Do you really want to drag our name through the mud because of your ego?"

My stance weakened as I thought about it. "Okay fine" I sigh, rolling my eyes at her emotional blackmail. She was good.
Richelle squealed like a hyena before pushing me down into the seat once more. "So now shut up and let me get to work!
We have less than an hour here!"

I shut my eyes as I let Richelle do whatever the fuck she wanted to do.
Minutes or what felt like ages past and all I could use to tell that Richelle was doing something were from the momentary thugs or pulls on my lashes, brushes coming in contact with my skin, things being sprayed on my face and pencils being drawn wherever!

"Tadaa!!!" She exclaimed from behind me.

My eyes slowly flutter open and what I saw in the mirror left me dumbstruck.

"I-i "

I couldn't believe it was my face I was staring at. I placed a hand on my cheek as I stared wide mouthed at my reflection that looked too good to be mine.

Damn...

There was no way this was me!

I watched as Richelle had this sly grin on her face as she did a little victory dance. "How is it!?"

"I-it's beautiful" I whisper my answer, afraid that if I spoke any louder I could wake up from this dream?

"Now for your hair..."
She hummed to herself as she looked over my hair.

Pulling out the claw pin that held my hair up, my curls came tumbling down in its messy glory.She placed it down in front of me and started working her magic.
I just placed my hands hovering over my closed eyes as I sat there for another hour or so, which I doubt was possible considering I had barely 5 minutes left when she started.

"Now get into this"

I got up from my seat to see her holding a beautiful black ankle length dress, with a split running up the left side. It had a deep V neck that would well expose my cleavage.

"There's no way you expect me to get into that" I stared at the dress wide eyed.

Number 1) I could never pull off such an elegant dress and 2) heck no! That's all the reasons I needed.

"Jasmine just got into the dress. After that if it doesn't look good we'll change it, deal?"
I grumble, snatching the dress out of her hands I walk into the bathroom

"I got to go!
Damon would be here any minute!"

"Wait! What!?"
I poke my head out of my bathroom door to see my room, empty!

**Fuck!**

**Just before I could curse more I heard the ding dong of my doorbell and I froze, this time I knew who exactly stood behind that door. I felt my heart palpitate in my chest as I walked out of the bathroom.**

**I slid on my black platform heels and wore my diamond stud earrings.**
**I guess I'm doing this!**
**Might as well go in style**

**I took in large breaths as I walked down the stairs, my eyes fixated on the door as the doorbell continued to ring. I gulped down hard as I flung the door open.**

**I allow my eyes to roam over his attire. I felt like all the air got knocked out of my chest. He had on a burgundy suit with matching dress shoes. As usual he had the first three buttons of his inner white shirt undone, leaving a patch of slightly tanned skin visible. He had his signature bed hair look, but somehow it looked sexier than I'd ever seen it. His intoxicating scent wafted through the air and I unconsciously took in his scent, totally unaware of the set of eyes on me. My eyes met with a pair of green irises as I looked up. I got lost in them. I could feel my heart thumping in my chest.**

# CHAPTER EIGHT

## Damon

I stare at her in absolute awe. I am a man with eyes for seeing and what stood beautifully in front of me was more than worth my attention.
She looked as beautiful as ever in a black body con dress with a split running up her left thigh, revealing her smooth, hairless leg.

I had to resist the urge to run my fingers up her thighs in sensual strokes.
I was getting hard just from the thought. Fuck. I let my eyes wander to her face, the first time I'd seen her with such makeup and to say she looked absolutely ravishing would be an understatement. Her milky brown curls cascade down her shoulders in their beautiful waves, a few curls coming to frame her gorgeous face.

My eyes darted to her cleavage that was on full display through the dangerously deep V neck of the black dress she had on. I gave them more attention than any other part of her. My eyes settled on her full coated lips and I felt the sudden urge to claim them in a passionate kiss and never let go. I never expected the dress to look so captivating on her.
Heck, everything she wore would look like a masterpiece on her.

"Tesoro". I spoke, my voice coming out a lower baritone than usual as I bit down on my lower lip, looking her over once more, how the dress clung to her like a second skin, her assets were making me go crazy.

I watch as her cheeks hold that red tint I always loved to see. "I see Richelle did a great job getting you ready". I acknowledged, finally able to tear my eyes off her glory and focus on her brown intoxicating eyes.

"She has great taste" A twinkle of something I couldn't decipher flashing ever so brightly in her brown irises as she spoke.

"Shall we?" I pick her hands and bring them to my lips. I hold her gaze as I place two soft kisses on the tip of her knuckles, her cheeks blazing pink as I lead her to my car, hand in hand.

… … … … … …


I stole glances at her as I drove through the dark streets of the city. She stared out of the window like there was something specific that peaked her interest.

I watched her turn her head as she stared at something. I watch her, not minding anything else. The noise blending into the background, all I could focus on was her right now. Her eyes met mine and she stared at me strangely.

"Aren't you going to get that?" she asks, a crease between her brows.

I blink out of my daze and just then I hear the monotonous sound of my ringtone.

"Mr. Black. I hope you haven't decided to reject my invitation at the last minute now"
His ever so ear wrenching voice came through the other end of the phone as I held it to my ear. I felt my grip tighten around the steering wheel, so tight my knuckles started turning white from the amount of force.

"I will be there Jace" I answer in an unamused monotone

"Good, I hope your PA dressed well for me" I turned to see Jasmine watching me with concern clear in her gaze.

"Don't you even think about it. If you want to keep those hands of yours, I suggest you stay far away from her". I didn't wait for his reply before ending the call and throwing my phone back.

I kept my eyes trained on the road as I could feel my anger bubbling inside of me. If Jace had the deranged idea, he could lay his hands on what was mine then I would make sure it's the last thing he ever touches. Fucking prick! I would be damned if I let him lay even a finger on what was mine.

I ignore the questioning gaze that Jasmine kept sending my way. I was too angry to acknowledge her concerns right now so I drove faster, ignoring the blaring horns from other drivers.

I stop the car, looking out my left I take in the unfamiliar tall building that was surrounded by valets and hefty body guards in all black suits.
I take in the beautiful gold and black of the tall building, the glass and marble walls give off that expensive mist. The rays of the moonlight bouncing off the walls, making them glisten.

Trust that prick to go all out.

I step out of the car, a cool wave of evening breeze sweeps through the air, the chilled feeling of it against my skin slowly causing my anger to dissipate. I walked over to the passenger's door and just when Jasmine was about to push the door I held onto it, catching her attention. I hold her gaze as I completely pull the door open and hold out a hand for her to take. I watch her exchange looks from my face to my hand before she hesitantly slides hers into mine.

I gently pull her out before pushing the door closed behind her. I hand my keys over to the valet and we walk in, side by side. Immediately the body guards stepped out of our way and we walked in, I felt Jasmine tense beside me as the sound of classic music filled the air.

We were met with the beauty of the ball room where different women and men dressed in elegant gowns and suits graced the floors. The hustling' and bustling' of the waiters, rushing from table to table with trays in one hand and napkins, placed perfectly 90° on their upper arm were covered by the sweet tunes of jazz music coming from an elevated portion of ground, where the band was stationed, playing their hearts out. As we walked further into the venue I placed my palm on the small of Jasmine's back, making her jerk. I stepped closer to her so my lips were slightly grazing her ear.

"Calm down tesoro. Just breathe and stay with me. okay?" I speak slowly to her as I wave at a couple that begin approaching us. "Just be careful with whom you share drinks with. I'll advise you to stay close to me, everyone here isn't as nice as they seem. Especially stay away from Jace, I haven't located him yet but I'm sure he's here somewhere" she noticeably tenses the more and I could feel her breathing becoming heavy, the red tint of her cheeks couldn't go unnoticed.

She gives me a meek nod in response. Satisfied I stepped away, but I remained close enough to her side as my hand resumed its position at the small of her back.

"Ahh, Mr. Black it's so nice to see you after so long. You're a splitting image of your father". Mr. Bruce roars, shaking my outstretched hand with as much vigor as his enthusiastic self could muster. I gave him a thin smile. Something about people mentioning my father left me feeling vague and out of place.

My father, The Late Mr. Andrew Harrison Blackwood was a nobleman, known for his brain, charm and charisma. He was a god when it came to business and other official work, he was so good he built the empire from the ground and for that I'd forever look up to him, but sadly he was never a father. Not like I really needed him, I got by by myself just fine and I took care of mom all by myself when he'd be travelling all around the world to gain favors and partners. I couldn't blame him though; he did what he had to do for his business. At least that was one thing in his life he paid close attention to.

"Mr. Bruce, the pleasure is all mine"

"You finally decided to come for one of these. As you can see Mr. Anderson never fails in upholding his name as the best interior designer in the city" Mr. Bruce smiles proudly, looking around at the handwork of his partner.

"I can see that" I deadpan, my face regaining its stoic expression.

"And here is the ever so beautiful Jasmine Scott, the sweet Personal Assistant to the man with the biggest empire in the city… " he draws tentatively, eyeing up Jasmine.

"Mr Bruce". Her sweet voice comes out from beside me as she accepts his hand.
He brings it up to his lips and caresses them ever so lightly with the pad of his thumb before placing smothered kisses at the tip of her knuckles. I felt the bile rise in my throat at the sight- how he completely ignored his wife that stood there beside him, watching the whole exchange with a distasteful face that she tried to cover with her sweet cheeky smile. Her disgust and feigned delight fighting to gain acknowledgement on her features.

I snake my hand completely around Jasmine's waist, pulling her slightly to my side, away from the old fuck that stood in front of us. Bruce smiles, exchanging looks from my hand around Jasmine's slender waist to my face and then hers.

"Enjoy your evening"
He excuses himself, understanding the daggers I had been sending his way.

He walks off with his wife remaining a few feet away from him. I growl as I watch their figures disappear into the crowd. I turn back to see Jasmine staring at me, her cheeks the same red tint.

"Come on tesoro". I speak in the same low baritone as I lead us further into the ballroom to settle at the bar, where I was sure I would have a full view of the ballroom, to catch that dick wherever he was hiding. There was no way he'd be late to his own party.

It's all part of his game...

# Jasmine

I pushed my small frame onto the barstool beside me, making sure I was properly situated against the cool, smooth surface. I directed my gaze to Damon, he stood backing me as his eyes raked the ballroom. I still felt tingles from the places he had held unto me, my cheeks were still burning and I really needed to calm down.
Only his presence was nerve wrecking and now this was all too overwhelming.

**Oh goodness
I just hope I manage to get through the night.**

**It felt like I couldn't breathe all the while Damon stood beside me,
with his hand at the small of my back.  The moment he spoke into
my ears I could feel my legs turning into jelly. If I hadn't gotten
myself seated then my knees would have probably given in by now.I
sigh, facing the bartender that just stood there, watching me.**

**I sent him a small smile.**

**"What will the pretty damsel have?"**

**I was a damsel all right, one who really needed a drink right now
A drink would definitely calm me down" Just a glass of wine
thanks" I hold his gaze as he smiles back at me, a little too bright for
my liking**

**"Sure thing, coming right up"**

**He excuses himself as he turns to get my order.**

**I had just downed the second glass and I already started to feel
myself relax.
I sigh, setting the half wine glass down on the black marbled counter
in front of me.**

**Was everything here dripping with expense? It was so bitter looking
around to see the expensive chandeliers that hung specifically from
the roof, its diamond extensions glistening. The gold velvet curtains,
the gold walls.**

**I had just realised how bright and ogling everything was, it was
making me sick.**

**"Calm down Tesoro, we don't want you drunk". He whispers into
my ear and I could feel my pulse rate quickening.**

"I... I won't get dr-drin-nk..." I drawl, barely able to complete my sentence.

Oh shit! I was tipsy
My brain felt fuzzy but I could still tell vividly where I was. The look on Damon's face would be the one thing I won't forget tonight.

"Okay tesoro, you're definitely drunk" he sighs, shaking his head at me with a rather gorgeous smile playing on his lips.

What was he smiling about? And why did my heart just do a cartwheel at it!!?
Okay I need to cool it with the wine. I watch as he snaps his head to a particular direction that had crowds of men in expensive looking tuxedos, his smile replaced with a scowl. "Just stay here tesoro, I'll be right back"

And with that he was gone. Like he had disappeared into the crowd with no trace.

I turn back to face my cup. I swirl the drink in my cup as I watch the red liquid twirl in its glass containment. I down the red liquid as I let it slide down my throat and settle, making me relax the more. I landed the glass clumsily down on the marble counter, a hiccup erupting from my throat soon after.

"Oh, excuse you Mia Bella". A husky voice cooed from beside me. I felt tense even in my relaxed state.

I turn my head to see Jace, grinning sheepishly at me, a set of his rather dull teeth on full display, rays of light bouncing on them. His ocean blue eyes held a glint of mischief and something I could see even in my woozy state.

"Oh now gorgeous" he started, eyeing me up and down like I was his next snack.
"Don't tell me that big bad stuck up boss of yours told you not to talk to me"

Another unauthorised hiccup left my lips and I instantly regretted drinking so much. I could barely focus on this perverted dude seated next to me. I shut my eyes tight, trying to concentrate my gaze on something in particular. Why did I have to drink so much??! I don't think I had that many drinks though.

"Can you get the lady another drink?"
I shook my head violently, for some reason my lips seemed unable to move.
I don't think I could get this tipsy just from wine.

I tried to blink myself out of the haze that kept blurring the corners of my vision.
I heard the brandy cup being placed in front of me, the sound of the glass against the marble unmissable.

"Have one more drink, gorgeous. Then you could come with me and I could take such good care of you" he cooed again, his voice laced, and hot with alcohol as he spoke directly into my ear. "I'll show you what a real man can do"

I shoved him away as much as I could. I could feel myself slipping in and out of it.
I got off the stool in an attempt to escape Jace's advances but I was caught off guard by the huge hand that wrapped around my waist, pulling me into a hard surface.
I crashed into Jace's chest, his hands snaked firmly around my waist, pressing my body into his.

Dizziness overcame me as I tried my best to wiggle out of his grip.

"L… let m-me g-" I drawled, my eyelids feeling very heavy...

"Don't worry love, I'll show you such a good time you won't need that son of a bitch anymore" his hot breath fanned against my ear making me shudder.

Before I could register what was happening his lips had latched on to my neck, nibbling and sucking on my tender skin. I jerked away from his hold, only to have him yank me back in place. Something was definitely wrong, it was like all my limbs couldn't function. I felt the energy being drained from me and I was left feely fuzzy and light headed.

I tried in vain to push him away from me, but his grip only tightened around my waist, leaving my body completely flushed against his. I felt myself being carried away.

I tried in vain to open my lips and call out for help but the words just wouldn't come out. Tears had started streaming down my cheeks. Couldn't these damned people see me getting assaulted here! My heart was beating in my ears as they began to ring, every other noise, even the sound of my own thoughts were blocked out by the ringing noise.

The only thing I could feel were the smothered kisses on my neck and collar bone. I cried out when he bit into my skin and tried again to jerk away but he held firmly. I called out the name that came to my mind "Dam-damon" it came out more like a desperate cry but to hell with it!

The next thing happened in a flash, I felt a force like no other pull me forward as Jace was ripped away from me, and I fell clumsily to the ground, my knees digging into the hard floors. I let out a cry, the force at which I fell evident on my bruised knees.

I tried to lift my eyelids to see what all the commotion was about but I couldn't, they were so heavy all I wanted to do was close them, succumb to the darkness, it's all I wanted to do.

# Damon

He was there, in the midst of those men in matching tuxedos. I would never miss his face in a crowd, his blood flaring face, eyes the colour I hated the most.
It was like I was chasing a shadow, and like one he was gone.

Just like that!

I looked around, not able to believe he had slipped out of my hands just like that.
I walked round the ballroom for a couple of minutes, searching for that rat but I instead got bombarded by old friends of my dad's who wanted to know the state of my empire and If I was running it like it was supposed to be run.

"Of course, I would expect nothing less from the son of THE ANDREW HARRISON BLACKWOOD". Mr. Coal Jones patted my shoulder, a hearty chuckle erupting from his throat.

"If you'll excuse me gentlemen, I must find my date"

Ah my tesoro, I'd left her in her drunk state. I couldn't help that familiar grin from taking over my features as I walked away from the men, memories of my tesoro's drunk state flooding my mind. As I neared the bar where I last left Jasmine, I heard a muffled cry coming from somewhere close by. The agony in the cry made a knot form in my chest.

For some reason I felt the urge to run and I did, till I was stopped dead in my tracks by the sight in front of me. I felt all the rage and anger burst in me, flooding my veins and blurring my vision

What happened next was like a flash. I was over there in a second, ripping Jace off Jasmine. I held the douche by his neck and pulled him off his feet.

"Fucking prick!"
I yelled as I tightened my grip around his neck.

"I told you to never make the mistake of laying a hand on what was mine, and now you would pay" I snarl, my voice devilishly low.

I felt myself going mad with rage and only one thing was in my mind right now was Jace must die.I felt my eyes turn into slits and darken.

I was going to break the hand he used to touch my tesoro.
I pulled my fists back, landing a punch square to his nose as the popping sound filled the air, bringing me an odd satisfaction. His cries filled the ballroom as they bounced off the walls. A crowd had gathered around us, watching the scene unfold, some videoing, others looking on with pity. Nobody had the guts to stop this, they knew better than to interfere when I was in such a state.

I hardly ever lost my composure, but when I did, people knew it meant only one thing.
Blood.When I was sure he had passed out I threw him to the ground.The music, dancing and chatter had died down, leaving the hall pin drop silent.

"Boss!". I heard Ray call from behind me, making me turn away from the douche below me. I ignored the staring eyes and rushed over to Jasmine, she was in Ray's arms shaking and crying.

Her tear stained cheeks made my chest heavy, like I couldn't breathe.

"T-tesoro, are you okay?" I stutter, the adrenaline still pumping through my veins, so hard I couldn't feel the pain from my bleeding knuckles.
I cup her face in my hands, looking over her small startled frame. She seemed fine physically, but I felt all the rage rise in me once more as my eyes settled on a hickey on her neck. I felt like beating the dick all over again but my tesoro was crying, she was more important.

"Tesoro, look at me. You'll be okay"  I tried to comfort her despite the anger building in me. The prick was going to pay in more ways than one, that I would make sure of.

She was still shaken up by everything and she couldn't even focus on me. I pulled her into my chest, wrapping my arms around her small frame protectively. "You'll be fine tesoro, I'm here" I whisper into her hair, her scent making my anger dissipate.
I felt her still and go numb in my arms.

I scooped her unconscious body in my arms, (bridal style) supporting her with my body. I walked out of the ballroom without looking back once, despite the noise rattling through the silence. All my attention was on her, only her.

# Damon

"The prick drugged her" I spoke through clenched teeth, my jaw tightening as I walked further out of the room and shut the door behind me, not intending our noise to wake Jasmine.

I doubt it would though. She'd been out for a good 12 hours now. I was beginning to worry but the doctor assured me she would wake up soon. The drugs that the son of a bitch used on her were very strong, the dosage had gotten out of hand so these were the effects.

I began my journey to my home study, Ray close behind me. "How much damage are we talking about here?" I let out an exhausted sigh, running a hand through my dishevelled hair.

"A lot of damage boss" his eyes held a lot of sympathy for Jasmine, I and the situation we were currently facing.

I deflate back into my seat, scratching my stubble as I brainstormed for ideas to get us out of this, specifically Jasmine. She wasn't used to this kind of life and I needed to keep her out of it as much as I could.

"Call a meeting with my closest associates, we need to discuss this matter as soon as possible" I announced while Raymond already started sending the necessary emails.

I grumble, I hated this kind of things, the media fucks up everything and they had managed to put up the one thing I didn't want on the tabloids.... Jasmine.
It all happened so fast and I was too angry to take notice of anything, of the media taking pictures of everything that was going on. Even if I could have seen them, there was little to nothing I could do about them, they are such a nuisance to the lives of every prominent person, but the thing was they have protection.

If they were abused or mishandled by anyone, it would cause a public uprising against he or she who dared to manipulate the public's need to be informed, and that ladies and gentlemen is why the press had such balls to do as they pleased and make all our lives a living hell.

Even if the information they carried was unnecessary and a total invasion of privacy they still felt entitled bitches who had the right to put all our private matters for the whole world to see, and it's exactly what they did. And for someone like me, whose life is hardly ever out there, this news spread like wildfire, covering all and every news channel in a matter of seconds. Every page, every vlog, every newspaper, every magazine had this on their tabloids;

*"FAMOUS MULTI-BILLIONAIRE DAMON IDRIS BLACKWOOD, SON OF THE LATE MR ANDREW HARRISON WAS CAUGHT ON CAMERA GETTING CLOSE AND PERSONAL WITH HIS P. A, MS. JASMINE SCOTT, WHO REPORTEDLY STARTED WORKING FOR HIM ONLY A FEW MONTHS AGO. THE TWO WERE SEEN HUGGING AFFECTIONATELY DURING A PARTY THROWN BY MR JACE ANDERSON"*

I sigh, remembering the headings and the millions of emails I kept getting from relatives, associates and others. I just switched off my phone and tossed it aside like I seemed to be doing to all my problems nowadays. I had no idea how Jasmine would react to this when she found out. Her safety was also on the line here, all at once. Her name and photos were all out there, on news channels, podcasts. Everyone was eating this up like hotcakes.

Such jobless douche bags, they had nothing better to do than stalk the internet till they got another big scoop to talk about and by the looks of it, this won't die down any time soon.
I sigh again, the idea of speaking to Jasmine after this slowly seems crazy to me. How exactly would I explain it to her, that her life is not going to be the same ever again, because the media saw it as entertainment worthy to put such false information about her on the tabloids and now it's everywhere. She would have to change every single thing about her now, she was at risk of the crazy paparazzi and I'm sure without a doubt, they are already raiding her home as I sit here, contemplating how to break such news to her.

I would even go as far as to lock her up here if it meant I could keep her away from all of this. I just hoped Gerald was able to get there before all her things were stolen or possibly destroyed.

The paparazzi were crazy and the worst part was they were never going to stop until they got what they wanted.

I just hoped it wouldn't cost me my tesoro.

# Jasmine

*"No! Please!! Stop!" I sobbed hard, but no matter how much I cried he wouldn't let go.*
*I could still feel his lips lingering all over me, it felt like I couldn't breathe and the next thing I knew he had his hands wrapped around my neck in a choke hold.*

*Fat tears dribbled down my cheeks, trailing down my neck and landing on my bare body. Just then I noticed I was naked...I stared wide eyed at my sperm donor.*
*I felt the fear creep into my spine, he had found me!*
*Like he always said he would.*

*He found me!*

*"I told you, you could never escape me, Cass"*
*His dark voice echoed all around, in my head I could hear him, he was still there, drowning me in the dark abyss. I clawed at my throat, fighting hard to swim to the top but I kept sinking. I was suffocating, dying!*
*I needed help!*
*I needed to get out!*
*I kicked and tousled but nothing was working!*

*Oh gosh! I squeaked as I felt myself sink further down, my eyes closing, succumbing to the weight.*

**I jolted up! My forehead is coated with sweat and my breathing is erratic.**

I placed a hand over my heaving chest as I tried to calm myself down, my cheeks still hot with tears. I shut my eyes tight, running a hand through my sticky and sweaty hair as I pull it back, trying in vain to get all the strands away from my face.

Everything came flooding back to me, Jace. It was all a big blur but I could still remember how helpless I felt. I let a few tears roll down my cheeks, I never wanted to feel as helpless as I did ever again.  I furiously wipe at my ears, refusing to obey my emotions and wallow in self-pity. My headaches, I felt worn out completely spent. Getting up I felt my legs hit a very soft material.  Only then did I take the time to look around the spacious and beautiful room I was in. The room looked bigger than my whole house, but that wasn't the surprising part, the surprising part was the color scheme of the room, it was my favorite color!? The part of it that was freaky was it was the exact shade I'd prefer it in, it was the shade I'd painted my room. The color calmed me down a bit as I stared at the way it mixed with the gold of the furniture, velvet curtains and lining on the walls. The color scheme was absolutely gorgeous.

I knew better than to let the beauty of this room deceive me. I needed to know where I was. I got to my feet and instantly regretted it as a wave of unsteadiness washed over me and I was almost knocked down, my head spinning. I slumped back on the bed, my head in my hands. It ached so badly, but I didn't have time right now to relax.

Let's try that again

I slowly rose from the bed. This time I was careful not to make any sudden movements. Once I stabilized myself I walked over to the door on the far left of the room, ready to open it and give whatever or whoever was on the other end a piece of my mind. When I flung the door open I just stood there and gaped at Ray, I didn't hesitate before wrapping my hands around his neck.

"Calm down princess" he cooed into my hair and I pulled away, only then noticing the tray of delicious smelling foods in his hands. He had everything from pancakes, bacon, eggs, mashed potato, waffles and a jug of what I assume was....milk?

"Almond milk to be precise"

He walked further into the room and set the tray at the bedside table, propping down on the bed. At least Ray was here so I knew I wasn't in danger, not yet at least.

"Would you just stand there princess, come sit" he gestures to the space beside him on the bed. I already started approaching him with my gaze fixated on the tray of food, my mouth already salivating. I come to a halt, pushing my hunger away and letting my curiosity take over. I ignore the dull pain in my head as I watch Ray dish out one piece of each type of food into a plate which I assume was for me.

"Where am i?" I ask with furrowed eyebrows. Ray turned his head to me, a look of panic crossing his features as he dropped the plate down.

"Don't bother princess" he waves me off "you'll know in time, just come and eat. I'm sure you're hungry" he covered up with a thin smile that looked less than genuine. I would know.

"I'm not hung-"
The unauthorized growling of my stomach interrupted my sentence midway. I fought the pink tinge that threatened to rise on my cheeks.

A small smile claimed his lips as he shook his head at me and got up, walking towards me with that same smile.
I could see through it just fine, after all it was the one thing I was familiar with, one thing I knew all too well about Ray, his left eye ticks when he's nervous or under pressure.

I found out during several important business meetings we had with top clients.
Ray was responsible for showing them our new strategy to get our goods on the market and raise their scales. His left eye kept ticking the whole time. It wasn't that noticeable though, but once you saw it, it was impossible to unsee.

"Just come and sit Jess"

His voice came out low as he avoided my gaze.

"What's going on Ray?"
I spoke in a softer tone, trying to get to his weak side.

"N-nothing Jess"
Cue to the tick- "Just come sit"

"Please Ray, what's going on?"
I spoke even softer as I took his hands in mine, caressing them with my fingers.
He was very emotional for someone who stayed as close to Damon as he did. He lets out a defeated sigh, his features softening.

"Where am i?"I asked with the same soft tone.
He held my gaze and I retained the adamant look my brown eyes held.

His head drops as he lets out another sigh.
"You're in Damon's house" he spoke so low I almost didn't hear him

Almost

I just gaped at him for a few seconds, waiting for him to scream it's a joke or something. I let the words sink in and when they did, panic and confusion rose in me at the same time.

"W-why am I in Damon's house!?" I whisper-screamed

"It's a long story Jess"

"I have time. Where is Damon?" I folded my hands against my chest as I stared hard at Ray.

"There is no need for that, I'll take you to him only after you eat" he regains his posture, trying to match my gaze but I hold my ground and refuse to let my confidence waver.

"Fine! " he snaps, throwing his hands in the air. "Follow me"

He leads me out of the room and into a beautiful hallway.

The walls were covered with white marble tiles and the color scheme was a gorgeous harmony of black and white. The hallways were beautifully illuminated by the gold lights hanging from the roof, creating golden-like rays streaming down our path.

We passed what felt like hundreds of black oak doors with the same designs and it felt like Ray was leading me in circles. The floors felt so cool under my bare feet and just then I'd noticed I wasn't wearing the black gown I was wearing at the party, instead I had on a black shirt that was two sizes too big for me and a pair of white tennis shorts that I hated to admit looked really cute. My eyes widen with realisation as I come to a halt in the middle of the hallway. The familiar intoxicating scent invading my nostrils.

"Is everything okay Jess?"
Ray asks, taking a step back.

"Who changed me?" I directed my wide gaze to Ray who stood there shuffling his feet.

"What do you-?

" Who changed me out of my dress!" I cut him off, the panic rising in me.

"I-it was D-"

That was all I needed to hear before I stormed off, to where? I had no idea. But all I knew was I had to see Damon right now!! I was wearing his clothes, in his house, with no memory whatsoever of what happened or how long I had been in that room I woke up in.

I fought back the embarrassing pink tinge that began revealing itself on my cheeks, the thought of D-damon haven seen me... No! I shake my head violently as I turn to another hallway.

"Okay what the actual hell! These halls look the same!"
I turned around to catch Ray before he ran into me.

"S-sl-low d-down"

He heaved, his breathing frantic. I roll my eyes and wait for him to catch his breath.

"You don't need to follow me, just tell me where Damon's study is"

"I don't even have the strength to stop you either" he blew out a puff of air and I rolled my eyes again like he could see me from his bent over posture. "It's the next door just down your right. You can't miss it, it's the only brown wood door on this floor"

I almost choked at his words. "On this floor!" Was he serious!
I cleared my throat and started my journey down the next curve, ignoring my urge to explore. I stand in front of the grand, brown, ceiling length, double fiberglass doors.
I wrap my fingers around the gold handles and pull the doors open.

Immediately I'm hit with the scent of old, or even ancient books and freshly filed papers. I stared in awe at the mahogany library, it looked like the library from Beauty and the beast. It had everything, the red couches, brown ceiling length shelves, filled to their capacity with hundreds or even millions of books. I gape at the biggest study I'd ever laid my eyes on.

I hear the clicking sound of an office pen and I snap my head to the direction.
There he was, sitting behind a large wooden table…in a white round necked shirt. The thin fabric flushed shamelessly against his mouth watering build, revealing his defined abs, his large hands practically struggling to come out of the sleeves and his big chests peeking out of the neck of the shirt.

His hair was in its natural disheveled glory as few strands came falling down his forehead, landing on his eye lashes.

It felt like all the air had been knocked out of my lungs and I couldn't breathe. As our eyes met I felt the heat creeping into my cheeks, leaving me probably looking like a baked potato. I immediately ripped my eyes away from the glorious being before I wouldn't be able to.

"I see you're awake tesoro. I hope you didn't have any issues"

"Why am I here?" I cut to the chase, not ready to beat around the bush. "And... in... Your clothes?" I look away from his gaze, not willing to see that twinkling look they held.

He looked like a devilishly hot being out of this world under the dim lights that illuminated his desk. I gulped down hard, trying to control whatever cotton feeling I had in my mouth. "Tesoro, we can talk about this later, for now go and eat something and get some rest" he diverted, totally ignoring the other things I asked.

"Plus, I think you look rather nice in my clothes, wouldn't you agree? " he added, I wiped my head up to see the playful smirk dancing at his lips. The way he eyed me up made my face flush and my mouth go dry all at once.

Stay focused Jasmine
Stay focused!

"I prefer being in my clothes, thank you" I deadpan "now why am I here?"
I wasn't matching his playful tone in the slightest, I tried to hold an unwavering stoic look.

"My clothes look a lot better, tesoro" he drawled getting up from his seat.

I tried to maintain my composure as I watched him take long strides towards me, my knees trembling a bit at the look his green irises held.
"If clothes are the problem" he started, gazing down at me with sinful promises in his eyes. I shrunk back at his deep baritone "then that could be arranged" he purred into my ear and I felt my knees turn into jelly as a shiver ran up my spine.
My brain went blank once I felt his hot breath at the nape of my neck. Goosebumps spread all over my skin, not only from the heat he was emitting but also from our close proximity.

Everything I had revised in my head to say, my confidence, my anger all dissipated and flew right out the window. When I felt his soft lips

latch into my neck I jerked back, my once closed eyes flying open as I shoved him away.
I stared at him wide eyed as he adjusted to his full length, a plain expression masking his features. My breathing was erratic as I just realized I had been restricting my flow of oxygen up until this moment.

"Boss, we've got them all together. The meeting will happen in the next few days."
I twirled around as the double doors came flying open and Ray came speed-walking through them. Damon and I remained quiet, just staring at each other while Ray hadn't even taken notice of me yet.

"Why is there an emergency meeting?" I glance away from Damon to Ray, who looked at me wide eyed, probably just noticing my presence

"I... uh" he drawled fiddling with his sleeve
"I thought you were going to tell her!" He whisper-yelled to Damon, as he turned away from me.

"I'm still here you know" I matched his tone, getting him to turn back to me. "What's going on here?" I glanced between the two men, noticing an odd energy and awkward atmosphere hovering around us.

"Ray?" I glanced towards his direction but he refused to meet my gaze.

"Hmm. Come on" Damon gestured for me to follow and for some reason my body compiled before I could think about it. I followed him out of the study, with Ray close behind us. We walk through the beautiful halls and stop in front of a slick, grey elevator door.
I held back my shocked expression.

He had an elevator in his house!!!!
I would be damned if I found a swimming pool here too

We all filed into the elevator before Damon put his finger into a glowing green slot I had just taken notice of. He held it there for a while before it turned blue and the doors closed. He punched in a code before the elevator started going down...

"You okay, you look kinda.... red"

I felt my already hot cheeks blaze the more at Ray's question.

I gulped down hard "Just peachy!" I squeak out

Did I just squeal!!???

"Where are we going?" I whispered soon after, hoping to forget that awkward answer.

"Wait and see," he whispered back.

We heard the audible ding and I just stared at Damon's back as the doors slid open and he walked out first, Ray second and I last. I gawked at what I saw in front of me as soon as I stepped out of the elevator. My feet were greeted with the fuzzy feeling of a furry carpet. I stared at the way the furs swallowed my small toes as I wiggled them, enjoying the soft and smooth feeling I was getting.

I gaze up to see a short hallway and a huge room, brightly illuminated.
I walked through and stopped dead in my tracks, my eyes coming in contact with the biggest flat screen television I had ever come across. It sat there, graciously above the beautiful stone fireplace, giving this place a homey feeling.
The color scheme was a gorgeous mixture of chestnut brown and gold. I gaze a few feet to my left to see a beautiful 'L' shaped couch, taking up half of the room, with single seated couches littered everywhere.


Bright lights were peeking through the velvet curtains of the ceiling length windows.
The marbled tables glistening....
The marble floors caught my attention and I followed my gaze to a door on my right, the white Oak door had a beautiful handle that

gave me the urge to pull it open and seek the wonders hiding behind it.

"You've heard it first folks, the infamous billionaire Damon Blackwood is suspected to be in a secret relationship with his personal assistant Ms. Jasmine Scott!"

I twirl around and stare wide eyed at the big screen. A woman dressed in corporate wear had a microphone in her hands as she spoke, a serious expression on her face.
"Mr Blackwood didn't entertain any questions on that night and left with his assistant in his arms"

I felt my eyes pop out at the image I saw in front of me.

It was me!

Damon was carrying me in his arms and of course it did not show why.
Many other pictures of him holding my face in his hands popped up, all over the screen I could see pictures of myself and Damon.
I felt dizzy all of a sudden and I dropped down on the couch that magically appeared behind me. I took in deep breaths to calm myself, I could feel my breathing becoming out of control.

I gaze up to Damon with wide eyes "what the hell!?"
He met my gaze but looked away soon after and I could have sworn I saw the guilt and sadness in those emerald green mists.

He sighs, "The media took those pictures of us and ever since then it has been the hot topic of gossip. Blasted paparazzi were let in" he balled his fists clenched and his jaw tightened.

"B-but you said the media weren't allowed to cover such e-event! " I was practically shaking, my voice coming out panicked and high

"They weren't! They weren't supposed to!" He defended with the same tone "that douche must have had something to do with it" his features soften when his eyes landed on my rattled form

"Calm down tesoro, it'll be fine. I'm working on it" he assured, coming closer to where I sat.

"How would it be fine!?My name, my face is everywhere. How bad is it?" I ask, knowing the answer but not wanting to hear the gravity of the situation.

"It's really bad. Your name and pictures are on every news channel. It's spread like wildfires" Ray added and Damon shot him a death glare.

Then it hit me!
Like a ton of bricks!
My chest tightens at my realization. I was everywhere... My pictures...Name...
Everything...
My sperm donor could find me now

He knows where I am....
H-he's coming f-for me!

My chest rose and fell as it tightened the more, I couldn't get enough air.
I needed air!!It was like the walls, everything was closing in on me and the only thing I could hear was the dark voice I always did in my dreams

"I told you I would always be able to find you Cass, I found you... " his dark and haunting voice echoed loudly and repeatedly in my ears, creating a deafening ring in them. I clasp my hands unto my ears, trying to block out his voice but it only became louder and louder!

"M-make it stop!!"
I heard myself cry out but soon a ringing noise covered my senses and I started feeling light headed. Fat tears dribbled down my cheeks as I tried so hard to fight, I wasn't breathing, the air was too thick.

"Please!" I gasp

I felt warmth consume me and large hands wrapped around me, pulling me into a hard surface "Tesoro calm down, you're having a panic attack. Breathe!"
I heard his voice so faintly and I tried to follow it and calm myself but the harder I tried the more i couldn't breathe

"Listen to me tesoro!
Take in a deep breath and release it!
Breath tesoro, breathe!" He yelled, violently shaking me while I sobbed the more.

# CHAPTER NINE

## Jasmine

He was coming for me. I couldn't deny it, whether I liked it or not.
He was going to find me sooner or later and I couldn't just stay here,
in this lavish penthouse waiting for my demons to catch up with me.

He could be on his way right now, coming for me. I couldn't go back
there, to that cellar. Where I died and woke up every single day.
A shiver ran up my spine at the thought. The damp cold floors. I
would remain there, starving and scared as night and day passed me
by.

I couldn't even tell how long had passed, there wasn't a single ray of
sunlight accompanied in the cellar, not even a hatch was there, nor a
window. Only a metal door that was only opened once every three
weeks and each time it was to be punished for my very existence

Would I say I deserved it?
Yes
Every painful whiplash I endured....
All of it

"Jasmine?" A calm voice peeked through a crack in my door "can I
come in?"
I sat up to see Ray's head peeking into my room, a nervous look on
his face.

"Sure" I gave him a lump sided smile, gesturing to him to come
inside further.
He pushed the door open, coming through in his full length.

"You never ate anything. Come on" He held out a hand to me, a thin smile encouraging me to follow.

I gaze away "I'm not hungry Ray" I lied. I didn't have time to eat. I had to leave, if he found me here.....
No,
He just can't find me here

Or at least I needed to find a way to leave here and never come back. I needed to clear my tracks again.

"Please Jasmine-" he softly pleated.
The more time he had here, the more the lump in my throat kept growing.

"O-okay. I'll be there just give me a minute" I croaked out, having absolutely no control over my tone.

My cracked voice betrayed me in every single way and Ray's features softened as he took in my shaky form. "Where's Damon?" I ask, redirecting my gaze to Ray

I had to resign from my job first, I wasn't ready to answer any of the questions I knew he would have. "He went out". The space beside me dipped as Ray sat down
"He's going to fix this Jasmine, he cares that much, he never wanted any of this to happen" he tried to console me as he grabbed a hold of my shaking hand in his, gently stroking the back of it.

"Everything will be fine" he offered me a thin smile which I tried to reciprocate.
I wish everything would be fine.
I wish none of this would have happened, but sadly I had to leave, despite the guilt weighing on my conscience.

But I knew no matter how much I wanted it to be alright, it could never be as simple as wishing it into reality.

"Shall we?"
I nodded and Ray pulled me onto my feet and led me out of my room.

I took in my surroundings for the last time as we proceeded into the elevator.
I watched Ray punch in the buttons and we began our journey down.


Pushing myself onto the island barstool, I set my hands on the marble. I watch Ray throw out some bowls and spoons in front of me.

"You cook?" I ask, an eyebrow raised

He chuckles "why, I don't look like one to cook right?" He smiles at me, pouring some things into a bowl

"No you don't" I mirror his smile. "Didn't think a guy who wore an Armani suit would be a familiar one with the kitchen" I snorted, earning a sheepish grin from him.

"You really need to stop your stereotypes woman"
He shot me a playful glare

"Okay, okay" I raise my hand in defeat and we burst out in hearty chuckles

"What are you making?" I inquire, poking my head further into what he was doing

"You'll see" he snatched the bowl away from me, turning to face the cooker. "No peeking" he gave me a side eye with a rather heartwarming smirk on his face

"Okay, mister chef" I retorted, snickering when I saw his feigned hurt expression.

"Ray can-"

I turned my head to the door as it swung open and he walked in, dressed in a three piece, black ...
You guessed it!
Armani suit

Gosh where did these men shop, they sure knew how to dress with class. I felt so underdressed in my simple... Oh wait, not simple in Damon's clothes.
I fought back the pink tinge that threatened to take over my cheeks. He exchanged looks between Ray and I before his eyes settled on what was brewing in the frying pan.

"Cooking again?" He scoffed, earning a glare from Ray.  "Thought you would give up after the pork fiasco" he snickered, shaking his head as small chunks of laughter spilled out and It just occurred to me it was the first time I'd seen him laugh.
His laughter sounded melodious and deep all at once, his parted lips revealed his perfect pearl white teeth. The scene was perfect and I couldn't help but get lost staring at it.

"I'll have you know I learned from that and now I'm a way better cook than you" Ray defended, hands wrapped against his chest with a pout

"Sure sure" Damon choked
"If you say so". His laughter died down as he stood straighter and directed his full attention to me, eyes meeting as I didn't have time to look away.

"Can I see you in my study tesoro?"
The atmosphere immediately became tense as Ray turned back to tend to whatever he had on the frying pan while I was left with Damon's usual stoic expression.

I nod and wordlessly follow Damon out of the kitchen.
As I walked behind him I tried to sum up my courage to bring up my resignation.
No matter how many deep and calming breaths I took in, it didn't ease the lump in my throat.

"Take a seat tesoro" He gestures towards the black cushioned seat stationed in front of his desk.

I propped down as I let my gaze follow him to the back of his desk, where I shamelessly watched him pull at the knot of his tie, leaving it

loosely hanging around his neck. He proceeded to take off his suit jacket, leaving his matching black vest on.
I gulped down, feeling the heat rising in my cheeks at the way his hands and back muscles flexed while he spread out his blazer against the back of his seat before he propped down, finally meeting my expectant gaze.

"Uh... you wanted to talk about something?" I begin, mentally patting myself on the back for not completely stuttering.

"Where do I start tesoro" he sighs, running a hand through his dark curls, partially pushing some back but they, without delay fall back unto his emerald eyes.

"If I say all this media shit isn't taking a toll on me then I'd be lying" he looked me straight in the eye "Everywhere, at every nuke and cranny paparazzi is there, making my life an absolute hell hole and I can't imagine how bad it would be for you"

I gaze away, the guilt swimming in his emerald gaze getting to me "It's not easy to have your face everywhere either and that's why I came to tell you.. " I trailed off, turning my gaze back to his scrunched up face, fear and anxiety flashing in his gaze

"Tell me what tesoro?"

"That I can't work for you anymore" I began, gazing away from his shocked face, pausing to let the information sink in

"It's all too much and I can't handle it. I'm going to leave this place and go live with my uncle, it's how it was meant to be. I was foolish to think it would go any other way" I whispered the last part, talking mostly to myself.

"I'm not used to this life Damon" I exaggerate to the entirety of this world I've been in for the past months "it's not for me, and I can't take it"

I bit down on my lip, waiting for his reaction but it never came. Instead he had his eyes closed as his chest rose and fell with an unusual rhythm.

His eyes slowly opened and he stared at me, an unusual demeanor taking over him "You do remember that the contract you signed states that you can't necessarily quit" he countered and my eyes went wide as I recalled the exact line in the contract that stated so. "I have to be the one to fire you and I am not letting you go tesoro"

"But-" I started, but he cut me off with a hand in my face

"But I do have a solution that will help the both of us, our lives and this situation we find ourselves"

I sat up straighter, my ears perked with anticipation.

"This contract" he began, pushing a stack of binder papers towards me on the table. "States that you, tesoro will be my lawfully wedded wife. Only for six months and within that time you will appear everywhere with me and you will have the protection from the media, like a full-fledged member of the Black Empire's inner circle and after the six months has elapsed if you still wish to go" His features softened and his eyes lost the hardness they held.  "Then you are more than free to do so" he continued.
"This contract makes the other one null and void, meaning you will face no lawsuits of any kind nor any restrictions at the time of your departure. Do you accept tesoro?"

I gulped down hard, trying to process his words as best I could.
I just gape at him, exchanging looks from the contract in front of me to his face

"It's the only way tesoro" he reasoned "All I'm asking is you be mine for six months"

I felt it getting harder to breathe as I tried to calm myself, the look of determination in his eyes making it even harder.
"You can't be serious" I squeak, my eyes wide

"I am tesoro, take a look yourself"

I started rummaging through the contract like a maniac and sure enough it was all there, written and drafted in ink.
I gaze at the different spaces that require my signature.

"You don't have to sign right away tesoro, take your time". He spoke, rising from his seat and coming towards me "And when you do indeed decide to sign, just let me know" he paused behind me and I felt the heat radiating off him as my cheeks bleached a pink tinge.

"You will be mine" he purred in my ear and I felt a shiver take over my body at his deep baritone.

With that he walked out of the study, leaving me all flushed and hazy

# Jasmine

"Ray! Ray! " I call out, making my way to the kitchen.

"Hey" he chirped, walking around the corner with a cookie in hand.

"I need your help" I began, snatching his cookie right out of his hand.

"Heyyy! " he wined

"Oh hush up and come along" I tossed the cookie into my mouth, gesturing for him to follow me to the elevator.

"What's this about?" He asked following behind me

I turn around to face him "I need you to take me back to my home Ray"

"What! Why! You haven't even stayed up to 3 weeks here yet and you want to leave!?" He exclaimed, his expressions hysterically tense

"I'm not going there to move back in Ray" I chuckle lightly "don't worry"

His features soften again
"Then why do you want me to take you back?"

I take in a deep breath, "I need to get something I left behind"

"No way" he shut me down, walking back to the kitchen

"What! What do you mean by no way!?" I grumble stumping into the kitchen right after him

"By no way I mean no way" he snickered at my scrunched up face. "Look, it's not safe for you outside here, the paparazzi are still on this case and they would eat you up like a pie during a market sale" he chuckled

He sighs, "It's not safe, plus I can't take you anywhere out of this building without Damon's permission" he shrugged, leaning against the island's marble.

Was he being serious right now! Damon didn't own me
I didn't need his permission to go get mom's last memory. I didn't need anyone's permission. I was going to get it whether that grumpy man liked it or not

I stormed out of the kitchen, determined to go out and get what I wanted all by myself. Anyway, I didn't need Damon or Ray knowing too much about my forgotten past, It was better left where it was. Forgotten
I paced impatiently around my room, momentarily peeping through the little crack in my door for Ray. I sigh, dropping down on the floor.

I had been at this for the past two hours.
I was waiting for Ray to walk out of his room before I snuck out the house.

"What could he possibly be doing in there?
Ugh!" I grumble, glaring at the path leading to Ray's room...

Footsteps pounding down the hallways brought me out of my daze and I quickly shut my door, keeping my ears against it.  I heard his footsteps fade down the hallway and after a few minutes of waiting I opened the crack in my door once again. Stepping out I looked side to side, making sure the hallway was completely empty before I came out fully and shut the door behind me.

I did a little booty shake as a victory dance and began my journey down the hallways leading to the elevator.
I wasn't sure where exactly Ray had gone to but I hoped he wasn't in the living room.
I crossed my fingers as I walked into the elevator, my palms sweaty and sticky as nervousness pinched at my skin.
I watched the numbers slowly go down and only then did I know how many floors this house had.
By my observations there were about six different floors in this house and I had only seen two, gosh I had to go exploring one of these days.

Once the elevator dinged and I was on the ground floor.
It all started....

# Jasmine

I made my way into my apartment, the door creaking open.
I jerked when I heard the door slam behind me, a chill running
down my spine.
I wrapped my hands around my body as I proceeded further into my
apartment.
I stopped and took in its disheveled form. Everywhere was untidy,
my pillows, cushions, everything was on the floor and everywhere
was pitch black.
It felt like a scene from a horror movie.

I shivered a little as I proceeded to find the light switch. Flicking it
on, the light bulbs flashed before going back off. I sighed, the
electricity bill must have expired. It had been due for quite some
time now.

I made my way up the stairs, watching my back every second, it felt
like someone or rather something was watching me. I shook my head
at my silly thought as I pushed my room door open, the familiar
scent wafting through the air. Making a little smile appear on my
face at the familiarity. I stared at the room I'd stayed in for the past
3 years. I scrunched down, reaching under my bed and pulled out a
brown wood box.

Caressing the intricate designs on the box I pulled the latch open and
smiled as tears pricked my eyes. I pulled out the little photo of mom,
the only one I had. I directed my teary eyes to the gold piece of
jewelry that sat graciously in the box.
I pull it out by its pendant, the smooth gold heart feeling ever so
familiar against the pad of my thumb.
It was the only piece of jewelry she owned, it only seemed fair that I
kept it, no matter how much it haunted me most of the time.
It was a gold chain necklace with a matching pendant, the pendant
had intricate vine designs. It was just like her, simple, beautiful and
graceful.

Securing it into my pocket I rose to my feet and began walking out, making sure to grab some extra stuff that Gerald forgot to bring for me.
I looked at my home, not my house, she wasn't here and wherever she was, I hope she's proud of me. Even though her daughter is dead.

I began my journey out on the street.
It was a cold night as the street lights dimly illuminated the path as I walked.
I kept my head low, my hood doing its job of shielding my face. I don't need some crazy stalker running up to me. Just when I was about to turn the corner I felt a strong hold on my wrist and before I could react I was being pulled backward.

I was shoved into someone's front; my hand being awkwardly twisted behind me. My hood was pulled down and I came face to face with Jace. He stared at me with crazy eyes and an evil smile on his face.
He chuckles, "Pathetic attempt at concealing your face my love" he came closer to my ear as he spoke, the scent of alcohol invading my nostrils.

"You're drunk!" I gagged, trying in vain to pull my hand away from his hold but he instead twisted it the more.
I winced, still trying to get my hands free.

"Don't you dare raise your voice, you slut!" He seethed in my ear, anger dripping off his words. "Because of the hold you have on that dick face Damon, he has sued my company and brought me to ruins! All because of a common worthless personal assistant" he clenched his jaw and his hold on my arm tightened.

I flinched, tears pricking the corner of my eyes, "Please just let me go" I begged

My heart was thumping hard against my chest as images from my dreams kept flashing in my head.
"What's so special about you..." he asked, moving his face closer to the crook of my neck, sniffing me like a dog

I jerk back, "Don't you dare!"
He pulled me into him, proceeding to twist my arm and I knew any second now it would snap.

"You dared to shout bitch, because of you my company has gone below the barrels and now you have the audacity to yell at me!" he screamed, shoving me down.

I fell, awkwardly landing on my foot as my scream tore through the pin drop silence.
I tried in vain to twist my foot back, the pain shot up my leg as I tried to stand, making me fall back. The pain was unbearable as I shut my eyes tight to subdue it, not willing to scream any more.

He lowered himself in front of me, " You are going to pay for everything. Just you wait and see. I will make your life a living nightmare" he whispered into my ear, making me flinch at his dark tone.

He abruptly stood, looking around like a crazed animal before running into the opposite direction. I stared at the place he ran to for a few seconds as I tried to calm my breathing. I tried again to stand and this time managed to get onto my one good foot but I soon lost my balance and slipped. I awaited my contact with the ground but it never came.
I felt strong arms wrapped around my small frame, holding me up against a hard surface. I kept my eyes shut, but as soon as I inhaled the familiar intoxicating scent my eyes snapped open and I came face to face with a horrific looking Damon.
His nostrils were flared and a vein on his head was throbbing, his eyes were emotionless or at least that's what I saw upon first glance, looking closer I could see a pool of emotions swimming in the depths of those green irises. The emotions were so intense I had to gaze away, my cheeks bleaching a pink tinge once I remembered we were still in that position, with my body flushed intimately against his.

I tried to pull away but he was faster. He scrunched down and wrapped his hand around my thighs. I felt my cheeks blaze red as he lifted me and threw me across his shoulder. I just dangled there, staring at the concrete floor of the sidewalk and his perfectly fine ass through his sweatpants.

I wiggled, snapping out of my trance "Put me down!"

"Don't even think about it tesoro, this is the last time I put you under Ray's care. The nitwit can't even keep an eye on you"

"You can't blame him, I snuck out" I defended. "And I am not a baby that needs to be looked after!" I snapped

"Oh I'm not blaming him and you are definitely not a baby, but you are mine" My face drops. "You are never to leave my sight ever again, have I made myself clear?" He didn't shout but the tone he used had my legs going weak

"Y-you don't tell me what to do" I stuttered, my face bright pink

"Oh, just dare challenge me tesoro, then you'll see how well I can dish out your punishment" his tone darkened and I felt the heat rising in me.

I wiggled again, this time more vigorously and I felt his hold on me tightening the more, the skin of his hand grazing my thighs.
I tried to take in calming breaths to avoid any possible scenarios creeping into my mind.

I groan, "Put me down"

He ignored me and continued walking, I huffed but kept quiet as a sinister plan formulated in my mind. I wiggled my legs, simultaneously punching his back.
I felt his grip loosening around my torso and I smiled, a sense of victory coming over me but it was short lived when I felt a stinging pain on my ass cheeks.


My cheeks bleached a pink tinge as my mouth yanked open
"D-did you just...?"
I glared at the back of his head with wide eyes

"Yes I did tesoro and make no mistake I will do it again if you don't pipe down"

I didn't dare to move again, the truth in his words making my
stomach churn with a foreign feeling.

I was brought low into his arms once again, my eyes meeting him
before he threw me down...Into a car? I adjusted myself further into
the seat, feeling awkward as he remained impossibly close, his eyes
staring deeply into mine. I noticed that same pool of emotions and
something I couldn't quite decipher swimming in his green gaze.
He pulled away and I suddenly felt empty, and cold, the heat he was
emitting leaving me immediately.
I turned away as he shut the door and my eyes stopped at a familiar
figure beside me.

"Richelle?" I whisper, not sure I was seeing properly

She turned around, a sheepish grin on her face, "Hey Jess, it's been
so long" she smiled

"Yeah, what are you doing here?" I ask, trying not to sound rude.

"Well, I am the head of the company's lead of attorney's so of course
I'm here" she answered in a  tone and my eyes went wide

Attorney!?
Richelle?
How did it never occur to me that I didn't know what role she played
in the empire?

"Anyways, there are some important things my expertise is needed
for. Someone is gonna pay" she had a grim smile on her face as if
thinking of what she was going to do.

She went mute the second Damon joined us in the driver's seat and I
took that as my que to get properly situated. I adjusted myself
against the cool seat only now taking in my surroundings. The black
tint of the interior and the gorgeous controls, blue lights illuminating
the dashboard and at the same time reflected on Damon's rings.

I watched him through the rear view mirror as the dim moonlight
reflected in his green irises giving them that dreamy out of this world

glow, I found myself unable to breath for a second as his eyes met mine and I immediately looked away, my cheeks bleaching.

The car started and I rested my head against the window. I watched the beautiful sky and how the stars burned with such an intensity.



I limped away while Damon was distracted talking to Richelle in the living room.

I didn't need him carrying me again, I didn't like the weird foreign feeling I got every single time he touched me. It made me burn up and I needed to avoid anything that meant I'd lose my composure. I had to focus on getting in contact with my uncle, I couldn't sign the contract before speaking to Uncle Tom about it.
I tried calling his line severally but for some reason it wasn't going through. It happened every time he went into "hiding". He would be out of reach till he came back and with his current mission I don't think he'd be back until he finds my sperm donor.

And I wasn't certain how long that would take so I had to make a decision on my own. For the first time I had to make a decision alone, without uncle or mother's guidance and I felt lost and confused.

Dropping down on my bed I groan once my tired limbs hit the soft, cool and smooth fabric. I stretch out and feel an immense pain shoot through my leg.
It stung so badly I winced.
Bringing my foot up I tried to massage it as best I could but the pain was too much.
I dropped down my foot and sighed, deciding to deal with the pain later on.

Pushing myself off the bed I limp over to the bathroom.
Sliding out of my hoodie and biker shorts I walk into the shower, a long,satisfying sigh escaping my lips once the hot water hits my skin, washing away all my pending worries and thoughts.

I lean against the shower wall, slowly sliding my fingers soothingly through my damp thick curls. Taking in deep breaths, enjoying this calm moment like it would be my last. Savoring each droplet of water against my skin. I walk out of the bathroom, a little towel wrapped loosely around my small frame. I hold it firmly against my chest, stepping further into my room.
I slip into a singlet top and a pair of biker shorts, happy I had gotten it over with I slump back down onto my bed.  I pulled my foot into my lap, slowly caressing my throbbing ankle, it looked purple, red and swollen.

I wince once I apply a little pressure on it.

"Tesoro?" I heard his voice and immediately my head shot up to see his gaze fixated on my injured foot.

I drop my leg, awkwardly adjusting, "Uh, wh-what are you doing here?"

I struggle to but manage to stand, wobbling every few seconds.
I pick at my lips, awkwardly shifting my gaze from his squinted eyes to his feet.
I felt my heart rate pick up as he stalked towards me, hands beside him. I shut my eyes tight, waiting for his next move but next I felt his hands on my shoulders and I opened my eyes, meeting his gaze. He pushes me down and I sit, his green orbs holding my dark ones. He crouches down in front of me, his algae orbs gazing up into mine.

I silently watch him cup my foot with his hands, bringing it up to rest on his lap.
I flinched away once his hands grazed the throbbing point. He looked at me with a strange emotion before he concentrated his gaze back to my foot, turning it around as he examined it.

I felt my skin burning under his touch.

"I-it's okay, i-im sure it's fine" I stutter, my cheeks a bright tinge

His eyes meet mine before he gets up and walks out of the room.

I let out a sigh of relief, but my relief was cut short as he walked back in with a first aid box. He resumes his position, holding a spray bottle and a roll of bandages.
He carefully sprays the liquid around my ankle and within seconds it begins to burn, making me bite down on my lower lip to suppress the pained moans that threaten to slip out. Muffled moans erupted as he proceeded to treat my ankle, all while my eyes were tightly shut.

The burn dulls as he proceeds to wrap the bandage around my ankle.
He drops my leg, looking over his work. I expected him to get up and leave but what he did next left my stomach doing backflips.
He leaned in, shifting all his weight to his hands as he placed them at each of my sides, trapping me between him and the bed. I gulped down hard, only now noticing that amount of rage filling his eyes.

"I-uh please leave, y-you have bandaged my ankle, it's all fine now. Y-you can go" I stuttered, i didn't like the way I was feeling around him. I could hardly breathe; the air was getting thicker the closer he came.

"What happened? Who did this to you tesoro?" He ignored my words, his eyes daring me to lie.

I pick at my lips, gazing away the intensity of his stare becoming too much, "I-i was returning when I f-fell… and I hurt my foot. There's nothing to it, I just tripped while running is all"

"I'm going to ask you again tesoro" he started, his face coming closer to my ear. "What happened to you and you better not lie to me because I am losing my patience"

I gulped down hard, visibly becoming tense once I felt his warm breath against the soft spot of my ear. I shivered slightly, only realizing now what he was doing to me.

"I-uh it was Jace! " I squeaked out, panicking once his nose came in contact with my cheek. I felt him freeze up before he abruptly pulled away, his cold eyes staring into mine. I could see they held anger in them

"Tell me everything that happened"

I proceed to narrate everything, intentionally leaving out the part where he promises to make my life hell. Only now did I recall everything he had said to me.
Damon stood, completely coming to his full length. His demeanor completely changed from the soft concern I had just seen to a cold and hostile one. He turned around and walked away with a clenched jaw and balled fists. I knew a war was coming and I was the center of it.

I sighed and deflated into the bed, covering my face with my palms, my cheeks still a bright tinge. I had to think of what to do, I had to make a decision quickly. I didn't know what would happen next but I was sure what I wanted to do. I had to take this step.

# Third Person

It had been a few weeks since Jasmine last saw Damon. He had stormed out of her room with murder clear in his eyes. She didn't know what to think. Would he finally do it?

Would he kill Jace?

She didn't know what would happen but she had made a decision. She wasn't going to keep waiting any longer. She had to protect herself, she had tried a few more times to reach Uncle Tom but all went straight to voicemail. She had gotten frustrated and made up her mind on what to do.

Strolling to his door she looked over the documents in her hands, her sweaty and sticky hands. Nervousness had become her best friend ever since she decided to sign the documents and come hand them over to Damon.
A lot of things were swarming through her mind; would she need to give him an heir, would they have to behave like any other married couple and...
Only the thought brought a fluttering feeling in her stomach.
She couldn't deny she was deeply troubled, and talking to Damon would be the only way to go about it.

Sighing she brought her hand to the door and placed three monotonous knocks. Her hands kept trembling while she stood there, waiting patiently for an answer.

"Come in" his deep voice came after a few seconds, making her heart stop.

She shook her head, pushing the feelings away as she pushed open the door, stepping in. She looks around the dimly lit room with furrowed eyebrows in confusion. It looked empty but she could have sworn she heard Damon speak for her to come in.

She spotted his figure perched over at the edge of his king sized bed. His silhouette showed he was bent over, with his elbows on his knees and his fingers intertwined. She gulped awkwardly, only now noticing he was completely shirtless.
She felt the heat rising in her cheeks the more she took in his glorious form.
He waved her over and she consciously took little steps towards where he sat, feeling a cotton feeling in her mouth.

She came closer, careful to keep a safe distance away from him.

"Yes tesoro" his eyes dropped to the stack of papers in her hands and he tried to fight the smirk from taking over his lips, knowing fully well why she was here. She had finally decided to sign the documents and that meant only one thing; she was his now, more than ever, only his and no one else's, and he'd be damned to let her go. The contract was just a well-crafted plan to keep her with him. He planned on eliminating all the threats and making sure she had nothing to worry about so she would have no reason to leave him.

She was his and he was going to use these 6 months to prove that to her and show her how much he had craved her for such a long time. She was in for it now... .

"Um- Here" she shoved the papers into his hands, her face a mixture of embarrassment and nervousness as she picked at her lower lip.

"Finally signed it tesoro?" Damon asked, a light and teasing tone in his voice.

"Y-yes and now what will happen next? ; will I adopt your last name for the next six months or will I keep mine?"

She nervously played with her fingers, not really knowing what to do with her body as she tried to focus solely on his algae orbs, anywhere away from his glorious torso.

"Not my last name tesoro" he began, getting on his feet, towering over her small build. She couldn't help but let her eyes travel down his glorious body.

His long tanned torso, his perfectly toned abs, huge arms and his big chest all came into her view and she couldn't look away. He looked like a Greek god straight out of the stories she loved to read, Hercules to be exact. Her eyes glued to his body as she swallowed audibly, feeling the cotton feeling overwhelm her mouth.

"Our last name" he whispered into her ear making her shudder at his deep baritone.

What happened next was like a flash, his lips met her throat, nibbling and sucking on her skin. Her eyes fluttered shut as she let out heavy breaths, feeling the heat overwhelm her. She bit down on her lower lip, not willing her moans to come out.

A few muffled moans slipped through her lips as Damon proceeded to kiss down her neck; to her jawline and back to the soft spot under her ear. She held firmly onto his broad shoulders for support as her legs were trembling like jelly, her head thrown back in pleasure.

She was in a moment of bliss and hated to admit it but she never wanted to leave, especially not any time soon. His hands held firmly onto her hips, securing her body against his, pressing his strong chest onto hers, leaving their bodies flushed intimately against each other's.
She felt the heat rising in her as her mind was on cloud nine.

"Damon!" Richelle's high pitched voice boomed through the hallway, making them both snap their heads to the door.
Audible groans escaping Damon's lips as he grumbled frustratedly and let go of Jasmine, stumping to the door.

She didn't know how to feel as his warmth left her all cold and numb.
Her breathing was erratic and she could still feel the tingling sensation from everywhere he had kissed her, her skin was burning and her cheeks were flushed and red. She pushed her chestnut hair away from her face, sighing deeply and gaining her composure before she passed Damon out of the room. Coming face to face with Richelle who took in her rattled and flushed form but Jasmine quickly walked past her and left them both standing at the door frame

# Jasmine

"Stop squirming you little weasel!" Ray teased, holding me down trying to push more flower unto my face

"Get off me your nitwit!" I cursed trying to push him off me, giggling uncontrollably.

He pushed a handful of flour onto my face, smearing my face, nose and cheeks.
He jumped off, making a beeline for the kitchen while I shot up, running in after him.

"You're gonna pay!" I roared racing after him.

I jumped him and we crashed on the ground, with me straddling him. I placed punches all over his face as he tried in vain to shake me off. I dumped a whole bowl of floor onto his face, smearing more and more into his hair as he giggled, sneezing all over the place. He grabs my waist and turns us over so I was underneath him. Taking the upper hand, he proceeded to tickle my sides, making me squirm to get away.

Gasp, "Ray, s-stop" gasp "Ray!"

I blinked tears away as he proceeded to tickle my sides making my stomach hurt as I laughed out the more.

Ray and I had become really close over the past few weeks I'd been here. We'd occasionally bake together, watch Netflix and make fun of each other. I had found a reason to smile after such a long time. Most times it was awkward but we made it work. He was bubbly, cheerful and enthusiastic, the exact opposite of me but we worked well together.

"Say it and I'll stop!" He grinned devilishly. "Say it!"

He tortured me the more as I gasped for air "Okay! Okay" I gasped "You're a better cook!" I squeaked out as he let go of me and just then the kitchen door flew open and Damon walked in. The expression on his face was dangerously grim and I could see his algae eyes turning a dark green as he took in our position and the state of the kitchen.

"What the fuck is going on here!" He growled, making me flinch. I had never heard such a deafening sound in my life. Ray rolled away from me and got up, helping me to my feet as I stared at Damon. I didn't know why but I felt guilty.
Guilty!? Fucking guilty? I couldn't look him in the eye

"Chill dude, it's nothing we'll clean up" Ray defended as he strolled out of the kitchen, possibly to get some cleaning supplies from the store room.

I gazed up to find Damon's eyes turn to slits as he stared back at me. I picked at my lips, gazing away from him. I was glad Ray walked away before Damon would lash out on him or worse, beat him up. Before I could open my mouth to speak Damon had walked out of the kitchen, leaving me confused.
I felt a tug at my heart, something wanted me to run after him and assure him nothing was happening between us but I kept my feet glued to the floor, not willing to come as vulnerable and dotting but I still couldn't shake away the feeling.

Pulling at my apron I throw it aside, trying in vain to dust off the flour from my clothes. I ran my hands through my hair, making it messier. My mind was all over the place and I didn't know how I was feeling towards Damon. His reaction shouldn't have made my chest tight but it did and I didn't like the feeling...

# Jasmine

I pushed myself off my push up position, sweet trickling down my face, forehead and down my back. I huffed out the air I had in my cheeks, bending over and resting my arms on my knees to take a break.
My heart was beating so loud I could hear it in my ears. I took a large gulp of water from my bottle and relaxed, slumping back down on my mat.

I looked around the gym, smiling to myself that I had finally explored and found a gym, a swimming pool, a home theatre.I couldn't wait to try it all with Ray but he'd been sparse lately. I called a few days back and he told me he'd been upgraded to a higher position in the empire and he'd be hardly available for us to hang out. Although I felt really bad I encouraged and congratulated him for his new position. He promised to visit but it had been a week and he hadn't come yet so I decided to keep myself busy, and working out seemed like the best way right now. It helped keep my emotions in check and my thoughts from running too far.

I used my sleeve to wipe my forehead, groaning at my soaked top. Irritation pinched at my skin and I needed a change before I proceeded with my day.

Strolling into the elevator I got extremely irritated at the way my top clung to my skin. I ran a hand through my damp stringed hair, pushing it away from my flushed cheeks. I pulled at my top, taking it over my head. I sighed in relief as cool air hit my hot skin.

I was home alone again so I didn't have to worry about Damon seeing me like this. The elevator doors slid open and I walked out, stopping dead in my tracks when my eyes stopped at a familiar figure on the couch.

"Ray?" I whispered, coming closer to the couch

"Jasmine" he got up and I watched his eyes drift downward but it hadn't occurred to me what he was looking at.I snapped my head to the side as Damon walked in. Shirtless.
He stopped as his eyes met mine. I watched his eyes travel down my body and I furrowed my eyebrows in confusion.


Was there something I was wearing..... Just then my eyes went wide as I realised what the two men were looking at.
I was in my bra. I felt the blood rush to my cheeks but before I could react. Damon had gotten a hold of my hand and was hauling me up the stairs. I tried in vain to keep up with his long strides but his long legs were no match for my little ones.

He threw me into my room, shutting the door behind him.
I watched in shock as his shoulders moved up and down with his unsteady breathing.
He sharply turns, catching me off guard. Turning us around he pushed me against the wall, towering over me.

"D-damon" my breath came out labored, I could feel myself getting hotter the closer he became.

"NEVER AND I MEAN NEVER let anyone other than me see you in such little clothes. Have I made myself clear tesoro?"

His husky voice dialed down by an octave as he spoke directly into my ear, making me shudder. His hand held firmly unto my hips as he pressed his bare chest against the thin covering of my black laced push up bra, forcing my back against the cold wall, goosebumps spread all over my olive skin.

I nodded, not really having much control over my body. He stepped back and I inhaled sharply, realizing I hadn't been breathing. "The mere thought of someone looking at what is mine makes me feel like killing that person right on the spot" he growled into my ear, making me shiver at his tone.

I stared at him, not knowing how else to respond. My chest was moving up and down as he moved his head to the crook of my neck. I let out a shaky breath, as his warm breath hit my bare skin.

"Your mine"
His lips met with my shoulder as he began to trail kisses up my neck to the soft spot under my ear. That had my brain spiraling out of control.
I shut my eyes tight, struggling to remain in control of my body as he proceeded to pleasure me. My eyes snapped open as his breath tickled the swell of my breasts and I stepped further into the wall awkwardly looking around, my flushed cheeks burning the more.

"Y-you should get going, Ray is w-waiting" I audibly gulped, waiting for his response.

He looked me over before his eyes came back to mine, "Put on a shirt and come down"

With that he left and I fell to my knees, steadying my breathing. My emotions were all over the place, I needed to get a grip and fast. I pulled on a cropped hoodie, discarding my sweat shirt in the laundry basket before I strolled my way out of my room and down the elevator.

I walked in on the two men seated in the living room having what looked like an argument? I couldn't really tell but they hushed down once I came closer.

I fiddled with my hands, "Did I miss something?"

"Not really Jess, just some work related topics. I'll be on my way then" he turned, gazing at Damon before looking back at me. "I'll call you"

With that he walked into the elevator and was gone.
I turned to see Damon refusing to meet my gaze as he played with his rings.
He stood up with a sigh and walked out, leaving me confused and worried.

Ray just came and he was leaving already. Something didn't feel right about the past events and I didn't like it one bit. Something smells fishy.

# Jasmine

I stroll down the hallway, not really paying close attention to my surroundings.
My eyes clued intently to the words in my book. I pushed open the kitchen door and walked inside, only for a foreign mixture of floral and vanilla scent to waft through the air, invading my nostrils.

I look up from my book to lock eyes with a pair of jade cat eyes staring back at me. I inhaled sharply at the welcoming and homey feeling they held. I felt a pang on my heart at the heart warming smile that graced her face, softening her features.

"Hi darling" the strange beautiful woman shone her pearly white role of teeth at me. Her light brown locks were tied into a low ponytail, her curtain bangs gracing her beautiful youthful face.
I felt my chest tightening, she looked a lot like mom.

"Hey" I all but squeaked out, awkwardly playing with the cover of my book.

"Te-". We both turned our heads to the door where Damon walked in. He stopped midway when his eyes landed on the woman in front of me. "Mother?"

"Hi honey" she chirps sweetly, walking up to Damon and pulling him into a hug. He bent to hug her properly with a rather hysterical expression on her face

That beautiful woman was his mother?

He pulls away, narrowing his eyes at her. "What are you doing here mother" he asks stoically, his tone rather serious.

"I wanted to come visit, is that a crime? " she batted her eyelashes at him innocently, earning a raised brow from Damon. She huffed, rolling her eyes "Ugh, I've been so lonely " she whined pouting up at Damon.

I could have sworn she looked so cute with her puppy dog-like eyes but Damon didn't seem fazed, instead his stare hardened as he narrowed his gaze at her. I could see that behind his hard glare was concern and worry for his mother.
I watched this mother and son in amusement. He definitely took her eyes and most of her features but her light and bubbly attitude definitely wasn't one of them.

"I also wanted to spend time with your wife" she beamed, walking over to me and throwing her arm over my shoulder "She's a pretty one. I always knew you had a thing for brunettes" she smirked

He groaned, pinching the bridge of his nose in annoyance "Mother..." he whined?
"You are supposed to be back home resting and not here playing mother in law"

She brought her hands to her sides, cocking her hips "Oh don't be such a spoilsport I'm fine" she turned to me, a small smile covering her face "is he always such a stick in the ass?"

"Yeah" I chuckled lightly and she joined in. I gaze at Damon to see him watching me, a simple smile on his face as he shook his head at us.

I felt my heart stop at how gorgeous he looked.

"Now come on, it's been a while since I've made something with my own hands so let's get started"

I blinked at Damon's mom as she rounded the island, stopping at the cupboards to pile out different ingredients one after the other on the marble counter.
"You two have fun then, I'll be in my study-"
"Not so fast Damon" his mom cut in, making him furrow his brows at her.

"You're helping"

"No, I have work to do" he explained, shifting his weight uncomfortably

"You're helping" she said in an end of topic tone and he groaned walking up beside me and watching over my shoulder as his mom proceeded to lay out more things.
"Wanna help Jasmine?"

I snapped out of my daze. Nodding at her I mirror her small smile, not wanting to come off as stuck up and rude.

Sincerely, it wasn't all that bad. We had just pushed the last pan of cookies into the oven when I was hauling over in laughter, clutching my stomach hard. Genuine laughter this time.
I was gasping for air while she chuckled on the barstool where she sat picking at a sweet wrapper.

"He always had quite the imagination as a kid" she had a distant look in her eyes like she was remembering all the memories of little Damon as a small smile graced her features.

She sighs, "But he had to grow up so fast" she shut her eyes regretfully "When his dad left he was never the same, his dad was already hardly ever there for him but when he left it was like the dam broke and he was never the same"

I hadn't really known her but for a short while when we talked while baking it felt like I'd known her forever and we were just reuniting. She flowed so well with me no matter how reluctant I was to react, she opened me up and it wasn't really hard to talk to her. I didn't feel cautious or wary that she would turn me down or judge me. She accepted me already as part of hers. She trusted me enough to tell me all these things and for someone like me who saw emotion as being vulnerable, her showing me hers only made me adore her more than I already did.

# Jasmine

"Cookies are ready!" She announced, beaming as she slid the trays out of the oven with mittens covering her hands.

She dropped them on the island and I couldn't help but smile as the smell of chocolate chip cookies and cinnamon wafted through the air, making my mouth water.
Tears blurred my vision at the familiarity, I'd been in this position so many times with mom baking the cookies.

I sighed, blinking my tears away, not willing to let them spill and come off as weak to Darcy. Damon had earlier slipped away and we were so caught up talking that we didn't even notice. She reached for one and I held her hand back "They're really hot" I reminded her and she scoffed. Swatting my hand away she took a piece and threw it in her hands, continuing to juggle with it as she hissed when the cookie came in contact with her hands every time.

She threw it into her mouth and shut her eyes tight, waiting for a few seconds till the burning stopped before she huffed out a breath of air.

"It's delicious" she cheered, humming excitedly to herself.

I just gaped at her with wide eyes. "What?" She asked defensively once she saw my face. "It's tastier when it's hot" she winked at me. "Want some?" She looked back at me and I smiled nodding.

I held one in my hand and felt more tears pricking the corner of my eyes as I looked over the cookie in hand. I laughed awkwardly as I sniffled a little, not being able to hold back my tears.

"What's wrong darling?" her face was laced with worry as she looked me over for any injuries.

She wrapped her hands around me, pulling me into a tight hug. I melted into her embrace feeling all my feelings come pouring down.

"I-its just my mom used to make these for me a-as a kid and I missed them s-"

I couldn't even complete my words as my chest tightened and I cried more into the crook of her neck. She didn't say anything but continued to draw big circles on my back soothingly.
We remained in that position as I tried to gather myself again but her scent made it even worse for me to control my emotions.
Everything about her- the warmth she emitted to her scent, everything reminded me of mom and I couldn't hold back my emotions.

I sniffled, pulling away from her hold "I'm sorry, i-its just lost it and"

She stopped me midway, pulled me into another hug "it's fine dear, feel free to vent and cry whenever you'd like. You keep too many things bottled up and I can tell you are really reluctant to let yourself feel things but trust me, everyone needs it from time to time"
She ran her hands up and down my bag as she spoke calmingly into my ear.

"Now come on let's pack up these cookies so Damon can't get his hands on any" she winked at me as I pulled away sniffling.

I was thankful she didn't press me for questions concerning mom. I wasn't ready to open up just yet but I felt safe with her

We packed the cookies into transparent glass containers. "Come on, we're dropping them in my kitchen. Damon can get really funny when he wants something" she chuckled to herself as we carried the jars to her suite

As we walked through the elevator and down her hallway I let my mind wonder where it always seemed to be drifting to... Damon. Darcy made me wonder how Damon really was on the inside, he seemed like he had this wall built up that no one could penetrate and she made it clear he was not always like this, so I was left wondering what could have changed him. Don't get me wrong he wasn't awful or horrible. He was just really distant and closed off. Especially with me these past few days, he'd hardly ever talk when he walked into where I was, he was always in his study or in his room or the gym, but we never bumped into each other no matter how frequently I went there.

He was clearly avoiding me and somehow it hurt. I couldn't help but think it was because of Ray and what happened when he walked into us, but there was nothing between Ray and I, we were best friends and that was it. I felt the urge to go and clarify things with him but always convinced myself against it as we were just married for only 6 months and it was all a ruse for my protection.
But even at that I felt a pang at my heart each time we locked eyes and he looked away from me.

"Thanks dear" she smiled at me as we reached her kitchen.

Her suite was a beautiful combination of a Royal Blue shade and cream. I gawked at the hallways as we passed and her kitchen was even more gorgeous and lavish.

"It's okay, the cookies were lovely" I smiled back at her as we walked in, dropping the jars in a cupboard. "It's so beautiful here"

"Yeah" she hummed looking around herself "Damon loves spoiling me" she smiled lightly as she turned back to me, taking my hands in

hers "I want you and Damon to come over for dinner" she announced smiling from ear to ear
"I want us to eat as a family"

I flinched at the word family but covered it with a small smile for her sake "Okay, I'll tell him"

"It's going to be so much fun!" She beamed walking over to the cupboard as she looked over her ingredients which I guess she brought here along with her. "I have enough to carry us for the next few weeks but we'll have to go shopping soon" she turned to me, the same face splitting smile on her face. "Girls day out?"

I smiled lovingly at her as she shot me a cheeky look before stalking back to me "Tell him it's by 8 and he shouldn't be late or else I'll pull his ears" she smiled grimly. "Oh and if you want you could stop by early and give me a hand. I loved baking with you so much I would love if you help cook dinner too"

I stared into her jade eyes that looked like they were pleading with me "Sure" I gave in, feeling my heart warm up as another cute smile graced her features. "See you then" she cheered as I walked out of her kitchen.

I stepped out of the elevator to see Damon leaning against the wall in front of me. He had his hands in the pocket of his sweat pants and he looked up at me through his thick eyelashes and that act alone sent my heart racing "Y-your mom says we should come from dinner tomorrow and-". His hair was in its natural messy glory and the thin layer of his white round neck flushed shamelessly against his perfectly sculpted body.

"She doesn't want me to be late" he finished for me, a small smile taking over his lips.

"Yeah" I studied his features as he pinched the bridge of his nose "You don't seem pretty glad about Darcy being here"

He sighed, "I'm not" he walked to the sofa and plopped down.

I followed his lead and sat carefully beside him, a wave of concern washed over me as I watched him drop his head in his hands "I want to take care of her. I left her to live with my cousin, I wanted her to rest and live her old age in peace, she's been through a lot" he looked into my eyes and I could see those vibrant emerald green eyes of his had gone dull, their look made a knot form in my chest "She just doesn't want to listen to me and take it easy" he sighed again, running a hand down his face

"I don't know Darcy as well as you do, but I have stayed a while with her and I know she will find more than enough peace here with you" I began, placing my hand over his comfortingly "She loves you and wants to spend time with you. I know you want to give her all she can ever want but I think what she wants is to really be with you, so please grant her that much" I smiled at him as he stared deeply into my dark orbs.

I felt the heat rising to my cheeks as he came closer and closer to me. Our faces were only inches away when I uncomfortably shifted backwards, breaking the moment. "Um... I'm going to call it a night then" I stood up and was about to leave when his voice came from behind me.

"Good night tesoro" he spoke so closely to my ear I felt a shiver run down my spine at his tone. I turned to watch him walk past me to the elevator.

# Jasmine

"Dice them well Jasmine!" Darcy all but yelled, throwing me a side glare from her position behind the pot she stirred.

I shivered at her strict tone. She was a beast in the kitchen, you could call her a perfectionist. She loved her things precisely and to the letter. "I am Darcy, gosh!" I exclaimed, chuckling after once I saw her eyes narrow into a glare.

"Are you laughing at my cooking instructions" she dared, glaring daggers at the side of my head

"Oh hell no, why would I? " I lied, feigning innocence, snickering quietly. I almost yelped when I felt something strong being thrown at my arm.
I stared wide eyed at the said ball of onion on the floor next to my leg. I stared shocked from the ball of onion to Darcy who looked at me with an evil grin on her face. "Did you just throw a ball of onion at me?"

"Oh hell no, why would i?" She grinned at me and I felt the sudden urge to mess up what she had told me to do, but as if reading my mind, she sent me another glare and I straightened up to continue my dicing.

I had taken her offer and stopped by her place earlier so I could help her get dinner ready. We spent hours reviewing what she wanted us to have and I remember gawking at the three course meal she selected. I doubt I could make a proper meal and here she was offering a three course meal.This woman was definitely something else, but I didn't want to disappoint her so I played along and it actually turned out better than I expected. Every moment with her seemed to fly by quickly and soon enough we were done.

I walked into the dining hall with the stack of plates and I helped to line them on the table according to her instructions. I was awed at how coordinated she was and how precisely she liked her things. Don't get me wrong I wasn't a messy person or anything, I just didn't tend to freak out when things weren't perfect but Darcy most certainly did. But honestly I found it cute. Strange.

We finished setting up but Damon hadn't arrived yet. "Your husband is so tarty"she commented, rolling her eyes in annoyance. "At least I hope you learnt how to make the main dish, it's his favorite. You could use it to bribe him to get you stuff" she winked at me and I felt the blood rising to my cheeks.

Did she really not know the basis of Damon and my relationship? Was she really not aware we were only together for another 4 months and after that I would be out of the city. I felt a tug at my heart thinking of Darcy's reaction when she'd eventually find out that Damon and I don't do the......things normal couples do. I doubt I'd be able to handle a scowl from her. But Damon should have informed her about our situation. I felt a wave of guilt wash over me, she may stop talking to me once she finds out or even worse, hate me.

My thoughts were interrupted when the dining hall doors came flying open and Damon strolled in. He had on his normal white t-shirt and his black blazer was hanging on his forearm. His shirt flushed shamelessly against his beautiful body and I felt the blood rushing to my cheeks once more as I gaped at his glory. He didn't have his tie on so I knew he had stopped by his suit to drop it off. The first three buttons of his shirt were undone, leaving a patch of slightly tanned skin spilling out.
He stopped midway when his eyes landed on his mother's scowling face. "10 minutes Damon, 10" she seethed, rolling her eyes and scoffing

"I'm sorry " he soothed, walking over to her and planting a kiss on her cheek, making her smile and blush like a high school girl. I just felt a smile covering my features at the scene, my heart squeezed watching them. For some reason I was happy Damon looked in better spirits today, maybe it had something to do with our talk last night. I had never seen him so.... should I say cheerful?
Yes we had moments where he wasn't always stoic or serious but he was on a role.

"Fine fine" she swatted his face away, turning to me. "Don't make your wife jealous now" she winked at me.

I looked up to find Damon staring intently at me before he walked over to the dining table. I was about to pull out my seat when a hand latched onto it, startling me. I almost jumped as Damon's figure appeared behind me, his breath tickling the hairs on my neck and I could feel the heat radiating off him as he stared at my face.
"Sit tesoro " he spoke slowly into my ear and I felt myself involuntarily shudder at his deep tone. He pulled out the chair for me and I meekly took a seat, fiddling awkwardly with my fingers as more blood rushed to my cheeks and ears. "Thank you" I whispered and he smiled before going over to take his seat.

I raised the fork to my mouth and I felt a bomb explode in my mouth once I bit down on the piece of steak. It was like a burst of flavors dancing with my taste buds as I moaned lightly, enjoying the sweetness that enveloped my mouth. "Oh my gosh, it's so good" I spoke with my mouth full, immediately feeling embarrassed once I noticed Darcy and Damon staring hysterically at me. The blood rushed to my cheeks as I bowed my head low.
From the corner of my eyes I could see Damon in his seat that was at the far left, he was picking at his lower lip, staring at me.

Darcy chuckled,"Thank you Jasmine" she smiled at me and I returned her gesture, still feeling my cheeks burning.

The rest of the dinner went silently, with Damon stealing glances at me and Darcy making little conversations. We finished up before bed time and I helped clean up while Damon remained in the dining room.

"Thanks for dinner Darcy" I smiled at her, giving her a side hug. "Also thanks for the tips" I winked at her, giving Damon a side glance as he uncomfortably shifted his weight. If I didn't know better, I would say he was... nervous??

"You could stop by for breakfast if you'd like then we can go shopping!!" She shrieked, beaming like a little kid. I smiled at her cuteness as we both directed our gazes to Damon, silently asking for his permission.

He sighs, shaking his head at us. "You two behave like if I refused you'd listen" he raised a brow, waiting for our response

"Well, at least appreciate that we asked" I shrugged, turning to Darcy who was watching us with a sheepish grin on her face.

"You didn't ask" he raised an accusing brow at me, pursing his lips.

I shrugged, walking out "At least you know where we'll be" I heard his mother snicker as I rounded her hallway "Good night Darcy! See you tomorrow!" I yelled as I speed walked to the elevator, ready to ignore Damon.

The doors of the elevator slid closed and I sighed in relief, knowing that I won't have to face him tonight. I squeaked when a hand interrupted the door's collision. The doors were pushed open and Damon stepped in, towering over my small frame.
The elevator door pinged and closed as we started going upwards.

I felt the air around me becoming thicker as his eyes travelled from my eyes to my lips and he bit down on his. His adam's apple moved up and down as his pupils dilated continuously, drifting from an algae hue to a dark emerald green. I stared breathlessly into his eyes, getting lost in their green depths and deep mists. My chest rose and fell as I tried to control my breathing and keep myself under control.

I blinked continuously like a doll as I chewed on my lips, feeling the blood rushing to my cheeks at our close proximity. The heat radiating off of him was making me want nothing more than to pull him close and feel his body against mine. My hormones were all over the place and I couldn't believe the thoughts running through my mind. I wanted to run my hands all over his body, through his big hands and down his toned abs.

His fingers caressed my sides as he placed a calloused hand over my head, trapping me between him and the cold elevator wall. He looked down at me with lustful eyes as he pressed his body against mine. Keeping in mind I had nothing under my oversized hoodie. His hard chest against my skin made me moan at the pressure. He trailed kisses from my jawline to the meeting point of my collar bone

and finally the soft spot under my ear, making me shiver. His hand gripped my hips, pressing my body closer to his, so there was no space left between us. He continued to kiss down my neck as my breaths came out labored.
"If you want me to stop tesoro" he began, nibbling on my ear lobe and I gasped. "Just say the word" he purred into my ear and I could feel myself going into overdrive.

Just then light spilled through the doors of the elevator as they slid open slowly. Damon must have realized I was breathless as he pulled away, panting as well. He brought his thumb in contact with my cheek, using the pad of his thumb to carefully caress my cheek and I couldn't help but lean into his touch. His rough but soft and gentle touch. It was like a trance as we stared deeply into each other's eyes, the algae hue of his staring into my dark ones.

"Jess?" I heard Ray's voice as he rounded the corner, stopping as he took in our position.

I had scurried over to the other end of the elevator with ragged breaths as my cheeks flushed with embarrassment. My hair was messier than how it was before our little... um... Act.

I smiled at him, "Hey" I tried to hold back my panting as he looked me over with a narrowed gaze.

"Hey...." he drawled, looking over at Damon who was also acting a little strange. I tried to hold back the laugh that threatened to spill from my lips.

He threw me one last glance before he walked out of the elevator, leaving Ray and I awkwardly watching each other. I still had my fake smile on, hoping it was enough to convince Ray.
He walked in and stood next to me, "You okay Jess?" He asked, looking at me with worry knitted at his brows

I waved him off, "Peachy!" I shrieked, throwing my mouth shut when I heard myself.
Oh geez was I this bad at composing myself!??
"I'm fine Ray. What are you doing here?" I asked, trying to direct the attention away from me.

"Oh, I found a way to report directly to Damon at home. That way I'd get to see you more often" he smiled down at me and I returned the smile, feeling happy I had gotten my best friend back.

"That's great!" I threw my arms around his neck, embracing him. "So! We start tomorrow after I get back from shopping with Darcy. Or if you'd like you could come with us, I'm sure she wouldn't mind" I offered, smiling hopefully at him as I pulled away.

"Are you kidding, hell no!" He exclaimed grimacing. "There is no way I'm following two females to go shopping, to see you selecting out dresses" he feigned a heart attack and I punched him. "Owwww" he whined.

"Oh shut up" I rolled my eyes and smiled.


# Jasmine


I padded down the stairs, grumbling under my breath as my lower abdomen aches.
I had found out why my hormones were acting up, I was on my period. I hated those things and it didn't help that I got them every month, but this one was a real piece of work.

I walked into the elevator, ignoring the dull ache at my lower abdomen. I wasn't going to let it stop Darcy and I from having a nice girl's day out.
I popped a few bars of chocolate into my mouth on my way down. I found the sweet burst of flavor in my mouth calming. The elevator

doors slid open and I began my journey through Darcy's suite. I crossed her living room and stopped when I spotted Ray, Richelle and Damon seated there, perched on the side of her couch. They were speaking in hushed tones and I couldn't help but let my curiosity get the better of me. I sneaked around and stood with my back against the cobalt blue pillar that was situated just a few feet away from where Damon, Richelle and Ray were.
"How's it going?" Damon asked, scanning a pile of documents in his hands.

"It's going great sir" Richelle began handing him another file. "Once every lawyer heard that he'd be going up against the most impressive team of attorney's in the city they backed out. Especially when it's head on with the best of the best" she spoke proudly, pumping her chest out and dusting off invisible dust from her shoulders.

"The court hearing is in a few days" Ray chimed in. "And I can assure you that he wouldn't be able to get himself together enough to come to the hearing, talk less of getting himself a replacement lawyer. He has backed down" he scoffed with a wide grin appearing on his face. "His business is already suffering huge losses and all of his investors are pulling out at a rapid rate. He will be too distracted to plan any moves' ' he leaned back, crossing his hands behind his head. "We got this in the bag"

"Gr-"

Damon began, but the sound of Darcy walking in interrupted him mid-sentence. I sighed and stepped out of my place behind the pillar. Pretending I had just arrived now I put on a small smile on my face to make it extra convincing.

"Did we miss something?" I asked, looking around to see the three people exchanging glances between Darcy and I.

"Of course not" Ray lied getting up and walking over to where we stood. He hugged Darcy and pecked her cheek. "It's been a while Wonder Woman. What have you been up to?" He winked at her and she pulled his nose, making him whine

"Oh nothing much," she waved him off turning to me. "You look so pretty Jess" she smiled and I felt the blood rush to my cheeks as everyone turned their attention to me once again.

I didn't think much of the blue fitted sundress I had on. I was too grumpy to really think much into my dressing so the compliment really struck a nerve.

"Of course she looks pretty Darcy" Richelle supported, walking over to me and throwing an arm over my shoulder. "After all she is Damon's wife" she winked at me and my face turned scarlet.

My eyes went wide at the realization. Richelle knew all along about the contract, I was stupid to think she didn't. She was the lead attorney of the Empire so of course she'd know about a transaction like this. From the corner of my eyes I could see Ray uncomfortably shift in his weight as he stared back at me. He probably didn't know until now and I felt a wave of guilt wash over me. We had been so close and I didn't tell him something so important. He must be mad at me or even hurt. I gazed away, feeling horrible that I didn't make it my duty to tell him.

I elbowed Richelle in the ribs and she hissed retreating her hands from my shoulder. "You knew!" I whispered yelled

"Of course I knew. I had known about the idea before you did silly things. Who do you think drafted the contract" she laughed awkwardly when I didn't match her playful tone. "Hey look at the bright side you have nothing to lose. I'd say it's a win win situation"

"You didn't tell Ray?" I whispered, feeling his lingering eyes on me.

"What? oh shit" she cursed, scratching the back of her head. "It was an open secret really so it wasn't my fault he didn't figure it out sooner. Besides you two really don't do a good job hiding you're" she cleared her throat "bonding sessions"

I felt all the blood rush to my cheeks and ears, making me look like a tomato. I groaned and covered my face with my palms.

"Don't worry your secret's safe with me till I get bored of it" she snickered in my ear and I glared at her through my palms.

"Shall we Jess?" Darcy's voice came, cutting my embarrassment short.

I nodded and followed her out of the room. But a familiar hand stopped me by my wrist. I turned to find Damon was holding onto my hand.

"Tesoro, I need you to please watch over my mother. She can get a little..." he pursed his lips thinking of the right words and I just gaped at him.

"A little wild, I know. Don't worry she'll be fine. I'll take care of her" I assured giving him a small smile as I walked off to meet Darcy in the elevator, feeling a pair of eyes on me as I did.

# Jasmine

We walked through the revolving doors of the mall. Goosebumps spread across my skin at the change in temperature. The place was what the outside read, lavish and pristine. The inside was a beautiful combination of white and gold, the marbled floors and walls made the place look extravagant.
I felt extremely underdressed and conscious of the staring eyes that were directed at me. I gulped down, feeling my throat being extremely dry.

Darcy gestured towards a row of white plush couches and we plopped down. She placed a careful hand on my knee, stopping it from bobbing up and down.


"Don't worry Jasmine, no one is looking at you" she assured, rubbing calming circles on my knees with the pad of her thumb.

I visibly calmed down, smiling back at her, "Thank you. Who are we waiting for? " I asked, my eyebrows knitted in confusion as I looked around.

"I think that's me" a calm voice came from above us and I looked up to see a beautiful woman standing above us with a straight pouting face. Darcy and I walked over to her and a small smile played on her face.

She had gorgeous straight black hair and she looks like a model from out of this world. Her high cheekbones, big plum lips were coated with red lipstick that made her pale complexion pop. "Hello Tailor" Darcy smiled at the lady-Tailor who returned her smile but the cold look in her eyes could be seen from a mile away, telling you her smile was fake.

"Hey Darcy. Please follow me" she waved us over as she started walking into an unknown direction.
Her cold dead Hazel eyes held a lot of pain behind them and I could tell there was a very sad story hiding in her icy gaze.

I felt my heart drop to my feet as I rummaged through my bag while we walked. "I forgot my wallet Darcy, I don't know how we'd pay"

"Oh don't worry" she waved me off. "Damon owns this place" she smiled, looking on.

I felt my mouth drop open. I took in my surroundings and to say I was dumbfounded would be an understatement. The beautiful marbled walls and floors, the multiple rooms we passed and rows and rows of shops displaying nothing but designer clothes. The countless elevators moving up and down throughout the mall made me dizzy.

All this was Damon's!!?
No freaking way!
My mouth was still hanging open after a while so I closed it and regained my composure.
We walked through a few more halls before stopping at a closed room
"Please wait here and change into the robes folded, you will he attended to shortly" with that Tailor left.

I nodded to Darcy and pushed the door open to see the most beautiful room I'd ever laid eyes on. Everywhere was stunningly decorated with flowers and other floral imprints that ran up the walls. Uv lights spilled a combination of purple, pink and yellow hues all over the room, giving it that calm and subtle aura.

I inhaled deeply, smiling to myself as the mix of different floral scents and oils wafted through the air. The place felt like it was on another planet as we stepped inside.

Darcy and I exchanged shocked looks. We spotted our robes nearly folded and kept on a marble step. I picked one and handed the other to Darcy who gave me a crazed look when she unfolded it. "Um... I haven't been to one of these and I know we are supposed to have a place to change"

I nodded and looked around. I spotted a room going to the back and pointed at it for Darcy to go in the first hole I waited for her.

While she changed I took the liberty of looking around the room. I only now spotted two four poster beds situated at the edges of the room. I felt the urge to jump on them and drift right off to sleep but I held back. As if on cue Darcy waked out all changed into her robe. She folded her clothes and dropped them on the same place we took the robes. I went in next and quickly changed, feeling weird that I had to pull my clothes. I walked out and found two men standing at the head of the beds. I looked at Darcy to see her staring wide eyed at me.

"Just calm down ladies, we're here to give you massages" the one with mocha skin spoke, rubbing his hands together. I gulped down hard, exchanging looks with Darcy.

The one with lighter skin smiled at me and I could see his dimples on full display. They were both hot men, don't get me wrong but compared to Damon they didn't have a chance.

I shook my head, embarrassed at my own thoughts. Did I just compare strangers to Damon!!??
I was definitely losing it, the heat here was getting to me.

"W-what are you guys going to do to us?" I asked, clearly shaking.

"Oh don't worry, we are massages. We help unlock and free the joints, giving you free movements" he informed, smiling sweetly at me. "Oh don't worry, it doesn't hurt that much" he assured me, noticing my panicked expression.

The other guy gave us more information and we felt better about attempting something so scary. We laid down as they instructed. I felt the heat rush to my cheeks as he placed his hand strategically on my body. He pressed a few places and I screamed once I heard a popping noise. "Oh my gosh!" I heard Darcy exclaim. "What was that!?"

*****

I signed as we walked down another path, carrying bags of what we bought. I felt like a noodle in soup and it made me smile. Other than that I was having a great time with Darcy. We both made our way through the mall, just window shopping as we didn't want to buy anything. Darcy asked a number of times if I wanted to get some clothes but I dismissed her immediately. I didn't want to come off as a gold digger and I didn't like any of the things they had on sale.

Darcy left me to go greet an old friend of hers so I used the chance to gawk at a pretty dress I spotted a while back. It was too extravagant to wear anywhere so I just took in all its glory for the last time before walking away to find Darcy.
It was a gorgeous dinner gown. It was a stunning maroon colour, with long beautiful sleeves with gorgeous studs all over it. The long slit that ran up the thigh made it look even more elegant, the off shoulder was deep revealing some cleavage.

I walked back to find Darcy on the phone talking slowly to someone. Once I neared she put down the phone and smiled strangely at me.

"How was your friend? Did I miss them?"

"Yes you did. Don't worry you'd meet them pretty soon but for now come on let's go get something to eat" as if on cue my stomach grumbled and my cheeks flushed a bright ting

# Jasmine

Groaning, I fell on my bed. Sighing when my tired limbs hit the soft and smooth sheets.

Darcy and I had a very long girl's day out and now all I wanted to do was crawl into bed and sleep till the gods of dreams wake me up. I was walking to the bathroom when fatigue took over me and I just had to lay down. After finding Darcy we ended up getting a few makeup things for me- which Darcy insisted I get.

I sat up, wincing when my body felt like it had been pulled through the entire year. I used my claw pin to throw my hair into one of its signature messy buns. Throwing my feet to the other side of the bed, I pushed myself up and walked over to the bathroom. Sliding off my current clothes I climbed into the bathtub. A satisfying sigh left my lips once my skin hit the hot water. I sunk deeper into the tub, submerging both my hair and face. I stayed there for a few minutes, letting my mind run wild. It drifted to Damon. He always found a way to leave me breathless but I still couldn't understand why each time it happened. If it was anyone else, I doubt I'd be okay with it.

So why him? Why was he different?
Why did my body seem to react to him?
Why did my body respond so eagerly to his touches?
And most importantly why did my heart squeeze whenever I saw him worrying or looking out for his mother?
All these thoughts were swarming through my mind like bees in a honeycomb. I decided to push the thoughts aside for now and get some well-deserved rest.

Sliding into my lace silk nightwear I was glad I'd gotten it over with. Now time for some sleep! Darcy didn't organize another dinner. We were both too worn out by the time we got back home a few minutes ago.

I heard a monotonous knock on my room door and I stopped. Sitting up I stared intently at the door, wondering who it could be by…... I turned my head to my wall clock to see it read 11:23pm. But this time?
I reluctantly walked over to my door and pulled it open.


**NEXT DAY…**


Pushing myself on the barstool I rested my hands on the island marble, worrying knitting my brows together.  Who could have dropped that box in front of my room last night? Darcy strolled towards me with two plates of our breakfast and I was brought out of my reverie.

"You seem occupied dear" she noticed, sliding me a plate of bacon, eggs and toast. "Something on your mind" she sipped on her coffee, pushing herself into the barstool in front of me.

I picked at my lips, wondering whether or not I should tell her about the mysterious box I found outside my room last night. It was just there sitting in front of my door, no name, nothing. Just a white box with a gold lace wrapped around it. Believe it or not I didn't let my curiosity run wild this time. Until now I hadn't opened the box. Call me crazy but I imagined the worst things could be waiting to jump me from that box. Yep I was definitely losing it. "It's nothing Darcy" I lied, lowering my gaze to the food in front of me.

"If you say so" she shrugged, giving me a knowing smile that I couldn't help but read more meaning into. "Damon didn't join us for breakfast?" She asked. I could hear the disappointment in her tone and I sighed deeply, having to be the one to break the information to her.

"Well Damon" I began, fiddling with my hands. "He went on a business trip yesterday and won't be back for another two days" as the words left my lips I could see Darcy's face dropping and her smile falter.

"He couldn't tell me that himself?"
The sad look in her eyes made my heart squeeze.

"He'll be back soon Darcy. Don't worry I'm sure he didn't want to see you sad" I comforted her, squeezing her hand slightly in mine. I also didn't understand why he just had to leave.

It was at the last minute he'd told me about his little trip and I was furious he didn't inform Darcy about it. I'd given him an ear full for the first time but I let him go because I understood his point of view too. Perhaps it was an unplanned trip.

She sighs, giving my hand a light squeeze, "Thank you Jasmine. I'll be fine " she smiled and continued eating.

I was at least glad she wasn't all too upset. We finished our breakfast and I washed up the dishes before coming back to meet Darcy at the lounge room. She had already gotten popped corn and a couple cans of soda ready for us.
She noticed my presence and turned, her face was a mixture of content and a cheeky smile played on her lips.

"Movie?" She asked, gesturing to the big screen.
I simply smiled and nodded. I made my way to her side, dropping down on the couch. She pushed some snacks in my hands and we hushed down as the movie started.
I had never watched the movie before.
It was Thor Ragnarok.

I watched Darcy closely, admiring the way her smile lit up her whole face. How close we had gotten and then it dawned on me that I'd soon lose her. Either by the 4 months is over or by the revelation of Damon and my relationship wasn't what she thought it was.

I picked at my lips feeling awkward.

I had to tell her we weren't a normal couple soon, so why not now. "Umm Darcy?" I called out as she turned back to look at me. "Damon and I aren't a normal couple. W-we got married over a contract that'll be invalid in the next 4 months" as the words came out of my mouth I felt a weight being lifted off my shoulders but at the same time I felt my palms become sweaty as I anticipated Darcy's reply and reaction.

She smiled and hung her head low, shaking it, "Oh Jasmine" she began, chuckling lowly to herself. "I knew about your relationship way before I came here. Why do you think I'm still here? I see the way my son looks at you, the way you two act around each other. You'll be a fool not to realize it"

I looked at her strangely, like she was speaking a foreign language. "I don't understand" my eyebrows were knitted in confusion

"Don't worry dear" she waved me off. "You'll have to realize it yourself but until then I'm here if you want to vent. When you do realize it you'll know and want to scream it to the woke world. You don't realize it yet because you don't feel like you deserve it" she turned, taking my hand in hers. "You deserve it all Jasmine. I don't know what made you feel that you need to keep your cards close to your chest at all times but I can assure you that you deserve happiness and you will get it. Just stop resisting it"

I was speechless. She just smiled and turned back to the television. I couldn't concentrate on the movie anymore.

# CHAPTER TEN

Jasmine

I sighed, resting my head back and taking in the calming feel of the evening breeze gliding against my skin.

It calmed my insides as I watched the sky. It had a dark hue and it looked like it was going to rain anytime soon, hence the calm and cold breeze that blew through my air, carrying my hair along with it.
Running a hand through my hair for the first time in my life I felt at peace. I had the bad feeling it wasn't going to last and I would be a fool to think it would. But what Darcy told me had struck a nerve and I decided to leave my sperm donor aside and just live life right now.

What did that entail?
I had no idea. But I was open to anything that came my way and I chose to tackle it with an open mind. My mind wandered off to the box that was dropped at my door yesterday. I was tempted to open it and when I did I was speechless. Inside the box carefully folded was the elegant red dress I was gawking at at the mall. After admiring the dress, I carefully kept it back in the box. Maybe it was a mistake. Who would have sent it to me? And it was the exact same dress I was admiring, but how??

Could it have been Darcy?
No way,  we left the mall at the same time and if she'd bought it I would've known. Who else would it have been then? Could it be some creepy stalker!? Was someone stalking me and keeping a close eye on me? I shivered at the thought.

Sitting up I looked around, feeling paranoia pinching at my skin.

I felt like the air was becoming thicker the more I thought about it. Thanks a lot for my over-thinking. I got up, feeling anxious. I made my way into the house, ending my little moment of bliss. I stumbled down the elevator to my suit. I didn't feel like making myself a burden to Darcy. I walked into my room only to find Darcy sitting at my bed. I walked further into the room, stopping a few feet away from her.

"This dress is so gorgeous Jasmine" she smiled, looking over the fabric

"I know. But I have no idea who bought it and how it ended up here" I confessed, my eyebrows furrowed.

"Hmmm," she hummed, seemingly deep in thought."Well, don't let it go to waste now. Go put it on let me see how you look in it" Darcy pushed the dress into my hands and I gaped at her. Was she serious?
"Go on" she encouraged, nudging me to the bathroom.

I reluctantly walked in. Feeling uncomfortable with trying on a dress like this. Don't get me wrong, it was absolutely stunning. Breathtaking even but I doubt I'd be able to pull off a dress like this. It was beautiful, lavish and glamorous. I had never worn a dress so eye-catching before.
I sucked in a deep breath and slipped into the dress. The smooth satin material felt devilishly good against my skin. I secured it around my body, my cleavage spilling out. Making sure the zipper was well in place before walking out. During my whole struggle I had to remove my claw pin, so my thick chestnut hair was flowing down my back in its natural waves.

"I don't think it's good on me-".

"It's gorgeous, " Darcy squeaked, literally running over to me. She pulled me in front of my full frame mirror.
I looked at my reflection and I couldn't help but smile as I admired the dress. It was seriously stunning. The dress clung greedily to my body, hugging my curves and my assets boldly.

"Come on sit" Darcy pushed me down into my vanity chair. She held onto my shoulders as we both stared at my reflection in the mirror. The little bulbs that surrounded the frame of my mirror brightly illuminated my face.
"You look absolutely gorgeous Jasmine" she complimented me and I blushed a little, lowering my head. 'Come on let's add some make-up"

I looked up at her in confusion. Worry knitting my brows. "Make up?" I asked.

She bit down on her lower lip, lost in thought, "ummm. Yeah makeup" she smiled awkwardly at me and I knew something was up. "Fine" she deflated.
"There's a surprise waiting so just play along"

I stared at her weirdly as she proceeded to cover my face with minimal makeup. I was never one to use too much makeup but I was pretty content with the work Darcy did to my face. It was very little, consisting of only eye liner, mascara, lip gloss, concealer and foundation. I was still confused; the dress, the makeup and everything. But I had to wait and see what Darcy was planning. She finished my look with a devilishly stunning set of jewelry; gold teardrop earrings, matching necklace and bracelet.

"Put on some shoes and come down" she whispered to me and with that she left.
Observing myself in the mirror I still felt something was up. The pit in my stomach kept growing and nervousness pinched at my skin. I felt a wave of uneasiness wash over me as I looked my dress over. I sighed, sliding on my nude stilettos and padding down the stairs to the living room in my suite.

Arriving at the bottom, I felt my cheeks flush when my eyes landed on Damon. He and Darcy were standing in the living room. Darcy had a huge grin on her face while Damon looked like he'd seen some treasure of some sort. I watched as his eyes travelled up and down my body, the look in his algae gaze unmissable. My face burned with embarrassment as I looked everywhere but at him.

"You look ravishing tesoro" his smooth velvet voice purred, making me shudder unknowingly. He took long strides towards me. Picking my hand, he placed soft kisses at the tip of my knuckles, making my face burn even more. I looked into his eyes trying to detect any hint of a lie but all I could see was sincerity and a hint of something else I couldn't decipher.

Darcy just watched the scene with that same sheepish grin. I was so confused. Damon had on an Armani suit, the cufflinks on them dripping with wealth, but that wasn't what caught my eyes. What caught my eyes was his blazer. It was the same color of my dress and that only meant one thing. Damon was the one who bought the dress from the mall. Does that mean he was following me?

"You two look so great together" Darcy cooed, bringing me out of my reverie. She held in her hands a camera. An actual camera. My eyes widened as she took a shot, a blinding flash invading my vision. Making me see stars. I shook it off, momentarily feeling dizzy. She took the picture as it slid out of the thin slot. She waved it off and smiled to herself, "This is going in the frame" she squealed.

"Frame?" I asked furrowing my brows.

"She keeps empty frames everywhere in her room. For what she calls "picture worthy moments" " Damon filled me in and I couldn't help the small smile that stretched at my lips. "Shall we tesoro?" Damon brought out a hand and I slid mine into his.

I couldn't deny how dangerously alluring I found him. His bed head looked extra ruffled today and his stubble was neat and smooth. I was tempted to run my hands down his chiseled jaw. His algae eyes twinkled with a hint of mischief and admiration. Admiration for me.

He walked me to the elevator and once the doors closed I felt my curiosity creeping in, "Damon?" I called out to him, making him turn to me.

"Yes tesoro?"

"Where are we going? And it was you who dropped this dress at my door wasn't it?"

A smirk covered his lips, "Are you really asking for my answer? I feel like you already know the answer to that question tesoro".

I picked at my lips, feeling uneasy, " At least can I know where we're going?"

"A party. Black Empire is hosting a party for our closest associates and as my wife" he gazed down at me and I could see something glisten in his eyes. "You are obliged to attend as well"

A wave of uneasiness washed over me as I felt my chest tighten, "P-party? Full of rich high class people!? " I shrieked, nervously fiddling with my hands, feeling them become moist.

Damon turned to me, worried about washing over his features as he took in my state, "Something wrong tesoro?"

"I can't be seen at such a party!" I began, my eyes wide. "I don't even look the part and now I'm going to be in the midst of the high and mightiest in the city looking like this"

Freaking out was an understatement. I was in full on panic mode. The air was becoming tight and it was like I couldn't breathe. I felt a large hand snake around my waist and I was pulled into someone's chest. I opened my tight squeezed eyes and gazed up, I was met with a pair of algae eyes, staring deeply into my dark chocolate ones. I felt my  pulse quicken as his eyes momentarily drifted to my lips and back to my eyes. His hand held firmly onto my waist, pulling my body flushed against his. My hands gripped onto his broad shoulders on reflection. His hard chest was forced against my breasts.

"You are part of the highest and mightiest tesoro " his smooth, deep baritone spoke into my ear. "You look like a queen. My queen and anyone there would frail in comparison to your beauty". The sincerity his eyes held made my heart melt. The blood rushed to my ears and cheeks as he pulled me impossibly closer and crashed his lips against mine. A gasp escaped my lips as he molded onto mine. My eyes fluttered closed and I kissed him back. The kiss sent fireworks erupting all over my body as our lips moved in sync. He bit my bottom lip and I gasped, a moan escaping my parted lips. He slid his tongue into my mouth, making me moan out as pleasure racked my whole body. It was like our tongues were molded together as I slid my hands into his hair, gently tugging at his curls. He moaned into my mouth making me arc my body against his, wanting more. His hand moved down to the slit that ran up my thighs and he began caressing my open thigh as my skin burnt under his touch. It was like fire erupted all over my skin as the heat rose in me.

Damon pulled away, sensing I was out of breath. He stared deeply into my eyes, bringing his hand to caress my cheeks. I was panting badly, my flushed cheeks red and glossy. My lip gloss was smeared all over his lips and mine. I held back a giggle at the sight; his messy hair, red swollen lips.
His eyes were a mixture of content and an emotion I could understand as he placed a lingering kiss on my forehead before pulling away from me, my cheeks coloring at his display of affection. I stared at him, still shocked at my boldness. I had just kissed him back. My cheeks flushed at the thought and I couldn't bring my gaze to meet his.

"Sir?"
I turned to see the driver standing at the elevator's parted doors and my cheeks bleached scarlet once again at the thought that he'd seen us making out.

# Jasmine

I spent most of the ride thinking and watching as we passed by cars and very tall buildings, going deep into the heart of the city where most renowned people resided. Damon's house was more of at the outskirts of the city, it was considerably secluded away from the hustling and bustling of the city. I admired how he liked his privacy.

Giving him side glances I couldn't help but watch his face. Under the moonlight it glistened, outlining his jaw line, pink plump lips and pointed nose and lastly his gorgeous emerald green eyes. In the moonlights others would look pale but his tanned skin looked radiant under the gentle glow of the crescent moon.

I felt a wave of uneasiness wash over me as reality dawned. I was on my way to a party of the highest of people. Me. Once a personal assistant and now the wife of the infamous billionaire Damon Black.

*"You are part of the highest and mightiest tesoro"'*
*"You look like a queen. My queen and anyone there would frail in comparison to your beauty".* His words played in my head like a song on repeat as I felt my cheeks flush again. The way he pulled me close and claimed my lips. Everything replayed like it didn't just happen hours ago.

I shook my head, trying to subdue the color of my cheeks and focus on the now. I was so engrossed in my thoughts that I didn't realize the car had come to a stop and the door had been softly opened. I turned to see Damon had his hand held out for me to take. I hesitantly exchanged glances from his hand to his face. He gave me a small nod and I slid my hands into his. I let him pull me out of the car, thanking him softly as he patiently watched me gather my dress.
I stared up at him to find him gazing down at me, a look of longing and deep emotions pooling in his eyes. His algae eyes twinkled with an indecipherable emotion. A small smile had cracked his lips,

making him appear much less menacing and more adorable and boyish as a few strands of his dark hair came framing his forehead finishing his look.

It didn't take a genius to see the clear look of happiness in his eyes, brightening the dark green hue to a light warm one. They were as clear as day even under the soft mood light. He was unmistakably happy I was here. Despite his melancholy state he seemed ever so alluring with his perfect smile and the eyes that had me transfixed. Pulling me in all the more I stared into them.

The cool evening breeze glided across my skin, sweeping my hair into the wind. I giggled as the cool air settled against my skin, continuously blowing my hair into my face as I battled to get it down. I felt a warmth like no other engulf me as a calloused hand wrapped around my waist, pulling me to a strong chest. I gazed up through my thick lashes to see Damon staring adoringly at me. He traced a finger down the side of my face, tucking a few stray curls behind my ear. His touch was ever so gentle, leaving goosebumps rising all over my skin as my cheeks bleached scarlet.
He let me go only enough to stumble to his side, where his arm snaked protectively around my waist. He rubbed calming circles at my side with the pad of his thumb.

"Don't worry tesoro. If you start feeling uncomfortable just tell me and we'll be out of there in a matter of seconds" he smiled reassuringly at me and I nodded at him, biting down on my lip. I didn't really know how to respond to this side of him.

He was showing so much affection and care that it made me flustered and unable to respond most of the time.
With his hands at the small of my back he steered me to the entrance of the building, where two bulky and intimidating looking men stood, hands behind their backs. As we walked up the stairs to them they both gave a curt nod at Damon, recognizing our presence. Damon had puffed his chest, standing out in his full length, his stoic expression back on. A contrast to the tender and affectionate side I'd seen a few seconds ago. Here he was the boss. A rich business tycoon. The sole owner of the biggest empire in the city. He wasn't Damon, right now he was Mr. Blackwood and I his wife.

We strolled in as the men pulled the grand roof high wood doors open. "You'll be fine, stay close to me but be free to associate. When I need you I'll call for you but if you need me just call and I'll come running" he smiled down at me, throwing me one last wink before he stared straight on, his neutral face coming back.

I gulped down the lump in my throat as the crowd and expensive aura smacked me in the face.
It was like déjà vu. The waiters ran up and down with trays in their hands, napkins perfectly hoisted at a 90° angle on their upper arms. Soft instrumentals soothed through the air, slightly soothing my nerves. Instruments like violin, saxophone, and many others could be heard through the distinct melodic sound. The place looked like some sort of ballroom from fairy tales but more grand. The tall wood roofs and roof night windows added to the grandeur of the ballroom.

A huge chandelier was positioned at the center of the Hall, light bouncing off, creating rays all over the room. The gold lining on the walls was dripping with expense and various paintings of what looked like babies in scarves filled the walls, giving off a heavenly aura. A spiral flight of stairs stood in the middle of the room, demarcating the two floors of the event Hall. I gawked at the expensive couches and fixtures that were littered all over the Hall. The white cushions make everything seem all the classier. I felt the bile rise in my throat, the extravagance making me sick.

"The place is packed" I whispered more to myself looking everywhere wide eyed at the many humans crowding each corner, more filling through the doors. I felt a lump forming in my throat as I gulped down hard, a wave of nervousness washing over me.

"Come sit tesoro" Damon must have sensed my uneasiness as he guided me to a nearby couch where I sat, the soft sofa dipping. He bent down to whisper into my ear, "I'm going to greet some people, join me when you feel better". He pulled away to stare into my eyes before placing a lingering kiss on my cheek, making them flush a bright tinge. Watching his back retreat I felt a presence beside me. Turning I watched wide eyed as a blonde girl, with eyes as blue as the ocean stared back at me. I adjusted away, feeling uncomfortable as she continued to watch me intensely.

"ummmm" I drawled, looking around for any sign of suspicion, or maybe she was lost or something. "Can I help you?" I asked, raising a brow at her.

"You are here with Damon right?" She batted her lashes at me. A hint of mischief hidden deep in her baby blue stare, and something else making me uneasy. "Damon Black?" She explained when I didn't respond.

I started getting up. The look in her eyes is a different tone from the unnerving smile on her face. I immediately started scanning the place for Damon. Her face held a calm and composed look while that of her eyes was a wild and dangerous flare, almost like a predator. Her gaze had something dark and sinister burning deep within it.

"Don't get your panties into a bunch" she started getting up. She came so close her nose was almost touching minc, invading my personal space making my breathing go haywire. "I know you are here with my Damon and let me tell you, he is mine. Don't get the foolish idea he'll ever fall for you bitch" she seethed, looking me up and down, judgement as clear as day in her blue gaze.

She was really pretty, gorgeous even. The black body con dress she wore showed off everything. The deep v neck of the dress had her cleavage spilling out, it was disgusting. She looked like she was going for a wedding with the amount of makeup she had on. Her dark dress is a beautiful contrast from her pale skin and vibrant ethereal eyes.

"He's been mine from the start and mine he'll always be" she smiled again, her gaze travelling downy body till it landed on the necklace I had on. "Oh Darcy must have given you this" she scoffed, her tone holding a slight mocking to it. "She must think you're the one. Don't let her fool you sugar. You will never stand a chance with Damon so stop dreaming". She came so close to whisper, "Oh and one more thing. This dress makes you look like a slut so do us all a favor and go back to the hellhole you came out of"

That was the last straw. I felt myself shaking with anger as it spread to my fingertips. I glared at her as she pulled away, the deceptive smile wearing her lips again. I pulled her in by her arm so her ear was directly at my lips. "Anyone ever told you jealousy isn't a good color on you?" I smiled when I saw a frown replace her smile. "And for your information it's Mrs. Jasmine Blackwood to you" I pushed her back enough to see the smirk on my face. "And I doubt my husband would appreciate your tone, bitch. So let me give you some advice" I moved closer, stroking her arm. "Never in your miserable god forsaken life ever call my husband yours or I promise it'll be the last name you utter. And if you don't want to be dragged out of here by those pretty extensions of yours then I suggest you walk away with the little excuse of a dignity you think you have intact" I growled, my eyes daring her to speak another word.

I pulled back, satisfaction washing over me at the deep frown that married her face. Her eyes held shock and anger. She scowled at me before walking off, trying her best to look good with her excuse of a hip sway. I rolled my eyes and turned around only to bump into someone's hard chest. I pulled away and looked up into a pair of mesmerising green eyes. They held a glint of amusement and pride.

"Are you done with your greetings?" I asked, biting down on my lip trying to take his mind off what he may have just heard and or seen.

A smile covered his lips, making my heart skip a beat. "My my Mrs. Black, I didn't know you had fangs that could bite that hard" he teased, snaking his hand around my waist as we began walking.

I rolled my eyes at his antics, a small smile forming its way at my lips, "I don't have fangs" I pouted

"You certainly do my wife" I felt a warm feeling enveloping me in his words. The way he called my wife made my stomach turn. "That's the first person that has been able to put Alisha in her place. Congrats " he cheered winking at me.

We walked over to a group of men all in expensive looking suits. Some looked ancient and others looked as young as Damon. I glanced around the halls, hearing giggles erupting from a particular place. My eyes landed on a group of ladies at a place giggling and smiling as they looked over at Damon and I. I just looked forward as we came to a halt.

"Mrs. Blackwood nice to meet you" a man with pepper hair spoke, his deep Irish accent unmissable. He brought my hands to his lips and gave my knuckles a lingering kiss before I pulled my hand back, smiling awkwardly. "Wow Mr. Back she's a real beauty. Looking forward to seeing more from you two in the future"

I smiled. Looking down at my feet. The future struck a nerve. There won't be a future for Damon and I, we had only 4 months left as a couple and after that the contract would be terminated. I felt a pang on my heart at the thought of having to leave everything and move away forever. But it was how it was meant to go. Right?

"So the saying is correct" a spout looking man with a deep Italian accent spoke, his words coming out groggy. "Behind every great man stands a woman. And may I say this one takes the cake" he smirked at me, making me uneasy as I scooted closer to Damon's side. I could feel his hands tightening around me on instinct.

"Please Mr. Giovanni. Let's talk business shall we?" Damon interrupted, bringing all their attention away from me and back to him. He had his stoic face back on and I couldn't deny how attractive I found it.
"I'll meet you later tesoro" he whispered into my ear and I nodded. I excused myself from the group of men and walked off. To where? I had no idea. All I knew was that I had to go somewhere to calm my nerves as soon as possible. It felt like I was suffocating here. My anxiety was acting up as panic kept rising in me. As I passed people kept stealing glances at me. Some were kind enough to look at me and look away while others, not so much as they just gawked at me like I was some alien.

I admit I wasn't blending in well with high society but hey couldn't they act like I wasn't here. Prude much. I felt a wave of relief wash over me as a familiar frame stood close to the bar, leaning against its marble chatting with the rather handsome bartender. I rushed over and immediately crashed into Richelle, throwing my hands around her neck. "Richelle!" I exclaimed, sighing deeply. "At least there's someone here I know" I pulled back to see a huge grin on her face as she looked at me.

"Babe you look hot" she bit down on her lip as emphasis and I rolled my eyes at her. "I'm sure Damon must be tripping so hard". This

time I smacked her arm, staring daggers at her and she waved me over to sit at the barstools.
"You look stressed" she observed watching me intently as she took a sip from her wine glass.

"Of course I'm stressed" I admitted blowing out the puff of air from my cheeks. "The last time I was at one of these I got drugged and assaulted so of course I'm anxious. The lavish everything is making me sick" I gagged, shaking my head.

"Okay you need to calm down" she soothed, rubbing calming circles on the back of my hand that rested on the cool marble counter.
"Hey" she called out and the handsome guy in a suit and a bow tie came out. He wore a boyish smile as a white cloth hung from his shoulder. I'm pretty sure that without that napkin on his shoulder you wouldn't be able to tell he was a barrister.
"Please get my friend a drink" Richelle smiled, glancing my way for approval and I nodded back at her.

"Coming right up beautiful ladies" he winked at us before turning to make our drinks.

"By the way everyone is really enthusiastic about you and Damon as a couple"

"Yeah" I smiled awkwardly. "Some more than others," I retorted. The bartender turned around, carrying a wine glass full of blue liquid.

"Your order" he smiled, dropping the cup graciously in front of me.

I picked it, staring strangely at the blue liquid swirling in the cup. I looked at Richelle and he gave me an encouraging nod. Bringing the cup to my lips I shut my eyes tight as the liquid slid down my throat. A burning sensation settled at my throat and I grumbled glaring at Richelle but soon the burning subsided and only a sweet, ginger taste was left lingering in my mouth. I hummed, smiling at Richelle.
"Tastes good"

"Told you so!"

And that's how the night started. Richelle and I chatted, catching up while we downed several cups of our drinks. I felt myself calming down once I reached the fifth cup. My shoulders and muscles had relaxed and I felt myself becoming quieter and calmer. I felt woozy as I slouched in my position, my body swooning, struggling to stay still.

# Richelle

"You know what, give me another cup" Jasmine slurred, giggling soon after while the bartender excused himself.

I watched in amusement as she struggled to keep still on her seat. The bartender came back seconds later with another cup and she downed it in a matter of seconds.

"Another!" She whined and the bartender went back for another. "Richelle I feel funny" she burped, giggling moments after. "Funny" she spelt out using her hands to count each word in the air.

My cheeks were about to burst with laughter as I watched her. Just then she shot up, getting off the barstool almost stumbling as she did. I had to jump off my seat and hold onto her. Okay this isn't good. I looked around for Damon but I couldn't see him in sight. He would chop off my head if he found Jasmine in such a state. I had to get her sober ASAP.

"Jasmine, I want you to sit here and not move, okay?" I spoke, hoping my slow and calm words would plead with her reasoning. She nodded frantically and I smiled, content I had gotten some progress. I hoisted her onto the barstool and set off to find Damon, putting the bartender in charge of her, hoping she wouldn't give him a very hard time.

Walking around aimlessly I searched top to bottom for Damon but no sight of him. It was like he had disappeared now that I needed him.

# Damon

Gazing around I searched for my tesoro everywhere but she was nowhere to be seen. I already craved her skin against mine, her chocolate pools that held a childish innocence as she stared at me through long thick eyelashes. Her pouty cherry lips that protrude every time I made her angry or teased her. Her flushed cheeks that colored anytime I expressed my emotions to her.

I couldn't hold back the grin that twitched at my lips at the memory; I bent, placing a lingering kiss on my tesoro's sweet cheeks, they flushed a bright pink tinge as she peaked up at me through those pretty eyes of hers.

Her sweet scent that engulfed me every single time I held her close. It was silly how I found every little opportunity to be close to my tesoro, every chance I got I'd hold her in my arms. Feeling her velvet smooth skin against mine.

How she smiled every time she cooked with mother. I'd stay at the door and watch her move ever so freely around the kitchen. Dreaming that one day she'll be in my kitchen, both of us moving around whipping up something for us and the kids to eat. It was pathetic how every time she'd smile at me I'd feel my knees going weak, wanting to buckle underneath me. This woman had no idea how she had stolen my heart. My soul, body, money everything belonged to her and she didn't even know it. Just from mere words if she'd command I'd lay down my life for her. Not able to withstand the pleading look in her gaze I'd obey her every wish willingly just to keep her smiling. That beautiful smile that stretched her cherry plum lips.

And her laugh. I felt my heart swell every single time I heard the melodic chime of her laughter. And when she touched me, whether by mistake or intentional I'd almost stumble at the contact. I'd think spending so much time with her would lessen my feelings but boy was I wrong. I found myself falling deeper and deeper in love with her. If I could call it love, love wasn't one sided; it wasn't selfish enough to trap the one you loved in a contract marriage. I felt my heart drop every time the thought of her leaving me crossed my mind. I couldn't help but wonder if she'd still leave me after everything. Why wouldn't she?
She had no reason to stay.
Someone as beautiful and as magnificent as her wouldn't want to be trapped with me. She'd want to be free and I'd be selfish to ask her to stay with me forever. Like I'd dream about; her in my arms, waking up to her beautiful face, her bed hair sprawled all over my pillows. I'd caress her cheeks and kiss her good morning and she'd respond groggily. She would scold me like she did about mom, whenever I'd make us late to anywhere. She'd look ever so delicate and gracious in nothing but a singlet top and biker shorts, her hair in a messy bun. She'd been my obsession for so long and now she was more than that, growing into something more than I'd want to admit to myself.
To have her reciprocate the untold feelings I had for her, to have her look at me with a swirl of emotions so strong I'd melt.

Having no idea if my advances were not clear enough to her was killing me. I needed to know if I'd made any impact on her or if I'd still failed in my mission to make her mine and make her see that she'd always be mine and me hers.
The way she addressed me as her husband made me go haywire, watching her defend me, her and our relationship had my heart doing backflips. I wanted nothing more than to hold her and beg her to tell me she meant every word she'd uttered. Make her confess to

me she loved me like she did her. I loved her, every fiber, every atom of my being adored her and worshipped the ground she walked on, but sadly I didn't know if she even liked me, I don't even know how she felt towards me.

The way she kissed me back in the elevator left me breathless. My insides are screaming for more. The sweet taste of her lips never left my mouth and my mind, how she pulled at my hair, pulling me closer to her. The way her body flushed against mine, every curve of hers against me. My body craved her touch again, her smooth hairless legs as I caressed them in sensual touches. Devilishly sinful thoughts clouded my mind as I continued to scan the area for my love. My tesoro.

I stopped in my tracks, spotting her at the bar. She was bent over at the counter, rambling to the bartender as he eyed her form. I felt the anger seeping through me, my fingertips shaking as I watched the bartender's eyes continuously travel down her body, hovering above her cleavage, his eyes clouded with lust. I stalked over, my eyes trained at the bastard who was about to have a broken nose.

I stumbled over and was about to pull the douche by his collar when a sweet scent invaded my nostrils. There she stood before me, staring into my eyes with a childish innocence in the pool of her chocolate glaze. She stood there bouncing on the ball of her feet, peeking up at me with an incredulous look on her face.

"Where were you?" she questioned, frowning at me. I had to hold myself from kissing her knitted brows apart. "I've been looking for you and you just left me here" she whined, pouting at me like a meek child.

"Why were you looking for me tesoro?" I asked, amused at the faces she'd been making. I watched her adorable pout twist into a cheeky smile as she grabbed my hand, thuggin me to the bar.

We stopped at the counter, her smile growing bigger, "Damy" she called, making me furrow my brows as a smile curved at my lips. What did she just call me? I stifle a chuckle at her nickname for me. "Meet my new friend Kevin, " she announced, gesturing to the dick face that stood behind the counter, smiling foolishly at my tesoro as she beamed at us. "He's my new friend. And you are my close friend so you two should be besties too" she reasoned, extending our hands so we could have a hand shake.

I played along, putting on a fake smile. I looked into Kevin's eyes and I could see a very foolish glint of mischief in them as he shook my hand with a smirk on his face. I pulled him towards me, making him grunt as his lower abdomen crashed into the counter that separated us. "Get your pretty little self far away from my wife or else you won't leave complete" I seethed, glaring daggers at him as I pulled away enough for him to look into my eyes, hoping he could see the blaze in them. I dusted off his suit as he trembled, flinching back at my touch. "Go" I tricked my head to the side, motioning for him to leave through the back. He nodded almost frantically scurrying to the back, not giving my tesoro a second glance.

I scoffed, turning around to meet my tesoro adorably glaring up at me, her lips stewed in an angry pout. "You just chased my friend away. " she glared at me, making a smile twist at my lips.

"Are you really that upset with me tesoro?" I asked, coming closer to her.

"Yes I am, he was really cute and you scared him off" she said, folding her hands against her chest.

"Oh he was cute?" I asked, staring down at her as she bit on her plum lips rethinking her comment.

"Yes" she said, staring down at my feet. I brought my finger to tick her jaw up so she was staring right into my eyes.

"If he's cute then what am I? What do you think of me tesoro?" I whispered into her ear, pulling away to see her cheeks scarlet as she bit on her lip in a failed attempt to conceal her blush. Using her drunken state to ask her this wouldn't be too bad.

"Damy?" She squeaks, fiddling with her little hands. "Damy. I-i think y-you're really handsome and attractive" she whispered the last words and her cheeks reddened.

I smiled, looking down at her. I pulled her into my chest, wrapping my hands around her waist. A wave of satisfaction washed over me, I finally had her in my arms where she was supposed to be. "Oh so you find me an attractive tesoro, is that so?"
She nodded frantically, biting down on her plum lips. I watched intensely, as she bit down on her lips. I brought my thumb to her lip, trailing the pad of my thumb over her bottom lip, making her release it. "Don't do that tesoro" I whispered so lowly that if she wasn't this close she wouldn't have heard me.

"I won't," she whispered, bobbing her head. I smiled at her childish innocence. "You have very beautiful eyes Damy" she blurted out, chewing on her lips as my eyes widened. A wide grin stretched at my lips at her words.

"Damon?" I heard a familiar voice from above me, breaking my gaze from my tesoro. I looked up to find Richelle staring at me, her breathing unsteady. "Y-you found Jasmine" she observed, laughing awkwardly.

I pulled back from my tesoro glaring at Richelle. No one else would have gotten my love drunk other than her. "You got Jasmine drunk?" I asked, narrowing my eyes at her.

"See I can explain everything" she started, her hands out in defense. "She was worried and panicking and I wanted to help her calm down so I suggested a drink but she went overboard" she slowed when her eyes met my hard ones. "And I didn't stop her," she whispered, avoiding eye contact with me.

I sighed, looking down at my tesoro as she played with one of my silver cufflinks. "Just tell the driver to bring the car in front. I'll take care of my-Jasmine". Richelle nodded and scurried off on her heels.

I looked back at the angel in my arms and she looked so adorable it seemed illegal for someone to look so innocent. "Ready to go home tesoro?" I asked, flicking her nose. She looked crossed eyed at her nose before rubbing it and pouting up at me with narrowed eyes.

"I don't want to go. I want to dance and have that sugar drink" she beamed, a deep frown replacing her smile when she didn't get an answer. "Fine I'll go but" she stopped, looking around. I brought my ear closer to her lips so she wouldn't have to raise her voice and in a split second she scrambled away from my hold and took off into the crowd. I stared at the place she ran to before I bolted after her. I pushed past the many people who just seemed to crowd me now I was rushing after my tesoro. I spotted her retreating back as she squealed. She noticed me and ran in the other direction, giggling hysterically as I came closer. I stumbled into an open space, frantically looking around but there was no sign of her.

I groaned, running a hand through my hair. This event hall was huge and god knows where my tesoro had gone. From the corner of my eye I saw someone in a red dress just like my tesoro's sneaking to the back of the hall. I took off without rethinking. Stumbling out to the back garden I looked around for her. I walked away from the wood porch and onto the pastures, narrowing my eyes in an attempt to analyze the little hiding spots she could possibly be at. Walking further through the tons of rose bushes, cover trees and shrubs I heard giggling coming from nearby and I knew it was my love. I reduced my pace, taking slow strides towards her form I spotted hiding behind a tree. I came up behind her, watching her adoringly as she peeped through the opposite side, probably attempting to see how clueless I was looking for her. I smiled at her childish mischief, coming closer to her. I cornered her, placing my hands on her hips, pressing my body on hers. Trapping her between myself and the tree. She peaked at me through her long thick eye lashes, her blush increasing as she stared deeply into my eyes.

I watched her melting honey eyes dilating, as they drifted from mine to my lips. I moved in closer, taking slow advances in case she'd want to refuse or push me away, but she didn't. She slid her hands to the back of my neck, pulling me towards her. I connected our lips, sighing in content. I trailed my tongue along her bottom lip asking for access and she moaned, parting her lips and I slid my tongue into her mouth. She settled her hands into my hair, her fingers intertwined with my curls as she tugged, making me moan into the kiss. Our tongues moved in sync, like they were molded together. Meant to be against each other. A burst or pleasure raked through my body as she slid her hands down, gently stroking my shoulders, her nails digging into my back. I allowed my tongue to explore every inch of her mouth. She tasted so sweet, a mixture of mint and something I couldn't decipher. All I could tell was I would never get tired of this taste. I ran my hands down her soft, thick curls, loving the feel in my hands. They were as soft as I'd always thought.

"Damon?"

Her chest rises and falls with the slow rhythm of her heart. I pull her closer to my chest, keeping her warm with the heat my body emits. She unconsciously nuzzles closer to me, wrapping her hands around my shoulders, burying her face into the crook of my neck. I shiver involuntarily at the contact.

Struggling to look away from my tesoro's beautiful face in my arms I almost bumped into a wall. Despite knowing this place from top to bottom I still couldn't concentrate. She looked so beautiful sleeping in my arms. She'd fallen asleep in the car on our way back and I couldn't bring myself to wake her. I didn't want to, she looked so innocent sleeping, light snores erupting from the back of her throat. I hoisted her in my arms and began our journey to my room where she'd sleep today.

Not knowing if she'd be okay in her own room I decided solely that she would sleep in mine. Also just wanting to have her close to me, where I could watch her beautiful face for as long as I wanted. Kicking my room door open I stumbled inside, going straight for the bed. I sat my tesoro down, using a careful hand to adjust the covers so she could lay on the soft velvet sheets... I looked her over. Her hair sprawled across my pillow, her beautiful eyes shut and her body cocooned, folding on herself.

Tucking a strand of her behind her ear I trail my hand across her cheek, loving the feeling of her skin against mine. "What are you doing to me?" I whisper so silently.

Pulling back I bit on my lower lip, feeling awkward about what I was about to do. I couldn't leave her in this dress. She'd feel uncomfortable and I also had to clean off her makeup. I rose from the bed and walked into my closet, stopping at the rack that held my shirts. I picked out a white t-shirt and came back out. Throwing it beside my love I gulped down hard, preparing myself for what I was about to do.

# Jasmine

I cuddled closer to my pillow. It wasn't what I was used to but the smell of this pillow was so intoxicating. It was hard and had lumps but I wasn't complaining. I felt so warm against it I never wanted to get up. Shifting closer and closer I couldn't help but inhale the scent and that's when it hit me. My eyes snapped open and I almost screamed at what I saw. Shooting up I almost fell back at the force I used to push myself away. I calmed down when my eyes met a pair of emerald green ones. They held amusement and a sparkle of content in them.

"Morning beautiful" he smiled at me and I couldn't help the traitorous blush from burning my cheeks. "Someone slept well" he smirked, gesturing to my hair. My eyes widened at his comment and I frantically tried to tame my hair by running my fingers through them while he just laid there watching me. I glared at him, and shrieked when my eyes landed on his bare torso. My hands flew to my face, covering my eyes from his blinding glory. I groaned into my palms picking up a pillow and throwing it at him.

"Put on a shirt or something!" I yelled and he groaned, huffing and throwing it back at me. I brought my hands down and caught it, regretting my actions immediately when my eyes fell on his well sculpted chest and large arms, my cheeks blazed with embarrassment. "Get out of my room Damon!" I yelled, shooing him with my hands. Gosh I just had to wake up with this! What was he doing here anyways?

He cleared his throat, making me glare at him, "You're in my room" he lied raising a brow at me

I looked at him like he was an alien. "How is this you're…. " I confidently started, looking around but my voice disappeared once I took in the dark interior of the room. The dark maroon and black colored bed sheets, the unsettling dark aura surrounding the room. The dark furniture, black walls and dark velvet curtains all screamed Damon in a weird kind of way. I felt all the blood rush to my cheeks and ears when I looked down at what I had on. A white t-shirt two sizes too big that was definitely not my own. I looked back at Damon to see a sheepish grin on his face that had my heart racing, "W-what am I w-wearing" I frown, scared for his reply.

"My T-shirt. I thought white was more of your color" he winked at me getting up and strolling to the door. My eyes twitched in annoyance at his blatant ignorance. I pushed myself off the bed only to shriek and cover my legs when I found I was wearing absolutely nothing under his shirt. No bra, no pants, just my underwear. I stared at him wide eyed and he refused to meet my gaze as he walked out of the room. I bolted out after him, screaming his name to stop and speak but he ignored me. I cursed following closely behind him as he walked down to his kitchen.

I stormed inside, my nose and ears flaring, my cheeks burning with rage. He turned, coming face to face with me and he smiled. His eyes slowly travel down my whole form and come back up to meet my gaze as he bit down on his lower lip. I watched his Adam's apple move up and down and my cheeks burnt at the look in his eyes, the way his algae colored eyes switched to a dark brewing green had my legs going weak, wanting to buckle underneath me. His hand snaked around my waist, pulling my body flushed against his. His eyes held my gaze in a trance. A trance I never wanted to break out of willingly. I got lost in the deep Mist of his dark emerald green eyes, the way they swirled with a pool of strong untold emotions had my heart wanting to melt. They glistened with untold tales and restricted feelings.

Blood rushed to my cheeks as I could feel his hard chest against my breasts. Knowing I didn't wear a bra underneath. I let out a shaky breath, feeling exposed and our close proximity wasn't helping matters. "D-damon let me go" I stuttered, failing in my attempt to sound serious.

"Or else what? I happen to like you in my clothes tesoro " he whispered into my ear, making me shudder. "You look quite sexy without underwear" he purred and I felt my legs turn into jelly as my cheeks burned with embarrassment.

Did he just call me sexy?

"I won't forget how sweet your lips tasted against mine. The way you pulled me in last night, how soft your skin felt against mine. I will never forget". My eyes went wide at his words. I had no memory of last night's events. How I ended up in his room, in his clothes with no freaking underwear. All of it, I came out blank. " How I wanted to claim you last night. Make you mine forever. But make no mistake, I wouldn't do that while you were drunk" he shook his head, his lips grazing my ear lobe making me shiver. "I want you to remember every second, every touch, every sensual stroke, every thrust. How sore you would feel but I won't stop. You will remember it all" his smooth, velvet tone had been replaced with a dark and husky tone, a glint of awaited desire and deep longing hidden in the depths of every vibration that flowed through me at his words.

I was drunk last night and I couldn't remember what happened! Nothing came to mind. His soft lips collided with my jaw, trailing kisses to my neck and back to the thin layer of skin that separated my collar bone,my breath hitched in my throat at his actions. He nibbled and sucked everywhere his lips touched, sending tingles and fire erupting throughout my body. Pleasure raked through my body as I moaned out, not restricting it. My mind was spiralling out of control as he proceeded down the length of my neck, stopping to nibble on my collar bone before coming back up to claim my lips.

He pushed me against the wall, ravishing my lips. The kiss was both passionate and hungry. I matched his energy, sliding my hand into his curls and kissing back with the same force and craving. I craved his lips. Since the last time we'd kissed I so badly wanted to taste the sour sweetness. How good it was to run my hands through his hair, tugging every second. His hands went under my thighs and I jumped, straddling his torso as I wrapped my legs around him. He forced my back against the wall once again, pressing his chest into me. I moaned out again, the excitement getting to me as the heat increased when his fingers dug into the tender skin of my behind, making me arc my body further into his throwing my head back in pleasure. My nails dug into his back making him moan and he continued to kiss down my neck, biting down at every spot he could as I shivered, letting out shaky breaths.

He pulled away. Both of us panting as he brought his forehead against mine, staring deeply into my eyes,"You're not ready. There's hesitation in your every move, in your eyes' ' he spoke, a deep longing and contradicting pain deep in his eyes. "But don't worry, I'll wait for you, my tesoro. I'm not going anywhere. You are mine and I yours so take your time".
He placed a lingering kiss on my forehead before letting me down.

"Breakfast?" He asked, sounding like a totally different person than a few seconds ago. He did so well. The hurt look in his eyes was gone and replaced with a calm and collected one. His dark green eyes had subsided and turned back to their normal algae hue.


"Yeah" I whispered, a small smile spreading across my lips. Tears sprung to my eyes in remembrance of his words but I was not willing to let them fall and sucked it in.

# CHAPTER ELEVEN

## Damon

"Sure sir, I'll call you later" Ray said, cutting the call. I dropped the phone, deflating into my seat. I sighed deeply, fatigue overcoming my sense of work at such a late hour, deciding to put it to rest and continue tomorrow I rose from my seat, packing up my papers and filling them properly.

Silent footsteps padding down my hallway brought me out of my fixated state. I shot my head up, silently listening for the sound again, but it only faded with each passing second. The hairs at the back of my neck stood. What if it was a kidnapper or a robber who'd thought it was a fun night to intrude the Black mansion.

Walking out of my office quietly I made my way through the hallways, careful to look both sides as I headed to where I heard light noises. I arrived down the stairs and stopped, all the blood in my face running cold at the sight. My tensed up muscles relaxed as I watched my tesoro. She was curled up in a ball, her knees held closely to her chest, her head buried into her knees as her shoulders shook violently with each sob that raked through her body. I felt my heart break into a million pieces. She was in one of my black shirts, it was two sizes too big, she also had fluffy socks on and little tights under, I tried not to find the situation cute. She just sat there beside one of the couches, on the floor, trying her best to be non-existent and make as little noise as possible.

I made quiet steps towards her, the sound of her sobs making my heart squeeze as I approached her. I knelt down in front of her, watching her silently cry her eyes out. I couldn't take it anymore and

I pulled her hands away, they were wrapped tightly around her legs and it made my insides turn the more as I took in her disarrayed form. She sniffles, her head rising and my heart clenched to see her pale,tired test stained face, her flushed cheeks, her red nose and eyelashes damp with more unshed tears.

I cupped her face, softly wiping at her under eyes with the pad of my thumbs. She didn't react, probably too worn out from all the crying her eye bags revealed she had been doing. She sniffled again, more tears falling freely onto my fingers. I couldn't stand the sight. My love in tears broke my heart all over again. If I just found out who was making her cry I'd make them pay. Without thinking twice I pulled her into my lap, holding onto her small frame.

I hoisted her up in my arm, settling on a nearby couch where I held onto her, allowing both her legs to drape down my left side while I tugged her even closer to my body, hoping I was able to provide a little comfort for my tesoro.
"Love please tell me what's wrong?" I whispered, rubbing calming circles on her back in an attempt to calm her enough to talk to me. "I promise I'll help as much as I can tesoro, so please tell me. Seeing you like this is killing me and I can't do a fucking thing about it".

She continued to cry as she kept mumbling something to herself. I kept quiet, trying to listen to what she was mumbling. "H-he's coming" she mumbled, shaking her head as more tears dribbled down her cheeks. "H-he's going to come back a-and take me back. I don't wanna go Damon please don't let him take me" she pleaded, holding tightly onto my collar, her voice breaking, her once warm brown eyes now full with sorrow and heart wrenching anguish it had me taken aback for a second. The amount of pain and fear I could see in her eyes broke me to the point I almost cried too. I didn't know who she was referring to as 'he' but if it troubled her this much then it must be important. Whether I knew or not I was going to make sure I'd protect her from whoever this 'he' was.

"I promise love, as long as I'm alive and breathing I won't let him come for you. I won't let him take you. You belong here with me and I will fight to my very last breath to keep you safe and here in my arms" I spoke into her hair, listening to her racing heart. My arms tightened around her at the thought of this man coming to take my tesoro away from me. "Don't worry love I'm here for you" I whispered, running my hands through her hair to further soothe her. Her sobs audibly died down, only quiet sniffles erupted from her as we stayed there, in that position, neither of us willing to move. I was satisfied there, with my love in my arms, where I'd protect her till my last dying breath. I'd make sure nothing ever happens to her. I promise.

Whispering more calming words to her I hushed down when I heard cute subtle snores coming from beneath me. I looked down in my arms to see my love, nestled close to me, fisting my shirt tightly in her little fists. Her eyes were lightly shut, her hair a mess. I smiled adoringly at her, despite how tired she looked she was still the most beautiful woman in the world. She was mine, my tesoro and I'd protect her forever.

Gathering her in my arms I walked up to my room and laid her down on my bed. I was about walking out when a small hold tugged me back to her. She laid there, eyes tightly shut, her brows were knitted together in angst, she held onto my wrist, silently begging me not to leave her side. And if my love wanted me beside her then that's where I'd be. I laid down beside her, careful not to make any sudden movements and disturb her much needed slumber. Once I laid down beside her she cuddled up to me, throwing a hand to pull her in closer to my chest, her head resting softly on my chest. It took me a few seconds but when I came out of my shock I wrapped my arms around her, pulling her to me further than she already was.

She snuggled closer to the crook of my neck and let out a deep breath of satisfaction, it made a smile twist at my lips that she found my scent comforting. I stroked her sides, wishing upon whatever higher being there was that she would always remain here with me. I'd wake up to this face first thing in the morning and sleep with it in my arms after a tired day. I just couldn't lose her, if there was someone out there who threatened her safety I had to find out who, why and where this person is currently. I'd make it my mission.

# Jasmine

"Come love, talk to me" he pleads, his eyes reflecting despair and sadness, a much greater sadness than mine.
I sighed, refusing to meet his gaze, he brought a hand beneath my jaw, nudging my face so he could have a good look at me. "You scared me so much last night. Since you woke up you haven't spoken to me. You haven't even told me what made you cry, it's killing me tesoro" I could hear the trouble in his voice, it broke my heart. But it wouldn't compare to the pain I'd feel if my dream came true. It just couldn't come true. It just can't. He sighed, deflating. He pulled me into his chest, wrapping his hands around my waist, I exhaled deeply, gently throwing my hands around his neck, nestling into his warmth. His hands held onto my much smaller form, pressing me comfortingly against his larger one.

It was hard to tell where I ended and where he began but I didn't want to move from this position. This was where I was meant to be, in his arms. I was unsure for how long but I'd be damned if I didn't cherish every second I got to spend with him. I never knew when it'd be my last and I dreaded it every single time it crossed my mind. I buried my head into the crook of his neck, inhaling his scent. I sighed satisfied. His touch, his ever so intoxicating scent, everything about him brought comfort to me. I don't know what Damon Blackwood exactly spelt the word comfort but it's what I had become accustomed to.

This big, scary, business man had become my safety blanket. I would be cocooned in his arms forever if I had the chance. But forever was a promise I wasn't sure I could commit to. It was an enchantment that meant for life, a bond and a desire so deep that coursed through our veins, the way we held each other close, we knew we'd want each other, forever, as long as we'd live but forever came at what cost? Neither of us were looking for the other but yet faith decided we needed to meet, and we did.

She played her cards well and we ended up here. In each other's embrace. Our deep untold desires consuming each other, our unscathed longing for one another growing with each second. It was a cruel game she was playing; a game that meant we'd die without each other. A game of possession, I was his, he always made that clear, but now he was mine too, but no matter how I tried to he would never be mine because his ethereal being, his very existence belonged to no one.

I was tied up, by chains binding me to the cold damp floor I had grown so used to. I almost gagged, the smell of old blood and debris filled my nostrils. He hadn't bothered to clean here.

Why would he?

It was where he liked to come and gloat about his new…. Toys. I'd be the first he'd try them on before he added them to his collection. He called them toys, I called them the very sick reminder of who I was and what I'd always be.

This time was different, this time we weren't in the cellars. I sat there, my legs in a heap beneath me, my limbs numb from my position. There he stood, with the darkness. He never had a problem blending into the darkness, he was one with it, they were so much alike, Opaque, dark, cruel, scary and haunting. He walked into the light that hung above us, coming so close his face couldn't be seen at the angle he stood. I heard the harsh scraping of something against the concrete floors, making me squeeze my eyes shut in hopes that it would stop, it was like my ears were bleeding.

A loud thump sounded, echoing through the deep, hollow room we were in. I looked beneath me, only a few inches away from me and my eyes widened, all the air was knocked out of me at the sight. My blood ran cold and my face went pale, all the colour on my face drained at the horrific scene that played out in front of me. Damon laid there, blood oozing from his freshly opened cuts, his body tied and gagged, his face was indecipherable, but I could recognize him anyway, his hair disarray, his body battered and bruised and he was barely moving. An ear cuddling scream tore through the silence. It was my scream. Tears free fell down my cheeks as my chest tightened, the scene in front of me seeming so horrific it could only be some fucked up joke of some sort.

I whimpered, scooting over to him as much as my tied up body could. I ignored the pain at the back of my head and the still opened slash wounds around my body from the whip lashes. I brought myself as close to him as possible, my eyes already hazy and more tears dribbled down my cheeks.

"This wasn't supposed to happen" I whispered, choking on the air I struggled to inhale. My heart hurt, physically it hurt, I could have avoided this, I should have kept him away from all this. He didn't deserve any of this, it was all my fault. I pushed myself onto my knees, struggling against my restraints to get my hands free but all to no avail. I fell onto my stomach, struggling to rest my head on his chest. My ear to his chest I frantically listened but there was no heartbeat. I stared at his face, it was blue and pale, his green eyes, the one I'd grown so fond of, the calm hue I'd started loving had gone still. His once red plum lips, the ones that tasted so immaculately tantalizing against mine had become chapped and peeled. His once radiating tanned skin had become pale and rusty looking and it hurt to see the deep gashes that were etched in his skin.

I sobbed harder. I could have prevented this if I had just surrendered myself. If I had then he'd still be alive, I'd still be able to see his emerald green eyes maliciously travel down my body, I'd still be able run my hands through his dark curls, I'd still he able to inhale his intoxicating scent, I'd still be able to feel his indescribable warmth surround me and tell me it was all going to be alright even if I knew it wasn't.

I felt myself being pulled away from him and I clawed, I kicked, I tussled , I screamed, "No! Don't take me away from him! No please! Please! Damon!" I shouted hysterically but his body kept fading away till I couldn't see it anymore.

I'd abruptly sat up from bed, panting.
My hands were outstretched in front of me. My breathing was erratic, my heart paste unsteady, my hair clung to my sweet clad forehead.
The scenes from my dream came invading my mind and I literally jumped out of bed. I needed his warmth, his scent around me, I needed his comfort. I ran into my closet, going for the rack of clothes I'd hidden his shirts in. I stopped as I spotted his black shirt, the one he'd worn me on my first day here. I stripped and threw it on immediately and once his scent hit my nostrils I broke down, crying.
I didn't want to leave him,
I didn't want that man to take him away from me,
I wished things were different,
I wished my demons weren't out you get me
I wish I was different
I wish I didn't have this constant fear hovering over me
I wished he could be mine, but at what cost? Certainly not in his life.

This feeling,
This empty feeling I was getting I wish I didn't have. It was indescribable, it was like my life was taken away in a split second and everything happened in front of me and I could have done something but I didn't. I knew this feeling, it was foreign, I never thought I'd get it ever again. I felt hopeless, I felt weak. I had started having hope, after so long I'd hoped my life would be okay, I'd hoped everything would be fine if I'd ignored it and focused on the present, but I wasn't given such a privilege.

# Damon

She wasn't talking to me. My love wasn't speaking to me, she seemed so sad and wouldn't let me go when she'd woken up. She clung to me, not letting me go to work nor get out of bed, I'd had to walk us to the kitchen with her straddling my torso, her head buried in the crook of my neck. I wasn't complaining, I loved having her with me every second but what bothered me was the constant look of fear I could see in her eyes. I'd catch her looking at me while I made us breakfast, momentarily wiping off lone tears that rolled down her cheek, silently sniffling, she wrapped herself up on the counter as she waited for me.

When I'd finished I'd tried my best to soothe her but nothing was working, she just wanted to stay close to me at all times and wasn't even speaking. It was killing me, not hearing her melodic voice, the sweet chime of her laughter, her immaculate smile, her ethereal vibrant dark brown eyes when they'd glint with amusement or laughter. Instead she looked dull, she had eye bags and she looked pale, her hair was a mess and she kept sniffling every second, revealing her secret cries she'd been trying to hide from me. My heart squeezed every time I heard her sniffle, every time her eyes shone with unshed tears and the amount of pain I could see behind her eyes, her dark orbs that were framed by her wet lashes, her flushed cheeks, glossy and red.

I help her close, taking in her scent, her very essence. I ran my hand down the length of her soft hair, rubbing calming circles on her back. We were so close, every curve and crevice flushed against each other.
I froze when I heard silent sniffling again, my tesoro's body shivered as her sobs broke the silence. I pulled away enough to look at her tear stained cheeks, my heart clenching at the sight in front of me. I frowned, deeply disturbed at her fragile state.

I walked us to the lounge, dropping us down on a couch. Pulling her into my lap, her legs draped at each side of my body, straddling my lap. I cupped her face in my hands, tilting her head so I could look at her very well. "Talk to me baby" I whispered, softly wiping away her tears with my thumb. I placed a soft kiss on her forehead, encouraging her to speak to me. I needed her to, I was running crazy at this point.

She sniffled again, bringing her slacked, long sleeves up to her nose to wipe it. She was in my sweater; it was two sizes too big hence the sleeve buried her hand deep.

"I-it's nothing, i-it's just h-had bad dream" she whispered, her voice coming out quiet and coarse, maybe from all the crying she has been doing throughout the morning. I nodded, encouraging her to go on, telling her I was listening. She squeezed her eyes shut, opening them again only for more tears to fall onto my hands, "In the dream" she started, looking away from me. "I lost you, you were lying lifeless in front of me and I lost you. I was taken away from you and I couldn't help you" she sniffles, more tears dribbling down her cheeks.

My heart swelled at the thought
How terrifying it was for her to see me in such a state. "I would never let you die on my watch, I would save you if it meant I would die, I can't let you go" she whispered, shaking her head at the thought of losing me. I sighed and pulled her into my chest, wrapping my hands comfortingly around her small frame. She was upset about losing me?
She cared that much, she was scared of losing me, just as scared as I am to lose her. If it came down to both of us I'd definitely choose her

over me and to know she'd choose myself over her brought a warm feeling to my chest.

I rested my jaw at the top of her head, smiling to myself as I continued to run my fingers through her velvety soft hair, "I promise you will never lose me baby. If it came down to me and you I'd definitely choose you over myself" I regretted my words as her head shot up, her glare so intense it had me gulping thickly, scared daggers would come out of her eyes and stab me. "Sorry tesoro, it would never come to that point don't you worry" I assured her, placing a gentle kiss to her forehead as she lay her head to my chest, snuggling closer like she couldn't get enough of me.

"You won't ever lose me, you belong here in my arms, where I can torture you with as many kisses as possible". She peaked up at me, her face a bright red and I winked, eliciting a scowl from her and I let out a hearty chuckle. "Or I could torture you in some other way"

She furrowed her brows at me, her lips parting to speak but before she could I flipped us around so she could be lying beneath me. I kept my weight off her with my knees, slightly propping myself up. She stared at me wide eyed as I maliciously smirked down at her. I attacked her, tickling her sides as she yelled, breathless giggles erupting from her lips. I continued my torture on her till she was a fit of laughter, roaring and shaking with each laugh that racked her body. I smiled at the beautiful sound reaching my ears. I didn't know when I stopped and was just staring adoringly at her until she had wrapped her legs around my waist and pulled me down to her. She cups my face in her hands connecting our lips. She starts moving her lips softly against mine, a moan escaping her lips as I trail my tongue along her bottom lip, biting down softly and tugging on it.
I ran my hands up and down her sweater clad sides, holding her firm beneath me as I continued my assault on her lips. I gently lick at her bottom lip and she parts them, granting me access. Sliding my tongue into her mouth I tasted every crevice, every inch of her, increasing the intimacy.

I couldn't get enough of her taste, enough of her. I was drowning in her, she was consuming me, the love I had for her was devouring me whole and I didn't mind, I let out a groggy moan as she tugged at my strands, not realising her hands had slipped into my hair. She continued to run her hands through my hair, driving me crazy. I left her lips, trailing kisses down her throat, licking the thin layer of skin that separated her collar bone from her shoulder eliciting a breathless moan from her and she clutched onto my shoulders. I took my lips to her ear where I continue to rain my torture on her soft spot as she shuddered under me, her nails digging into my bare back making me moan as well.

# Jasmine

Every second I spent with him, every time he made me forget the need for oxygen. My brain was spiralling out of control as he continued his rain of torture on my throat, biting and nibbling anywhere his lips touched. Breathless moans escaped my lips without permission as I arched my back against him, wanting to touch every part of him. I ran my hands down to his chest, loving the smooth feel of his skin against my hands. I proceeded to feel every inch of his body, his muscled back, tight abdomen and big arms. My hands itched to have him closer to me, to pull him into me

He stopped at the nape of my neck and licked it, making me shiver, the need for oxygen becoming dire.

"You're so beautiful. I love you" he whispered into my neck and I froze, his breath gliding across my skin. My muscles tensed and I slid my hands down to my sides, away from his body. He must have noticed my sudden stiffness as he pulled away, studying me.

His emerald green eyes crinkled with sincerity, a desire so deep it had my stomach turning, a love so strong it made me breathless. He did love me, he just admitted it but the debt in his eyes told me he had these feelings deep within for a long time. He rolled away, giving me space to prop myself on my elbows. I watched him as he ran a hand through his hair, sighing deeply. When he looked back at me I could see the hurt in his eyes but it was gone with the blink of an eye. He stood, bringing forth a hand for me to hold, I slid my hand into his and he pulled me into his chest, making me crash ungracefully into him. A small yelp left my lips as his hands latched at my waist, holding me tightly to his chest he stared into my eyes, a swirl of emotions glistening in his.

"I do love you Tesoro," he said, making my eyes snap to him. There was no trace of lies or jokes in his eyes, only a deep burning passion as he studied my reaction. "It's not now that I started loving you. From the first day you walked into my office accidentally I knew you were mine, you had to be mine. Your pure ethereal beauty, your effortless innocence stunned me, the brown pool of your eyes kept pulling me in deeper and deeper until I had no escape. For the time you worked with me I had to control myself from taking you with me and never letting you out of my sight, it took the most amount of self control I have ever exercised not to have you in my arms every second. You had no idea

"You still have no idea you own my heart" he confessed, staring at me with such strong emotions it brought tears to my eyes. "You stole my heart and took it along with you everywhere you went, without you I couldn't concentrate, you were always on my mind and when you were with me I found myself unable to look away" he caressed my cheeks with his knuckles, smiling adoringly at me. "You own everything, my body, my money, my mind, all of it belongs solely to you. If you ask I'd give you my fortune, I'd give my life just if you'd ask me to".

He spoke with such depth I was stunned. Damon was never someone I'd think would feel so deeply and hearing he felt so much for me made my heart melt.

" I'd protect you till my last dying breath, I'd save you from the world and anyone who would try to hurt you. I swear to you my love. I never expected you to come into my life, before you I never and I mean never entertained the idea of any serious relationship with any woman" the mention of other women made my fists clench and unclench in anger. He brought his hand down to my balled fist and slid his palm, dissipating my fist and intertwining our fingers.

"But the moment my eyes landed on you I knew you were the one, I knew you'd be the one for me, you were sent to me and I'd be damned if I let you go. I promised to keep you close. This contract was a way to ensure you'd remain with me, we have 3 months left and I don't know how you feel but I was too selfish to keep you with me without asking you. But I promise tesoro, if you still want to leave I won't stop you but please give me the chance to love you till my lungs give out"

He rested his forehead on mine and froze when he saw my teary eyes, "Baby why are you crying?" He panicked, cupping my face and looking me over for any injuries.
"Did I say something?"

"N-no
It's just" I sniffle, gosh I was so tired of crying and I'd been so emotional for the past few days it was tiring. Damon was the only one who managed to bring out so much emotion in me. "You feel so deeply for me, how can you feel for me with such intensity when I can't ensure I'll be able to be yours" I dropped my gaze, rubbing my nose with my sleeves.

"You are mine, you've always been mine, and you will remain mine whether you like it or not you are mine. I would never have it any other way". He sealed his confession connecting our lips. This kiss wasn't hungry or lust driven, it was a kiss with pure emotions, an emotion a man had for a woman. Damon had for me. "I'll make sure anything that keeps you away from me is destroyed. You will always be mine"

I wanted to be his, so badly. I knew I was already; I'd fallen for him so hard it was painful. It hurt because I couldn't risk his life, he would kill Damon if he knew I was in love with him. I couldn't let that happen, even if it meant I wouldn't get to see him ever again, at least I'd know he was still alive.

The pit in my stomach kept growing, an unnerving feeling pinching at my skin. Something was going to happen and I had to prepare. He wasn't so dumb to leave me for so long, he was sick and deranged he could do anything and at any time. We weren't safe.

# Chapter Twelve

## Jasmine

Towel drying my hair I walked out of the bathroom, my towel flushed against my bare body. Tiny droplets made their way to my skin, dripping to the floor as I walked further into my room. I threw my towel aside, walking into my closet I couldn't find what to wear I didn't feel like wearing my usual singlet top and shorts, ever since I'd gotten into Damon's clothes I had a distasteful taste for any of mine. His clothes were drenched in his scent, they were so big, homey and comfortable, my favorite type of clothes.

I groaned, nothing appealed to my new taste of clothes. Sighing I turned away from the closet and walked into my room, sitting frustrated on my bed.

"Tesoro"
My head snapped to the door where Damon walked in, stopping dead in his tracks as his eyes fell on me. In nothing but a towel, my face turned beet red as his eyes travelled down the length of my person, hovering on my legs that were on full display due to the short length of my towel. I swallowed down the lump in my throat, looking everywhere but him. His eyes had turned a dark green and he began stalking towards me seductively, his eyes darting to mine as he covered the distance between us in an unbelievable amount of time. His deep desire and fiery passion was so evident in his gaze it was coming off in waves, making me shiver avoiding his gaze, the intensity getting to me.

Although I was nervous I couldn't move, I was rooted to the ground. He stopped in front of me, studying me, his gaze ran across my face before travelling further down my body. I felt my skin burning under his intense gaze, he licked his lips, scanning me thoroughly before he closed the distance, wrapping his hands around me, eliciting a small yelp from me at the speed in which he used to push me against the wall, towering over me as he placed his hands above my head trapping me between him and the wall. I stared into his eyes wide eyed as he lowered his head to my neck inhaling my scent deeply, "Delicious" he spoke, his voice coming out huskier than usual.

"Jasmine!" I heard Ray call out from behind the door. Panic rose in me, I couldn't let Ray see us like this, I was in a freaking towel! I placed my hand on Damon's chest, attempting to push him away but he instead tightened his grip on me. His nose grazed the bare skin of my throat and I shivered, trying my best to control my breathing which was futile.

"D-damon, R-ray's going to walk in and see us" I spoke breathlessly

"Let him come in, you can warn him if you'd like" he spoke into the crook of my neck before he began trailing kisses down my throat, licking and nibbling on the tender skin. I struggled to keep my breathing in check as I watched the door over his shoulder. Breathless moans escaped my lips as I tried in vain to push him off me all while trying to control the sounds of pleasure that threatened to spill through my lips, my body shivered in delight as he bit my skin and I moaned out. I watched the door open and Ray came through only to turn beet red when his eyes landed on us at the far end of the room, he faltered in his steps, walking backwards as his eyes looked like they were going to pop out of their socket. It was like Damon knew he was watching because what he did next left my cheeks blazing with embarrassment.

He slid his hands down, grabbing my behind and I squeaked, hiding my face in his shoulder squeezing my eyes shut, for a split second I wished the ground would open and swallow me whole. The door slammed and I looked up to see Ray had gone, my face was still scarlet and I was at least thankful Damon was huge enough to cover my towel clad body from Ray's eyes maintaining my little dignity. I pushed against his chest and this time Damon pulled away enough for me to see the smirk on his face and the amused look in his eyes.

"Seriously?" I frowned, pushing past him into my closet glaring daggers over to him.

"You seem angry baby, if I remember exactly you were the one moaning a while back" he responded, and although I wasn't looking at his face I could tell he had a smug smirk on his face making my face bleach red.
I groaned, pulling out one of my cropped hoodies and a pair of bicker shorts and walking out. I was still happy I didn't have to wear most of the clothes Damon had gotten and filled my closet with, I was still keeping to the clothes George brought.

I passed him and was about walking to the bathroom to change when he gripped my hand and pulled me to his hard chest. I glared at him while he smiled amusingly at me, "Oh you look so adorable pouting baby" he teased, flicking my nose with his finger.

"Let me go" I frowned, trying my best to sound intimidating and angry despite the embarrassment I still felt. I would never live that down. "I'll bite you" I snarled, hoping I sounded the least bit intimidating.

"Oh I have a few places to suggest" he teased, bringing his face closer to mine. I just stared at him as my cheeks blazed.
Ugh!

"Get out of my room Damon" I ordered, swatting his face away. Ray didn't deserve that, he was already upset I didn't tell him about Damon and my marriage contract and now he walked in on to see me after many weeks of us not speaking to see this.

"Do you really want me to love you?" He spoke into my ear, his voice coming out a deeper baritone than usual, as his breath tickled my ear lobe I shivered pulling my head back.

"W-what you did to Ray wasn't right Damon " I said looking him straight in the eye hoping he could see I was being serious.

He scoffed, sliding his hands into his pockets letting me go "What part of it wasn't right exactly?" He asked rhetorically, raising a brow at me. "He didn't knock before entering, you are a married woman aren't you? You need your privacy and he should knock next time, I was just teaching that to him" he shrugged nonchalantly making me gape at him.

"But I'm not technically your wife" I spoke quietly looking down at my feet

He didn't like that as he pushed me against the wall, pining my wrist with one hand above my head.  He looked down at me, anger clear in his green gaze as he stared at my wide eyes, "let me make this clear love, you are mine and I am yours. You are my wife, that contract is crap. Even without it you have always been mine so remember that and now you are my wife so if I deem fit I will show that to anyone who ever looks at you ever again" he spoke the truth, his eyes reflecting how serious he was about it. His gaze travelled to my lips and back to my eyes. He brought his free hand to trace my bottom lip slowly pulling it apart when I tried to press them together in angst, "I own these tantalizing lips of yours" his eyes travelled around my face and he brought his knuckles to slowly caress my cheeks as he spoke with so much passion it had my heart leaping, "and your gorgeous face is also mine to adorn and worship, your ethereal beauty, a beauty only worthy enough to be possessed by a queen"

He trailed his fingers down the length of my arm, caressing my cold skin, torturing me with sensual strokes that cheated me up instantly, "Your velvety soft skin, it's intoxicating scent" he brought his nose to my neck inhaling my sent deeply as he continued, "it's all mine" he brought his free hand to cup strands of my hair, running his hand through it, tugging all the nuts out, "your hair, the scent so enticing I wish I could bathe in it forever. All of it is mine and I worship it all"

He gazed into my eyes, a passion so strong it reflected in his gaze, his desire so deep it told a tale so old and pure. He closed the distance, slowly connecting our lips. He moved his lips so passionately against mine, it told me the amount of love he had for me couldn't be measured, his want for me would forever be unquenchable, his desire to have me goes deeper than he can possibly say. It wasn't a hungry kiss, it wasn't rushed, it was just perfect, slow and passionate. I tried to get my hands loose to run them through his curls but his hold on my wrists only tightened telling me he wanted full control here. He pressed his body completely against mine eliciting a moan from me. He pulled away enough to look into my eyes as if asking for permission and I nodded. He grabbed my under thighs and I jumped, wrapping my legs around his torso, straddling him as he held tightly unto my ass making me moan as he connected our lips once again.

He walked us out of the room, not breaking the kiss. I felt us enter the elevator to his suit as he continued his sweet assault on my lips. I should have been worried about Ray or Richelle seeing us if they happened to be on any of the floors but my mind wasn't going there at the time. I was currently in a world of pleasure as Damon bit my lower lip, tugging on it as I gasped, running my hands through his hair, tugging slightly eliciting a moan from him. He started walking again and I was thrown down on his bed. I looked into his eyes, both of us panting, our breathing erratic as the need for air became secondary to our need for each other.

He climbed on top of me, using his hands to hold his weight, enough to hover over me. He raked his eyes down my towel covered form, the look in his eyes if only they could strip me they would have a long time ago. He pressed his lips to the crook of my neck trailing kisses down my throat as his hand travelled down, stopping between my legs. My breath immediately hitched when his hands dipped and began rubbing me roughly. I moaned out, my chest rising and falling as I gripped the sheets trying my best not to lose my mind at the amount of pleasure I got just from the thrust of his fingers into me.

My mind was spiraling out of control as I drifted in and out of consciousness, the pressure building up in my lower abdomen as he increased the paste of his thrusts. My mouth hung open, breathless moans escaping my O shaped lips as my face flushed. He pulled out his fingers and I felt myself calm down, catching my erratic breathing but it was cut short when I spotted him lowering himself, his head dipping between my legs.

Another loud moan escaped my lips as he started teasing me with his tongue, sliding it deep into my clit. My chest rose and fell as I gripped his curls with one hand, my other gripping at the sheets. The pleasure that raked through my body had me arching my back off the bed and my toes curling upward. He pulled out, licking his lips as I watched him drowsily. He crawled up to me, connecting our lips once more, my taste mixed with our lips left a feeling of ecstasy.

# Jasmine

As the soft marshmallow melted in my mouth I groaned, loving the delightful taste on my tongue. My taste buds were dancing with the devilishly tantalizing sugary flavor that burst in my mouth. At this point I should be diabetic, the rate at which I devoured sugar coated sweets and foods would have any normal person worrying but since when was I normal?

I munched down my last packet, grumbling when it finished. I threw it aside, shuffling about to pick my can of whipped cream and spray a swirl in my mouth, humming in content as it melted into my mouth.

I giggled as a shiver raked through my body at the cold temperature of Darcy's room. I'd snuck out here while she went out with Ray to buy some supplies for tomorrow's breakfast. Ray seemed really excited to go push a shopping cart around while Darcy educated him on all the stuff she threw into it. However, he enjoyed it was beyond me but at least I'd gotten her room all to myself.

I grimaced as I took in the condition of her room, already imagining the scolding I was certain to get when she'd come back. Her bed had wraps and wraps of chocolate, gummy bears, marshmallows, cans of soda. I shrugged it off, my gaze fixated on the big screen in front of me.


"Tesoro?" He called out, walking into the room and falling silent.

I turned my head, throwing a marshmallow into my mouth. I blinked at him, watching his eyes take in the state of his mother's room before it landed on me, a small chuckle escaping his lips. He walked over to the bed where I lay comfortably on my belly; at the foot of the bed, a pillow propping up my chin.
He got in beside me, making me sit up to face him, by brown furrowed in confusion.

"You're-" my breath hitched in my throat as he brought his face to mine, startling me so badly I almost fell off the edge. My cheeks flushed as he licked the corner of my lips, pulling away to completely lick my plum lips. I stared at him wide eyed as he pulled back and settled on his knees, staring at me with a smirk on his face, a glint of mischief in his gaze

"At least I know why you like whipped cream so much," he acknowledges, running his tongue across his mouth like he was savoring the taste of my lips. "But I admit I prefer this tasting method better" he spoke looking straight into my wide eyes as I swallowed thickly, my cheeks still blazing.
"Come on we're going out" he announced, sliding off the bed. That was enough to bring me out of my shocked state and I tumbled out of bed too, pausing my show first of course.

"Out?" I asked, making him turn to stare at me, the look in his eyes suddenly making me lose my breath. "I-uh where to?" I blurted out, stuttering like a baboon.

"To get something to eat of course" he called out, walking out of Dacry's room and I followed behind, trying my best to keep up with his long strides.

"What? If you're hungry I can make something" I suggest and he abruptly stops, catching me off guard as he turns swiftly, eyes wide and mouth twisted in a cheeky smile. I stared at him in bewilderment, was he doing okay? A crinkle of excitement sparked in his green eyes, an excitement so childlike I couldn't say no to it.

"You want to make something together?" He asks and I nod without really thinking it through, the childish glow in his eyes had me hypnotized to do his every bidding just to keep that glow. "Come on"

I squealed as he bent beside me, one hand going below my knees and another around my waist as he hoisted me up in his arms, jerking me up as I screamed, throwing my arms around his neck to ensure I didn't fall. Although I knew he would never drop me. "What are you doing?" I asked, staring at his smirking face with wide eyes. "Put me down Damon, I can walk" I protested, tapping his chest lightly for him to let me down but instead he pulled me even closer, tightening his bolt on me as he shook his head in disapproval of my request.

"Not happening, just hold on tight" he winked down at me and I diverted my gaze to the ground, a blush covering my cheeks as he began walking, his eyes fixated on my face.

In no time we'd reached his suite and although I had requested him to drop me since we'd arrived he still declined, insisting on dropping me only when we'd gotten to the kitchen. Kicking the door open, he walked us into the kitchen. I waited for him to put me down but he walked over to the marble counter depositing me there, my legs dangling off the edge. I just blinked up at him, as he positioned himself standing between my now parted legs and his hands resting at my sides, his face only inches away from mine. "How am I supposed to help cook like this?" I asked, my brows furrowed and my mouth stewed in an angry pout.

"Oh that's the thing tesoro, you're not" he said walking away and I opened my mouth to protest but he was already back with a jar of Nutella and a big spoon. He handed it over to me and I took it in my hands, staring confused at his face. "You will help, don't worry my sweet but only after you've finished this jar of your favorite treat" he winked at me and I couldn't help the smile that stretched at my cheeks.

He'd known I loved Nutella? "And I'll make your favorite, breakfast for dinner" he smiled proudly and I couldn't help but giggle at his endearing charms.

"You seriously went to check out all my favorite things just to charm me didn't you?" I asked during fits of giggles.

"Well if that's your way of saying I did a good job then thank you"

"Well get going would you?" I swatted his face away and he glared at me, playfulness twinkling in his eyes as he walked back to the shelves and started filling out ingredients.

I watched him adoringly as he mixed the pancakes batter and turned on the gas like a pro, all the while there was an appreciative smile plastered on my face. He walks up to me, placing his cheek before me, tapping on it to give me a clue on what to do as I stared at it bewildered for a moment before getting the idea and placing a kiss on it. He smiled cheekily before walking off again. I couldn't help but stare at the way his back muscles flexed, tensed and relaxed with every movement he made.

I sighed in content as I dug a spoonful of Nutella and deposited it in my mouth, groaning when the sweet, gooey goodness hit my tongue. I continued to fill my mouth till I had the goodness all over my mouth, littering the corner of my lips. I felt his presence and peaked up away from my jar to see him staring at me, his face so close to mine. I swallowed thickly, biting down on my lower lip.
He moved in closer so his face was barely a hair strand away from mine, he buried his head to the side of my face, licking my lips, every corner, from my top lip to my bottom lip, exaggerating each glide of his tongue against my lips like he was savoring the taste while my

heart thundered in my chest, my cheeks burning a bright tinge at his actions. He pulled away, running his tongue over his lips while he stared at me, "Still my favorite feeding method, ravenous" he spoke, his voice coming out huskier than usual and we both knew he wasn't talking about the Nutella.

# Jasmine

Running my hands on the smooth covers I smiled to myself as I waited patiently for Damon to come out of the bathroom. He'd told me to wait for him after his workout session so we could go get something to eat. I was ecstatic to finally leave the house after so long and I really had a strange liking for take-out food, especially the unhealthy ones.

My cheeks still burnt in remembrance of how hot and sexy he looked while working out. I stole glances at him from the position he'd dropped me, the way his back muscles tensed and stretched as he threw punches at the punching bag continuously, sweat trickling down his forehead from his hair that had stringed into tiny strands due to the amount of sweat his pores had produced. I watched the way his body glistened under the light rays bouncing off his sweat clad torso. I found it interesting how he'd exercise without a shirt on, but I wasn't complaining, I loved the view. His body was really a work of art, something only possessed by the Greek gods themselves, a body so magnificent only the sight made me swallow harshly at how devilishly alluring he was. It was such a sweet torment to my eyes, my hands itched with the craving to run them down his beautiful tanned skin, feeling his tight muscles against my palms. Appreciating their sinful beauty.

He stopped abruptly, turning to me and throwing me a wink. My cheeks flushed on the realization he'd caught me staring, I pressed my lips together, avoiding his gaze. He stalked towards me, stopping before me he pulled me into him, my hands landing on his moist chest and I squealed, "Ewww, you're sweaty" I whined, feigning a gag and he chuckled, shaking his wet hair in my face making me giggle, trying to push him away. Beads of sweet sprinkling onto my face

"You like me sweaty" he teased, flexing his chest muscles making my face flushed more as I stared at their movements. "Come on kiss me" he drawled, bringing his lips closer, them up, ready to kiss me and I squealed, slipping out of his hands and making a beeline for the double doors, running away giggling once I came through.

I turned to see him running after me, determination and excitement flashing in his eyes, a sinister smile curving up his lips. I screamed, flying up the stairs and running the full length. I pushed open any door I could find and held it closed, placing my ear against it. I heard his footsteps padding down the hallway and I sighed in relief, I was safe. I turned around to see I was in the laundry, I walked further in, admiring the carefully folded clothes, the washing machines and the dryers that were placed so strategically.

I jerked when I heard the door fly open. Turning sharply, I stared wide eyed at Damon as he strolled in, a malicious smirk marrying his face. His eyes darted from my face down my body. He covered the distance, pulling me into his chest as I squealed, swatting his pouty lips away, ", don't!" I giggled, pushing him off my only to lose my balance and fall flat on my back, blinking a few times to make sure this was actually happening.

Damon jumped on me, pinning both my wrists above me head, using his other hands to trace a loose strand of hair that clung to my sweat clad forehead. He looked at my face like I was the most beautiful little thing he'd ever seen, his pupils were dilating in admiration, the more he stared down at me and my cheeks didn't fail in exposing my embarrassment. He lent down slowly, his eyes darting to my lips that I had pressed together. He trailed his tongue over them, making me release it from their hold before he connected our lips, moving his slowly against mine, waiting for me as I joined in a few seconds behind. His free hand that wasn't holding my wrists trailed down to my exposed belly, where my shirt had risen from our tussle. He slowly drew circles with his thumb making me hum into our kiss, appreciating his touch. He used his knuckles to caress from the length of my stomach down and I gasped, feeling the electricity running down my spine.

"If you weren't wearing these shorts right now" he whispered into my ear, tracing his hands along the waist of my denim shorts, slightly tugging on it. "Heaven knows" he swore, his eyes darkening to the dark green hue I always got lost in. I stared deeply into his eyes, my cheeks flushing, the blush covering my ears. My blush increased when my stomach growled, ruining the steamy moment. His eyes brightened with amusement

"I'm hungry" I whispered, not able to look away from his eyes but feeling the tension in his gaze.

"Famished" he said, his eyes travelling down the length of my body and coming back up to my eyes. I couldn't look away, the depths of his eyes held a passion so deep, a desire so devouring it left me bewildered. I swallowed thickly, understanding very well we weren't talking about the same thing.  He chuckled, shaking his head and smiling down at me, he released my hand and got to his feet. Helping me up he pulled me into him again, placing kisses all over my face eliciting a fit of giggles erupting from me.

"Come on, we'll go out for takeaway after I take a shower" I beamed up at him, smiling from ear to ear as he flicked my nose.

A click sounded and I whipped my head to the direction of the sound. I immediately regretted it when my eyes landed on Damon, he was in nothing but a towel. It hung lazily around his waist almost falling off, my wide eyes darted to his face. His dark curls clung to his forehead, tiny water droplets falling from them and landing at his feet. He had a towel draped around his neck and a smile framed his face when his eyes met mine. I stood, walking over to where he was and taking the towel from his neck. I used it to dry out his hair as he wrapped a hand around my waist, pulling me closer to him and I giggled as little droplets spilled onto my face from my ruffling his hair.

# Jasmine

"I'll have a large cup of raspberry bomb and curly fries, big size" I smiled, looking over to Damon to see him staring at me, an incredulous look on his face. "Oh and a big pack of chicken nuggets and Waffle fries chick-fil-A's" I finished, thankful I didn't miss anything from my favourites.

"And you sir?" The lady taking our order asked through the slightly parted windows, her sweet smile so sweet it could give a toothache. I sent a glare her way, reading her intentions through her soft eyes that carefully roamed my Damon.

"Just a mini burger and large cup of coffee" he smiled and drove away when we were sure she'd gotten our orders.

We drove to an open field, Damon getting out of the car to go collect our food while I came out to lay on the bonnet of the car, resting my back softly against the windshield.

"Do I have to come up there?" I heard a deep velvety voice speak from my left to see Damon looking up at me, a little smile on his face.

"Mhm" I hummed, adjusting and patting the space beside me. "Come on, I'm hungry" I pouted at him, making him groan, giving in. He mounted himself up beside me and set our food between us. He brought out my food, handing it to me I immediately started digging in, not minding the eyes I knew Damon had on me. "Stop staring" I glared at him with my mouth full.

"You just look so beautiful while you eat I can't help it" he defended but I could hear him stifling a giggle.

We stayed there for a while, neither of us saying anything, just enjoying the silence and each other's company. I softly shut my eyes, taking in the feel of the cool evening breeze gliding across my skin, taking my hair into its wings and pushing it everywhere. I giggled slightly, feeling a bit ticklish. Feeling a pair of eyes on me I directed my gaze to the side to see Damon staring intensely at me, a swirl of emotions so intense it had my heart racing in my chest, so fast I was afraid it would come out and best right in front of us.

"You're so beautiful" he whispered under his breath, tucking a dark stray of hair behind my ear, tracing his knuckles over my flushed cheeks. I stare at him, his eyes dilating from their algae hue to a dark emerald green shade.

I turned away, my cheeks burning a pink tinge, "Did you just ask me on a date Mr Blackwood" I teased, smiling up at him

"Uh-i" he stuttered, awkwardly rubbing his neck and avoiding my gaze. I stared wide eyed at the biggest business tycoon in the city stammering right in front of my eyes. "The truth is, I've never actually ever taken a girl on a date before" he said, his voice so quiet I wouldn't have heard if we weren't so close.

"Really?" I asked, dumbfounded

"Yeah" he turned to meet my gaze, a pain surfacing in his eyes. "I spent my teenage years taking care of my mother because my father was too busy running his business" he spat, venom dripping off his words as his fists clenched and unclenched. I could see the pain, regret and sadness in his eyes, it was so deep it made my heart clench in my chest, the urge to comfort him overwhelmed me as I dropped my hand on his clenched fist, making him turn to me, his eyes sad and dim. "I could have done better to make him proud enough of me to be there" he said, the sadness in his words so great it brought tears to my eyes. "He never saw me as worthy enough to even be there. He wasn't there when I learnt how to play football, he wasn't there when I learnt how to ride a bike, he wasn't there to teach me how to fall and get back up, I learnt that all by myself" I thought he'd look up at me but he kept his gaze fixated on his shoes. The need to comfort him and tell him he didn't need his father became dire as I heard small sobs coming from him. My eyes widened as the situation registered in my head.

I pushed myself off the car's bonnet, getting to my feet. I hold onto his hands and pull him down, his glassy eyes following my every movement as he obliged. Once we are on our feet I pull him into a hug, my chest aching as I hear his sniffles. The sight of such a strong and influential man breaking in front of me was unnerving. But he was mine to comfort and I'd be damned if I didn't make him see how great he was. I wrapped my hand around his neck, holding onto his as he continued to cry, his head buried in the crook of my neck and I momentarily heard his inhale deeply, using my scent to calm himself. I pull away enough to cup his face in my hands, staring at his tear stained cheeks. I softly wipe at his bottom eyes with my thumbs, placing kisses all over his face to try to soothe him.

"I don't know why I'm crying" he choked on a sob, laughing at himself.

"It's okay, I know it still hurts" I tell him, knowing all too well what the pain felt like. I continued to rub calming circles on his cheeks with the pad of my thumb, hoping he would feel a little comfort from my actions. He held onto my waist, pulling us closer as I rested my forehead against his, our breathing in sync, our eyes staring deeply into each other's, a full on conversation going on through them. "Your dad is the one who should feel bad, he missed out on raising such a beautiful child, your mother did a great job, and your dad wasn't here and although I know he never told you or expressed it I'm sure he was very proud of you, only a nitwit wouldn't be" I giggled and he chuckled at my excuse of a curse. "You're a great son Damon" I whispered to him and his eyes shone with unshed tears. "You love your mother so much and want nothing more than to protect her, she couldn't have asked for a better son, so don't doubt yourself. You learnt the hard way yes but if you had to go through all that to be this man in front of me, the one I deeply admire, then I'm sorry to say you shouldn't regret it" I smiled up at him, placing a little kiss on his protruded lips, but I didn't have the leisure of pulling away as he pulled me back, connecting our lips.

His lips moved softly against mine, expressing the passion, love and desire he had for this one woman in front of him. I moved my lips

against his, our lips moving in sync. I kept my hands on his face, loving the feeling of his skin against mine.
His tongue glided across my bottom lip and I moaned, parting them, giving him access as he slid his tongue into my mouth, tasting mouth, making me moan into the kiss. It was like our tongues were molded together as they danced together as he stroked my tongue, massaging it gently with his, a moan escaping my lips at his actions.

He pulls back, eyes searching mime as I gape at him breathless. "I love you" he whispers, the truth in his eyes making me even more breathless.

He really loves me. I should say it back, but I won't burden him with what comes with my love. I could never do that to him, regardless I do love him and I would continue to whether I'm with him or not.

# Jasmine

"Damon! Damon!" I called out to him, walking into his room but there was no response. I looked around the empty room, confusion knotting my brows together.

"In here!" I heard his deep voice yell from behind the closed bathroom door. My brows furrow as I approach the door, stopping before it to listen intently

"What are you doing in there!?" I ask, earning an exaggerated whimper from him.

"I forgot my robe" he whined, making me roll my eyes at his expense. I looked around and finally spotted his black robe sprawled out on his bed. Walking over to it I pick it up, temptation getting the best of me as I bring it up to my nostrils and inhale deeply, smiling when his scent floods my senses.
"Please bring it for me" he begs, I knew he had a pout on his lips and his eyes were wide in his attempt to look all innocent when he was actually a very perverted lil nut case.

I rolled my eyes and walked over to the door. He pulled it open with a crack, the space enough for my hand to fit and for his to take the robe. I pushed my hand inside the crack, expectantly waiting for him to take it but he didn't. I wiggled my hand trying to let him know I had it but he still didn't take it. I frowned, pushing my hand deeper, my lips parted but before I could get a word out a hand latched onto my wrist, pulling me with such great force I let out a yelp, my eyes flying shut.

I blinked a few times, glaring at his frustrated gorgeous face only inches away from mine. He held me close to his bare chest, his wet strands of hair clinging to his forehead, a wide grin on his face. I so wanted to use the can of dry shampoo behind us to whack that grin off his face. "Seriously?" I ask, raising a brow at him. His hands held firmly onto my waist, making sure I had no way to wiggle away and run. He leaned against the wash sink, his perfect body angled in such a way that his waist was touching mine and he was only wearing a loose towel that dropped lazily around his waist, making my cheeks color

"What?" He asks, feigning innocence. "It's not my fault I missed your lips" he says, his eyes darting from mine to my lips as he ran his tongue across his.

"Damon, Richelle is downstairs we were having girl time" I whine, frowning up at him

He scoffs, a pout resurfacing, "But I miss you. Richelle's stealing you away from me" he widened his eyes for more effect, his lower lip quivering and I had to give it to him, his acting was spot on and I couldn't stop myself from giggling making him narrow his eyes at me as I reigned apologies over and over again. "Okay, just give me a kiss" he reasoned, pouting up at me with feigned innocence but I knew it wouldn't end at just a kiss, it never did when it came to him.

"No" I turned down, shaking my head. "It won't end at just a kiss and you know that" I say, looking up at him. "Especially not when you're like……this" I demonstrated to his stature and what he had on, my cheeks bleaching when he wiggled his eyebrows at me.

"Ohh… you find me attractive" he teased, grinning at me.

"No I don't" I lied, looking away from him.

"Just one kiss" he repeated, somehow sounding so much more convincing and I nodded meekly. He brought a finger under my chin to nudge my face up so he could have a good look at me. Leaning down he connected our lips, moving his hunger against mine, torturing me with his immaculately delicious lips. I matched his starved, raw paste, moving my lips hungrily against his as his hands slipped from my waist to my hips. I slipped my hands into his hair, interlacing them with his curls, tugging slightly as pleasure raked through my body. He pulled away, his lips connecting with my jaw and he trailed kisses along the line to meet my ear as he bit down softly, making me moan out. He bit and nibbled on my throat, tracing the conjunction between my jaw and my collar bone. I arched my back into him, wanting more, my breaths becoming labored as I panted for air. He continued to kiss down to the patch of chest that was revealed atop my shirt. He came so close to the swell of my breasts, my breath hitching in my throat as he undid the top buttons of my shirt with such ease, the rest bursting upon. His lips connected with the cliff of my left breast and he sucked, making me throw my head back as pleasure raked through me, his hand held firmly onto my right, massaging it through its cup as I moaned out, my breathing erratic.

"Jasmine?" My eyes snapped open once Richelle's voice came from behind the door, interrupting my euphoric bliss. I stared wide eyed at Damon as he stood straight, a smirk claiming his lips as mischief danced in his eyes.

A gasp threatened to slip from my lips as Damon flipped us, holding me against the wash sink, my back to his front as I faced the large mirror that hovered above the sink. He dipped his head to my neck, beginning to nibble on my throat as I threw my head back, biting down on my lower lip to suppress my moans from drawing Richelle's attention towards us.

"D-damon" I called out breathlessly

"Mmmm" he hummed, biting down on my skin. As I stifled another moan.

"R-richelle would hear-ohm" I couldn't help but moan mid-sentence as Damon's hand gripped my breast harder, gently massaging me as my mind spiraled out of control. Pleasure wracked through my body as the need to let out my moans became dire. My heart hammered against my chest, my breath labored as Damon let go of my breast, leaving bites all over my throat.

"You can tell me to stop any time tesoro" he whispered in my ear, his voice coming out huskier than usual, making me wet instantly. "Just beg for me to stop"

Another unauthorized moan left my lips as he slipped his hand under my skirt, pushing my underwear aside he dipped two fingers inside me, rubbing furiously. I couldn't help but let my moans slip as my body shuddered, the pressure building up inside me as my legs trembled, shaking harshly. I gripped the edge of the sink, trying my hardest not to lose myself

"Gosh baby, you're soaked" he whispered seductively into my ear, his voice so surreal it made another wave of pleasure wrack through me.

"D-damon I'm going to- " I moaned out again, cutting my sentence short. The pressure building in my lower region as I trembled.

"No, hold on," he commanded. "Don't release until I tell you to" he said in my ear as my legs trembled, my release on its surface.
I bit down on my lower lip, trying my hardest to hold it in but I could feel it coming.

"I'm going to cum" I spoke, my voice coming out more of a moan than a warning.

He shook his head, thrusting his fingers deeper, his fingers curling up as I shouted out, my whole body shaking with my release.

"One more"
He whispered and my eyes went wide.

# Jasmine

"How do you watch this stuff?" he whined, his jaw massaging my head as he spoke from his position above me.

"Shush" I shushed him, turning my head to glare at him through my narrowed gaze. He gave me a lump sided grin and I rolled my eyes at him and continued to watch Tarzan.

We had been in this position, on the couch in his suite. I sat in between his legs, my back laying on his chest as he wrapped his hand around my stomach, resting his jaw on my head as he focused on my scent instead of watching the movie. We sat there on the couch, our snacks between my parted legs as I munched softly, my eyes glued to the screen, my undivided attention on my favorite character.... Tarzan

"He's so hot" I said, staring admirably at the way his back flexed as he climbed, swinging on the vines.

"What!" Damon exclaimed. "That bush weasel!?" He accused me, making me gasp as I turned to face him. His playful gaze met mine as his lips were stewed in a pout, his frown deep.

"How dare you call my Tarzan a bush weasel you nut case! " I glared at him, packing a fist full of popcorn. I threw it at him, earning a glare from him and an even deeper frown.

"What's so great about that ape man?" He asked and I chose to ignore his insult.

"See the way he carries Jane in his hands" I pointed out, gesturing towards the television displaying how he held onto her in her yellow dress, swinging on vines and climbing. "I don't know I think I have a thing for guys with an animalistic primal side to them" I hadn't realized the words had slipped from my lips as I was too fixated on the movie.

I let out a loud yell as Damon spun me, hoisting me in his arms like Tarzan carried Jane, bridal style. I stared at him wide eyed as I held tightly onto his neck, pulling myself closer so I wouldn't fall. The wild look in his eyes had my heart racing and my sense of danger going through the roof.

"Damon put me down" I told him, my voice coming out high pitched and startled quite far from the serious tone I had in mind. He jumped off the couch, my screaming filling the whole room as he jumped onto another couch like a barbarian. "Damon!!" I screamed, kicking my legs frantically for him to stop. "Damon, Damon please let me down" I begged, giving him my big puppy dog eyes; widening my eyes to make them look more persuasive.

"Okay" he said with a shrug and a smile immediately washed over my face, my heart calming down. "But" he started, cutting my relief short. "You have to say Damon is the sexiest and way better than Tarzan" he reasoned and I just blinked at him, seriously?

"Never" I snared and immediately regretted it when he threw me in the air, making me scream out like a frantic chicken and I landed in his arms, my eyes wide. I think my heart was still yet to land from the height he'd thrown me. "Damon please don't do this to me" I begged, using all the persuasion techniques I could but nothing was working.

All of a sudden I was thrown to the couch, my eyes wide as I stared at Damon, his large figure hovering above me. Mischief danced in his eyes, a wide grin on his annoyingly gorgeous face. And it was then I knew I was in trouble. He attacked my sides, tickling and torturing me as I screamed, scrambling beneath him. I laughed out like a mad woman as he continued his humorous torture on me. I gasped, "Damon!" Gasp "please" gasp

Tears began to prick my vision and my stomach hurt from all the excessive laughing but he didn't stop, with him it was always such sweet torture. "Say it!" He commanded and I shook my head despite my frantic movements. "Okay then I have another way to get it out of you". He stopped and I was finally able to catch my breath, but it wasn't long after when his lips collided with the corner of my lips, his body bringing mine back down. He continued to kiss down my jawline, nibbling and sucking along my tender skin.

He licked over my throat making me shiver beneath him, my breathing going haywire. He proceeded down the length of my throat, stopping at a point to bite down on my skin making me moan. His hands went to the buttons on his shirt I had on, undoing them, a gasp left my already parted lips as he had traced the bare skin of my twins, making me regret not wearing a bra under his shirt. He began teasing me with his fingers making it harder to stifle my moans, his erotic touches making butterflies erupt throughout my body, my arousal at its peak.

I arched my body against him, a light moan escaping my lips as he moved his lips down to latch onto my breasts. I throw my head back in pleasure as he sucks on my nipples, rubbing his tongue across its pinkish brown. My chest heaved as he continued to run his tongue along them, showing each of them equal amounts of attention but focusing more on my right one, my core already dripping wet.

"Say it" he spoke against my bare skin, the heat from his lips making it worse. "Say it" he repeated, I couldn't wrap my head around what he was saying, my mind was too scrambled. My hands itched to touch him but he had my wrists pinned above my head, pushing them down against the cushions. "Say I'm so sexy" he cooed in my ear and it was like I was in a trance, the pleasure had me floating on cloud nine, all my sense of stubbornness had gone through the window and the need to obey him became dire. My rational thoughts had dispersed being replaced by my lustful ache.

"You're so fucking sexy" I breathed out, coming out more of a moan than words. He brought his lips to my ear again, smiling against it as he proceeded to tease me with his hands

"Good girl"
And that right there was my breaking point as my mind went blank, the pleasure wracked through my body, his words making me crave for him. For him inside of me, the need was scraping at my skin. I wanted to pull him towards me, feel his body against my hands so I tried pulling them away from his restraints but he , shaking his head at me. "Don't be a bad girl now, you stay right there and let me worship you the way you deserve"

✳★◆★✳

I rested on his chest, mine heaving as I still tried to calm my breaths after releasing three times.
My knees were at his waist as I straddled him, his hands around my waist and mine on the wide expanse of his chest. I pulled back, finally coming back to my senses, my euphoric bliss subsiding.

"Was this why you wanted me to wear your shirt?" I interrogated, narrowing my gaze at him

"No" he said, his head thrown back as he peaked down at me through his hooded gaze. "You just happen to look so devilishly good in them I can't help it" he grinned and I rolled my eyes at him. "Someone seems grumpy," he teased. "Is it because I'm so sexy I seduce you? " He asked, wiggling his silly brows at me and I scoffed, turning my head away. "Don't be mad love, not everyone has my charms" he bragged making me raise a brow at him challengingly

"Oh is that so?" I ask, folding my hands over my chest.

"Yes in fact it is so, no one has been able to do it " he nodded

"I bet I can seduce you in less than 2 minutes". He just gapes at me before erupting into a fit of laughter, my body shaking with his movements.

"Try your best tesoro, but don't worry when you fail we'll eat ice cream to make you feel better" he teased and I grinned, knowing exactly what to do.

He watched me as I connected our lips, leading the way. Gliding my tongue across his lower lips he granted me access, parting his lips for me as I slipped my tongue into his mouth. He moaned out as I massaged his tongue with mine, going ahead to let my tongue roam his mouth, tasting every inch and crevice of him. His tongue chased after mine in an attempt to take control but I didn't let him, I liked being the one in charge for once and boy was I going to use this to my advantage. I pulled away panting, his breathing erratic as well. I began trailing kisses along his jawline, stroking it along the tender tante tan skin of his throat. I nibbled on some spots, earning a subtle moan from the back of his throat and I smiled, knowing he'd been trying to hold it back so my work was halfway done. I connected our lips again, dominating the kiss in every single way as he tried to keep up, responding rather well for my control. I let my hand roam the wide expanse of his broad chest going to undo the buttons of his shirt. I pull back, staring at him with my intentions clear in my eyes. I bit down on my lip, knowing well his eyes were following my every move. I pulled his shirt apart, revealing the huge ropes of his biceps.

His chest was huge, oozing masculinity and sex. Everything about him was sexy and breathtaking.

After admiring the beautiful creature that was Damon I started trailing kisses down his chest, stopping to let my tongue glide along the skin and I could feel his muscles tensing and his breath hitching in his throat as I ran my tongue along his nipple. I tugged on it softly with my lips, going to almost suck on it as he finally let out a breathy moan, gripping harder onto my hips. I proceeded down to kiss his tight abdominal muscles, making them tense and release beneath my lips. I stopped at the V shape dipping into his trouser, the top of it visible due to how lazily his trouser hung on his waist. I sucked on the spot eliciting a husky groan from him and I smiled, well feeling the huge bulge underneath me.

I moved back up, pushing myself up so we could be face to face. I watched him panting, his chest rising and falling as his iron hold was still on me. His face was flushed, his green eyes dark with lust and his lips parted to aid his breathing. I placed my hands on his chest, pushing myself so my lips grazed his ear, making him groan. "Congratulations Mr Black, you've been successfully seduced "I smiled into his ear, pulling back to see his hazy stare on me

"You drive me crazy my little seductress" he breathed out and my cheeks blazed and I tried to get up but he held me close. I tried not to stare down at how huge his bulge was. "Stay" he spoke under his breath, his voice still husky from his moaning and groaning.

"No way" I denied, pushing his nose in like a button, earning a pout from him. "You're handling your arousal on your own. That'll teach you never to underestimate me" with that I rocked my hips against his bulge and he groaned, going to grab me but I pushed myself off, staggering to my feet, my legs asleep but after a while I stood better. I felt my will breaking  as I saw his outstretched hand, pouty lips and big eyes. He was motioning for me to come into his arms but I shook my head, giggling hysterically as he moved to grab me but I made a beeline for the stairs, hearing him grumble something along the line of, "cold showers again"

# Jasmine

Curled up like a ball on her couch I threw more pieces of popped corn into my mouth, enjoying the new Captain Marvel movie with Darcy.

"You'd think her hair would be longer as she transformed as well" she rolled her eyes making me giggle and snort, actually liking her hair.

"So how are the party preparations coming?" I asked in a hushed tone, not sure if Damon was back and would hear us. "Have you chosen a venue yet?" I inquired

"Yes, it's a big Hall that's a few minutes away, it's huge and we'll decorate it with Damon's favorite colors. His cousin is coming over with her baby after the celebrations" she beamed, smiling from ear to ear at the mention of Damon's second cousin. The joy twinkling in her eyes as she continued, "when will you two give me a child" she asked making my cheeks flare and I looked away, my mouth suddenly going dry at the thought

"In due time mother, in due time" Damon's voice chimed in as he walked into the living room in his suit. I had to admit he looked really sexy in it, the way his first three buttons were undone and the material flushed against his god-like body was making me unwilling to look away. "Trust me your daughter in law is so irresistible we may give you a baby right now" he winked at me and my cheeks burned the most. He pulled me off the couch into his chest, his hands wrapping securely around my waist while mine landed on his chest, my eyes wide in disbelief that he was doing this in front of his mother.

"Did you miss me, wife?" He asked, mischief sparkling in his gaze as he smirked at me.

"D-damon let me go, mother is here" I whispered to him, hoping he'd see the desperation in my eyes.

"Oh don't mind me" Darcy waved off my words, getting up. "Anything that gives me a grandchild sooner" she shrugged, walking out of the living room.

My eyes widen as I stare at her back till she disappears. My gaze flickers back to Damon, his eyes fixated on my face, as if savoring my looks. He inhales deeply, "Gosh knows how much I missed you" he said, satisfaction washing over his features as he rested his head into the crook of my neck, inhaling my scent and sighing deeply.

A small smile tugged at my lips, he was such a baby. "I missed you too you big baby" I teased, he pulled away enough for me to see his gaze narrowed in a glare. I giggled as he blew raspberries at me and nuzzled his nose back to my neck.

"Fuck baby, for you I will accept being a b-big baby" he whispered the last part, his nose scrunching up in distaste. "That sounds so bad" he whined, making me giggle. He pulled away, looking at me with pouty lips.

"Are you crying?" I asked, cupping his face, stroking his cheeks with the pad of my thumbs.

"No" he denied

"Oh, if you were crying I would have kissed you. But since you're not" I began pulling my hands away but he placed them back shaking his head frantically.

"No, no I'm crying, I'm crying see" he pouted, widening his eyes for more effect and I couldn't help but burst out laughing. Smiling, I place kisses all over his face and multiple on his lips to seal it. He beamed, his smile stretching up to his ears, "You're my best stress reliever" he sighed, kissing my palms.

"Oh so you have others?" I retorted, and shook his head, looking up at me a smirk making its way on his lips.

"No way, you're my one and only" my cheeks turned beet red at his revelation. "Everything about you relieves me, makes me forget about all my sufferings and stress. I wouldn't have it any other way"

He was right. He was my drug, I was addicted, addicted to him. His kisses made me feel as though I was drunk. He made me forget about all my demons, drowning in our passion, every other thing like thoughts, fears, they all became secondary to our love and need for each other. Somehow along the line he had become my safe Haven, my comfort blanket, the air I breathe, I would die without him but I would die happily if it was for him.

# Chapter Thirteen

## Jasmine

"Happy Birthday!" I cheered, running up to him and throwing my hands around his neck. His hands wound around my waist, my feet off the ground as he spun my giggling form around.
I looked down at his face, his hands still lifting me up. I could see the happiness in his eyes, his algae orbs looking ever so radiant.

"Thank you love" he placed a lingering kiss on my lips and I giggled against his. My legs now wrapped around his torso, straddling him while his hands held firmly to my derriere "Where's mother?" He asked, making me bite down on my lower lip.

I was supposed to keep Damon busy till exactly 6:00 pm, then I'd get him dressed and take him to the venue, all while making sure he had no clue about it. How on earth was I supposed to do that? I didn't know but I had to pull it off somehow.

He raised his brows, urging me to speak.
"She had to go see your cousin, she needed help with the baby. But she left you this" I placed three kisses to his cheek and he chuckled

"Just like my mother" he smiled

"Oh and this" I pinched his cheeks and he flinched

He groans, "Just like my mother", rubbing his cheek, making me giggle.

"Come on" I urged, squeezing his cheeks and he pouted. "What are we going to do today?"

He pressed his lips together, racking his brain, he looked so adorable.
"Well we could stay in bed all through and watch more of those .... movies" he grumbled and I raised a brow at him.

"How about a spa date" I suggested, his eyes lighting up at the word 'date'. "I'll be back" I said, I was about to pull away when he pulled me back to himself, frowning.

"Where are you going?" He asked, his voice high pitched

"I want to change into my robe" I giggled and he shook his head. "Damon" I warned

"Wear my shirt" he pleaded, his eyes big and glassy, he was getting good at this. "Please" he begged and I nodded, giving in. He beamed like a child and carried me over to the closet where he set me down and walked in deeper, leaving me to watch his retreating back fade away.

He came back, holding a big black round neck shirt, three sizes too big. I gaped at him as he handed it to me and I smiled, shaking my head. I got up from my current position on the bed, walking to the bathroom he pulled at my wrist, bringing me to a stop. My gaze met him and he shook his head at me like a puppy, his dark hair bouncing along with his movements. "Change here"

"No way. If I do then you know we won't end up having that spa date" I said, shaking my head and giving him a knowing look. His eyes travelled down my body as he nibbled on his lower lip, deep in thought. He pulled me into him, his hand slipping underneath my top and caressing the curve of my back, my bare skin burning under every stroke making me falter, my breathing coming out laboured.

"I don't mind" he spoke into my ear, his voice coming out huskier than usual sending tingles down my spine. "As long as it's you" he whispered. His hands slipped down, gripping the hems of my singlet top and tugging upwards. I raised my hands, allowing the piece of cloth to slide up my body. I stood there, bare chested as Damon's gaze was fixated on my twins. My cheeks flushed, the urge to cover up was getting stronger but the look of pure desire and want in his eyes made my urge to cover up become secondary to my want for his hands all over me. His head dipped to my collar bone as he pressed a lingering kiss to it making me throw my head back, a shaky breath escaping my lips.

He laced his hands around my waist, pulling my body closer to him as he continued to kiss from my collar bone to my shoulder then to my throat. He nibbled on the skin, inhaling my scent as he hummed in satisfaction. He came up to my face where he placed a kiss to the sides of my lips, my jawline, my cheeks, my eyes. My whole body itches to have his body against mine, have him claim my lips, he was going slower than usual, it was torture.

My hands had slipped into his hair out of reflex. He sucked on my skin, running his tongue along the smooth conjunction, eliciting a moan from mc. Hc brought his face to my flushed one, his eyes filled with an unwavering amount of love, so much that it had my heart melting despite its fast beating. He connected our lips, moving his softly against mine and I matched the same pace and passion. He ran his tongue along my bottom lip and I obliged to his tranquil command and parted my lips. He slid his tongue into my mouth, stroking it against mine, the feeling making me moan. He continued to taste every crevice of my mouth, his tongue wandering around. He pulled away, the need for oxygen becoming dire. He leaned his forehead against mine, our breathing ragged and erratic as we both stared into each other's eyes. Our eyes speaking words neither of us could utter.

He pulled away, pulling his shirt down my small frame, the material stopping mid-thigh. I smiled up at him, "I know you don't like lavish celebrations but I hope this is enough" I spoke chewing on my lip anxiously. I pulled out my left hand, raising my ring finger. He stared at it with wide eyes, his gaze fixated on the inked name that resided at the very position a wedding ring is placed. His eyes flickered to mine, an emotion I'd never quite seen in his eyes filling them to their peak. He picked my hand, raising it to his lips he placed a lingering kiss on the tattooed name, his eyes welling up with pride and love. "Now as the ink stays on my skin, so will your right over me always remain, whether I wear a wedding ring or not your name will always be close to my heart"

He pulled me into a hug, burying his head into the crook of my neck as I smiled over his shoulder. "Thank you" he whispered.

****

"Put this on Damon " I commanded, pushing his clothes to him while rummaging through mine for something to wear. I turned with a dress in my hand, silently asking for his opinion and he stared from me at the dress, a smirk gracing his lips.

"It's gorgeous, baby. Although anything you wear would look ravishing on you, my favorite color has never looked better" he smiled and I beamed at him turning to go put it on. "You better be dressed by the time I'm out" I spoke before shutting the door, sending him one last warning glare.

It was 30 minutes to 6 and the venue was still a few minutes away and we couldn't afford to be late. Damon still had no idea we were planning a party for him, he believed what I told him; we had dinner reservations at a restaurant, Darcy's gift to him. He couldn't refuse so he had to go. I had to hurry before he got a whiff of what we were planning.

I slipped into my spaghetti strapped dress, loving the smooth material against my skin, the gorgeous cobalt blue (Damon's favorite color) looking devilishly good against my mocha skin. I stepped out after applying minimum make up, nothing too much but simple and beautiful. I was stunned at the business man that stood in front of me, he looked so immaculate in his all black suit. He had inside a black turtle neck long sleeve, black blazer and black suit trousers. My gaze flickered to what he and on his wrist, the black color blend in so well with his suit.

"Is that-" I trained off, gesturing to the bra strap bracelet he had around his wrist, my eyes wide.

"Of course it is" he smirked at it, flaunting it about. "I'm going to wear it and show everyone I'm taken and no one can match up to this goddess in front of me" he winked, pulling me into his chest. His eyes travelled down my body. "Fuck tesoro, are you trying to make me lose control and shred this dress apart?" his voice came out husky as he bit down on his lower lip, his Adam's apple moving up and down.

"Well I have to show you are taken by someone so sexy so the rest would cower away, am I right?" I winked, giggling at his open mouth and big eyes. I swatted his face away, pulling back.

I walked over to the bed, bending to slide on my shoes, knowing his eyes followed my every move. I smiled to myself, turning him on intentionally would be a dangerous game but I was in the mood for it. I straightened my posture, saying my hips as I walked to the door pulling my bag from the handle. I felt large hands grip onto my waist, forcing my behind to his front. My eyes widened as I could feel his bulge behind me.

"Feel that?" He asked, his lips to my ear I nodded, his voice deep and husky as he spoke. "That's what you do to me, you drive me so fucking crazy, I get the urge to do so many sinful things to you every single time I lay eyes on you. But now you are testing my patience tesoro" the lust in his voice was sending shivers down my spine, my inner thighs trembling. "You look so devilishly alluring. If we weren't going somewhere I wouldn't mind slamming you against that wall and thrusting so hard into you, you will climax over and over again till you pass out."

My eyes went wide as I shuddered. My plan was failing miserably so I did the only thing that came to mind. I arched my upper body forward, letting my behind hit his bulge as I pushed against it, his hold loosening on me as he groaned. Before he could hold onto me I scurried off, giggling, leaving him standing there, aroused and stunned.

# Jasmine

"I never took you as the kinky type" Damon teased, a smirk on his face.

My cheeks turned beet red and I shook it away, leading him into the venue. I had to blindfold him in the car so he wouldn't see anything and spoil it.
I led him towards the door, my heart thumping in my chest.

"I'm just going to keep that information safe for later" he said and I couldn't help the shiver that ran up my spine at the thought.

I pushed the grand doors open, stepping in. The place pin drops silent. I walked in with Damon and stood at a place. "Take off your blindfold" I told him and he obliged, pulling it off his eyes and scanning the place, an unknown emotion taking over his features. I also gaped at the beautiful decor, it was absolutely breathtaking. The way the blue fabrics danced along with the chandelier was absolutely magical.

Gold draped the walls, giving off that dreamy look. The tables and chairs that were stationed at strategic places to avoid interruption of movement were beautifully adorned with blue covers, white lilies and gold table cloth.
I turned to him, going on all ten toes I pecked his lips, his eyes following my every movement as I smiled, "Happy birthday"

"Happy Birthday baby" Darcy cooed walking towards us, her hands extended.

"Mother?" Damon asked, confused as she pulled him down for a hug. He had to bend but it was still cute. He pulled back and she placed kisses all over his face, smothering his cheeks and nose while I giggled from my position beside them. "Mother this is beautiful, but you shouldn't have bothered-" Darcy cut him off, a dangerous glare sent his way.

"Oh don't worry it was no bother" she waved him off. "Now shut up and enjoy your day" she commanded with a stern expression which changed as she pressed a kiss to his cheek once more.
Like that Richelle, Ray and many other relatives filled up to wish Damon a happy birthday. "Happy Birthday brother" Ray and Damon hugged, patting each other on the back.

"Thanks" Damon said, nodding as they pulled away

"You really deserve it. After taking care of this one" he gestured to me. "She's a real pain in the a-" I cut him short with an elbow to his rib and he winced, laughing awkwardly and waving at us as he walked away.

Many other relatives came forward, I could tell Damon really appreciated it but he was getting uncomfortable so Richelle and I stole him from the crowd of people.

"Your wife here did most of the work" Richele gestured to me. "You're a piece of work" she finished, earning a glare from Damon.

"It wasn't that hard" I winked at Damon, reminding him of my teasing. "He's my husband after all" I giggled, ignoring the raised brows he directed my way. Pervert


Damon gestured for Richelle to leave and she excused herself. I turned to him and immediately his possessive hands reached out, tugging me to his chest.

He smiled down at me, the look in his eyes making me smile back.
"Thank you so much my love" he said, pressing a kiss to my lips

"It was nothing," I shrugged. "You deserve it" I kissed his lips back,
for a longer time. I pulled away before either could get more heated.

"Want to dance?" He asked and as if on cue the music changed to a
slow and romantic one making me smile, nodding. He pulled me to
the center of the Hall, everyone's attention on us now. I felt my
cheeks blaze, my gaze fixated on my shoes.
Damon used a finger to nudge my head up so he could look into my
eyes. "Just look into my eyes, focus on me and you'll be fine" he
promised, the sincerity in his eyes assuring me that he'd not let me
fall and he'll be right here, holding me tight all the way. I nodded
proudly, slipping my hands around his neck while his wound around
my waist, pulling me completely to his chest. No space left between
us.

We glided across the Hall, our movements completely in sync. My
eyes never left his and the amount of joy I could see in his eyes gave
me butterflies. Everyone around us was cheering but all I could
focus on was him right now. It was like everyone else had faded away
and it was only the two of us. It was like we told the other what to do,
the next step to take all through our eyes, no words, no need. The
warm pool of emotions in his eyes made my heart melt. His eyes told
me how much he loved me, how much he'd cherish me and how
much he truly wanted me, mind, soul, body.

The end of the song was coming so Damon dipped me and when he
pulled me back up our lips met, his hands tightening around me.
Fireworks erupting in my body at the contact. Everyone cheered,
Richelle louder than others. He moved his lips softly against mine,
and I bit on his lower lip, slowly tugging on it as I pulled away, his
eyes wide as he stared at my lips. The urge to kiss me again was clear
in his eyes. I giggled running off the floor leaving him standing there
looking flushed and startled.


🦋 🦋 🦋 🦋

"The Bahamas are great this year" Richelle chimed in, making me groan into my palms, my cheeks still blazing.

"No that's nonsense" Darcy dismissed. "Hawaii is more romantic" she sighed, smiling into space, Richelle and I bursting into laughter.

"Ughhh" I groaned, both of them staring at me confused. "You two are planning for something that you haven't even fixed a date for" I reminded them

"That date can always come later" Darcy pointed out

"Yeah but the location is what's more important" Richelle backed up. "We could let Damon choose, I'm sure he'll choose a very good place" she winked at me and I almost threw her the china plate that sat in front of me. "Hey hey don't get all violent. Don't worry we'll keep thinking"

I parted my lips to speak but the ringing of my phone brought both mine and the two women's attention to the sound coming from my purse. I pulled it out, "You two go ahead I'll be back" I stood and walked out of the Hall.

Settling outside the grand doors I stared at the screen, it was an unknown number. Weird. "Hello?" I spoke, bringing the phone to my ear.

"It's been so long, Cass. How are you? "my breathing stopped, my eyes went wide and my face drained of all the color as I blinked profusely. I brought the phone down from my ear, my hands shaking as I looked over the number. "Don't tell me you don't recognize me, love" his dark voice peaked through the speaker and I brought it to my ear, my eyes welling up with tears as my hands shook uncontrollably.

"I-it can't b-be" I barely got my words out, I felt my heart beating in my throat, the lump in my throat growing. My chest tightened, my lungs unable to accept the basic necessity. Air.
The very face of my nightmares was back, I could feel my palms become clammy, my head was spinning and my lungs felt like they were closing in on each other.

"A little too late for a family reunion isn't it?" He asked, his voice sending chills down my spine, the familiarity in it making my knees go weak. "Your foolish uncle thought he could hunt me down and find me. What a waste of time I may add"

I was shaking with fear, my legs giving in as I slumped on a chair I found outside the building. "It's not possible" my voice came out in barely a whisper, I couldn't believe he was alive.

"You look so beautiful, just like... Rose" the way he called her name with such love made me almost. I shut my eyes tight, all the memories connecting mom, Cassandra flooding my mind. Tears dribbled down my cheeks as I remembered her scent, her touch, her beautiful long hair.

My eyes snapped open at the realization, "How are you seeing me?" I asked, not really wanting to know the answer.

"That's the thing Cass, you don't need to know that my love, I've always had eyes on you, you just never noticed. What you need to know is that I have come to collect". At the words my heart stopped, fear sipping into me.
"You forgot what you are, you forgot what I made you into and that is unacceptable. Come back now Cass and I leave everyone else"

My heart sank to my stomach.

"Your beloved is right there; I have an aim. I don't think he'll like playing laser tag" a sinister laugh broke through the silence and I knew what it meant.

Hurrying to my feet I looked through the window. My eyes scanned everywhere before they landed on Damon, a small laser on his chest, totally unnoticeable as he spoke to his guests, completely unaware of the gun being pointed at him.

"No!" I screamed, tears free falling as I gripped my mouth to stop myself from making more noises. "Please" my voice broke and I sobbed harder, my resolve shattered

"You love him" he chuckled, the hidden intentions behind his laughter making my stomach churn. The darkness and the evilness in his laugh brought so many memories back.
"You forgot you are nothing. You don't even deserve to be alive and I will make sure you suffer every second " he sucked in a breath, an ear splitting scream slicing through the speaker. "I almost told him to pull the trigger" he laughed out, making more tears spill from my eyes.

I was done for. All my nightmares were coming true and there was nothing I could do. He can't hurt Damon. "Please no!" I beg, sobbing the more. "I'll do anything, anything but please don't hurt him please"

"That's better" he chuckled. "Now my love I want you to do something for me okay sweetheart" the names made me almost throw up, but I answered in the affirmative. "Good, good" he cooed. "Now once I end this call I want you to walk out of the venue, there is a black car waiting for you. I want you to get in and keep your mouth shut, any foul play and your beloved goes tik tik tik... Boom! " he screamed and I clutched my ears. "Now go, you have 15 minutes and you know daddy doesn't like tardiness" a sinister laugh echoed and he cut the call. I broke down sobbing.

It was all over, everything I'd experienced in the last 4 months was over. I stood on shaky legs, staring at Damon through the window. I wanted to touch him for the last time if I could. I'd be able to go in peace

I wiped at my eyes, cleaning my tears. If it was the last time I needed to touch him just once again then I'd be content. I ran into the Hall, ignoring people's questioning eyes on me. Spotting him I lunged at him, wrapping my hands around his neck and burying my face into his collar. I heard the relatives he was speaking to awkwardly excuse themselves so he could attend to me.

"Tesoro?" He called out, wrapping his hands around my form

I tried not to let my tears slip as I inhaled his scent, unwilling to let go. I didn't want the moment to end, I never wanted it to but forever was a promise I know I could never keep.

I stifled a sob, willing myself not to cry. I wore a fake smile, pulling away. As much as I'd hate this was the last time I was going to see him and I didn't want to spend it crying, I was going to spend it savouring everything in him that I loved. He looked confused and without a word I connected our lips, moving mine slowly against his. He followed my movements, wrapping his hands around my waist as I slid mine around his neck deepening it. A lone tear slipped, rolling down my cheek as I pulled back enough to place a lingering kiss on his cheek before leaning my forehead against his, our eyes staring deeply into each other's. I could see confusion in his eyes, I could tell he noticed something was off with me and I couldn't put him in danger.

I had only 5 minutes and just like that I whispered the words I'd never thought I'd say out loud, "I love you" I whispered, tears leaking down my face silently. I kissed his cheek before scurrying off, quietly sobbing as I ran out the venue and straight into the waiting vehicle outside.

I held myself, pulling my legs to my chest I curled up into a ball and cried, my body shaking with each tear that wracked through me. My heart shattered, the pieces hurt so fucking bad. He always said I'd never be free, he had all the control and I was a fool to think I could finally have it all.

"Welcome back birdy"

I looked up through my teary eyes but before I could register anything I felt something heavy being swung at my head, a stinging pain spread through my scalp, my vision blurred before my eyelids succumb to the darkness.

# Chapter Fourteen

## Jasmine

Pushing myself into a sitting position was futile as I choked, coughing profusely till I filled my mouth with saliva and spat it out, blood coming out as well.
I had no idea how long I'd been here but I could feel myself growing weaker. The air smelt like blood, dead bodies and what I can only pray was rotten eggs. My nose felt like it was on fire, my sense of smell deteriorating with speed.

My body felt numb and so was my heart. I hadn't seen Damon for what felt like decades to me. I missed him, I missed his scent, the feel of his baggy clothes that were three sizes too big for me. I couldn't cry, I had long run out of tears. I remember the night I got here I cried till I couldn't and then passed out. It was like that till I felt nothing but self loath and pity for myself. I didn't even flinch when I was whipped anymore. It was something I'd gotten used to and no matter how scarred and ugly I knew my body was I didn't care. My will to live was gone, it would be stupid to think I'd ever get to see Damon again so I had nothing left to look forward to, I had to keep him alive and the only way to do that would be to stay away, as long as he was safe then I would be content with whatever torture or condition I'm put in.

That was the funny thing about hope. Once you have it and it's taken away from you, it goes with every other thing and leaves you feeling numb and empty because you were dumb enough to have it. It was a cruel lesson I had to experience first hand. I asked myself why it had to be me, why it couldn't be someone else but then again I knew the answer, it was because of him. No matter how far or where I ran to I could never escape him, he was like my shadow because deep down he was part of me, he was my demons and whether I'd like to accept it or not it was my fate. To be nothing but his prisoner.

The heavy metal door was pushed open, making a screeching noise that made my ears bleed at the high pitched assault. I shut my eyes tight, hoping for whoever it was to leave me to my misery or better come to end it and let me go meet mom and tell her how sorry I was for letting all that happen. I was sorry, I'll always be.

I felt myself being lifted off the ground and I didn't flinch even when my deep open wounds were touched. I just stayed still as I was thrown over someone's shoulder, my weak form dangling as I stared at the floors, not even the urge to look up or ask where I was being taken came to me. I just wanted to be put out of my misery. I was already dead on the inside and emotionally so why not finish the job.

I was dropped real gracefully onto the ground. Note my sarcasm. My body ached as I just lay, looking up at the ceiling. I was kicked on the ribs to sit up, the pain soaring through me as I winced, obliging, they felt broken.
I sat up with much difficulty but I had to rest my back against the wall to be able to keep myself up in the position.

"Now my love, don't give me that look. I have great news for you" he cheered walking to me and kneeling in front of me, pressing my cheeks together with his thumb and four fingers on each cheeks as he raised my head to meet him. "You look so much like her it's repulsive" he spat and I winced at his dark tone. "It's a very big surprise" he gave me a toothy smile making me flinch at the gold color of his teeth.

"Come in Sir" he announced and a man walked in. He had grey hair, dirty skin and a cigarette in his mouth. I scrunched up my nose at the smell of alcohol wafting through the air.
"Mr Vince this is her " he gestured towards me and the man pulled down his dark glasses allowing his eyes to travel down my barely dressed form. His eyes were red and it told me he was a drug addict meaning he was one of my sperm donor's close associates.

"She'll definitely go in one bid, no matter the price" he smirked, playing with the cigarette pipe in his mouth. My eyes widened in realization at the words bidding. They were going to s-sell me?

"So there's no problem there then, take her off my hands" he dismisses, waving me off

Everywhere became dark as a bag was thrown over my head, blocking my vision. I grunted as I felt myself being lifted by a strong pair of hands, my ribs cracking with the pressure, telling me it was definitely broken. At least I was left to hope my new owners would do the job and finish me off.

Destiny was playing such a cruel game with me just like mother was sold to my sperm donor I would probably be sold as a sex slave. I almost gagged at the thought but then again I could just have myself poisoned when I got there so it would all be over soon.

I felt myself being thrown into a trunk of something and I groaned as my body hit the hard surface. I tried to stay as still as I possibly could, my body ached, every muscle throbbed with unimaginable pain. I felt the ground underneath me begin to shake and rumble. I could only believe we were in a vehicle, to where? was what I didn't know and dreaded. If I was indeed being sold then I had to prepare myself to be transferred into the hands of another devil. I could do nothing but pity my faith, a traitorous tear dribbling down my cheek at the thought of what Damon would have gone through after not finding me for so long.

"Good morning, coming to you live from the station we bring to you the morning news on the 14th December 2020" the radio spoke and my eyes went wide. I had been gone for over a year. My stomach clenched thinking of how worried everyone would have been for the past months.

I shut my eyes tight as we stopped moving, my body being lifted off the ground. Before I could register what was happening I was thrown over someone's shoulder, I almost gagged at the force exerted on my abdomen. I didn't have anything in my stomach, I had been starving for days on end only given a bottle of water every two days. How I survived I had no idea but I didn't survive to be treated like shit.

I winced when I was thrown down, my rib paying the price. I heard a metal door being pushed closed and I knew I was in yet another cellar. With much difficulty, muscle exertion from my side I pulled away the bag on my head and gasped for air, choking from the speed I used. I let my eyes adjust to my environment and when it did my heart dropped. I was in a dark cellar, I couldn't even see the walls, nothing. I hated the dark, absolutely detested it and now I was to stay here for only god knows how long. I tried to calm my racing heart and control my erratic breaths but it was futile, my chest tightened and I gasped for air, tears pricking my eyes, rolling down my cheeks. My vision became blurred and I felt darkness overtake me as I passed out.

# Damon

It's been A year, 8 months, 2 weeks 10 days and 15 hours since I last laid eyes on her. Her beautiful face, her birth marked cheek, her sweet scent. I replay the moments every second in my head. The way she pulled me in and kissed me, when we stared into each other's eyes I could tell something was off, something was wrong and I couldn't do anything about it. I let her whisper the words that haunt me till now "I love you" and I let her slip through my hands like sand.

I missed her. Not a day went by where I didn't hate myself for not holding onto her hand and asking her what was wrong. I knew something was off, there was fear in her eyes, she was scared about something and till now I didn't know what that was. When I had finally realised something was wrong it was too late. I couldn't find her anywhere after the party ended. Mother, Richelle and I checked everywhere but she was nowhere to be found. I immediately knew something was off and I don't know why but my chest tightened. We went back home and I ran to my room but she wasn't there, none of her belongings were anywhere to be found in her suite, it was like she had never been here.

I almost went crazy with fear and anger. I tried calling her but I was told her number did not exist. My heart shattered into a million little shards when I found a single piece of paper under her pillow.

I ran away, please don't follow me

Something was wrong, Jasmine would never just leave me like that, especially not after confessing her love to me like she did. She would never do that. Not only was this writing rough it was also not Jasmine's, it peaked my suspicions even more. I knew it wasn't Jasmine who did this, something was up and I needed to get to the bottom of it. My love wouldn't do this, I knew her better than that. The fear I saw in her eyes was another thing I knew meant she didn't leave willing.

All of a sudden everything came tumbling down on me. The time I found her crying, she was afraid she'd be taken away from me and now she had been. I promised her she wouldn't leave my side, she would remain in my hands where she belonged but I lost her. I lost the woman I loved, the one who owned my heart and now I was left a shell of a man without her.

I missed the sweet chime of her laughter, the way she'd blush anytime she was embarrassed, the way her hair was always messy whenever she cooked, how engrossed she was in all the movies she watched and the way she'd yell at the characters when they'd do something stupid. I almost felt like breaking down again, because of me I didn't know what state my love was in. I didn't even know if she was still... alive. The deranged madman whoever he was that took my life away from me would pay and I'd make sure of it.

I had searched top to bottom of the city for her but nothing, I didn't get any leads nor any sight of suspicious activity and I was going crazy. For the past year sleeping has been so hard for me to do, eating or even anything other than work just reminds me of her. The

way I'd hold her in my arms as she slept, all my dreams coming true all because of her, the way I'd cook and she'd savor every last bit of it would always flash into my mind and I'd feel so horrible I'd want to destroy everything.
The one thing I had to do; protect her I couldn't even do it. I didn't deserve her, I would understand if she'd not want to stay with me after this and I'd let her go, no matter how painful it would be but I needed to save her first. If she was truly in the amount of danger, I was left to believe something had to be done.

"Boss?" One of the security guard's voice cake through the telecom

"Speak"

"There's a man here, he says he's here for Jasmine" he breathed out, his voice going quiet immediately he heard my cursing.

"Send him in" I ordered, turning off the telecom and running a hand through my hair in angst. There was only one man who was left to find out about all this. Jasmine's uncle, Tom. He'd disappeared and I hadn't even heard from him in such a long time and now he would hear his niece was nowhere to be seen.

My office door swung open and in came Thomas, his stern and his muscles tensed.
He abruptly stopped in front of my table, his eyes searching mine before he sighed, pulling out a bag I only now took notice of. He pulled out a tablet and a sheet of paper that looked like a map?

"What happened?" he vaguely asked but I knew what he was asking about. I just looked away, too ashamed to tell him I'd let her slip right through my hands. "She was taken was she?" He asked more clearly and my head shot up, my gaze flickering to his.

"How did you know?" I asked, confused knitting my brows. "Were you-" I trailed off, glaring at him to explain himself. I could tell he was hiding something and if it had to do with the whereabouts and what happened to my tesoro then I wanted to know every last detail.

"Damon, if my niece hasn't told you then I will respect her decision and wait for her to do so" he began but I cut him off with a loud bang of my fists against my office desk as I stood, blood pumping through my veins, anger surging to my fingertips.

"Bullshit! If what you have to tell me has to do with where she is then fuck yes I need to know!" I yelled, my jaw clenching and my fists tensing. "She has been missing for a freaking year with no sign of her anywhere and it was like she never even existed, like she was wiped clean and you come here with information and you are not willing to share!"

"Who exactly are you to my niece that I'd be willing to share even the littlest bit of information to you?" He challenged, raising a brow at me, his hands folded against his chest.

"I fucking love that woman, not knowing where she is is killing me, I saw her last before she freaking disapeared and she told me she loved me back and poof she was fucking gone!" I yelled, expressing the amount of pain I'd been keeping in for the past one year. "I promised her every time she had a nightmare that she'd always remain in my arms where she was supposed to be but what an idiot I was, I couldn't even keep her safe " my voice broke, deflating, my eyes softening as I slump back into my chair. A wave of grief and sadness washed over me as I dropped my head in my palms, my shoulders shaking as tears dribbled down my cheeks. My chest tightened with all the memories I had of her, it physically hurt, I couldn't keep anyone safe, the empty shell of a man I had become spilling over. The one who dealt with my demons, she wiped away my tears, she taught me how to live, I learnt how to make her favourite meals just so I could have her with me in the kitchen. Now I couldn't even be with her because I wasn't involved enough in her life.

"I'm such a failure" I croaked out, a shudder running up my spine. I felt a comforting hand placed on my shoulder and I peaked up through my lashes, my eyes landing on Thomas.

He sighed, "I won't tell you what my niece hasn't, she would do that, It's not my place but I will tell you what we need to do to get to her before it's too late"

I raised my head, meeting his gaze as I blinked away the rest of my tears, feeling stupid for crying the way I did. "Too late?"

"Yes" he started, walking in front of me to where he had the laptop. He pulled it to me, pointing at a red dot that was barely blinking. "This is her," he said and my eyes widened. She was so far away but somewhere at the borders of the city. "I put a tracking chip in her when she was leaving for this city, knowing who she was and who was after her I had to do it" he said, "Don't get me wrong I'm not overprotective or anything" he defended after seeing my facial expression. "I just wanted to be able to save her if need be and now it is definitely needed. If my suspicion is correct, her current location-"

"The borders" I finished for him and he nodded humming, a known smile covering his lips as he studied my now serious expression.

"It means they want to sell her or they already have and are planning to ship her off to another country anytime soon" he tells me and my eyes widen, wanting to pop out of their sockets. I wanted to ask so many questions but I knew it wasn't the time so I pushed them down and nodded for him to proceed. "Normally a shipping like that, human trafficking would take close to a month or so to be properly carried out without suspicion and I trust they have had more than enough time to do that. But supposing they haven't already shipped her yet then it means they only just found a buyer and we have less than a month to get to her. If we fail then" he trailed off, gazing away

"We won't fail" I said, standing. "What do we need to do to get there?" I asked, getting into the situation.

"Well first, if you want to help which I know you do you'll have to know how to use this" he pulled out a suitcase which I again had no idea he was holding till now. He put in a pin and pushed it open, he smiled down at the contents before pushing it to me and my eyes shone with surprise at the gun that sat in the case. I picked it up, inspecting it. It was firm, mobile and light.

"Perfect" I smiled, looking back at him

"You've used one?" He asked, sensing my little experience, maybe from the way I inspected it, pulling out the bullets to check the amount.

"More like I've pulled one or two triggers in my life" I smirked, popping the bullets back and dropping the gun, it was the best. Small, mobile, light. Perfect.

It was one of the most traumatic experiences of my childhood. The first time I'd ever held a gun at 15.

"We will move out in the next three days," he said, showing me the plan he drew up. "We will get there in a day or two and then we map out the areas and strategize. Once we do it's a walk in the park from there" he finishes, looking up at me as if asking for my opinion.

"I have no problem. As long as we get my tesoro back with me then it's fine" I said, my eyes watching as the red dot blinked. "And you will have to give me the chance to put a bullet through the brain of the man who took her from me" I gazed at him and he nodded, understanding in his eyes as he nodded and packed up his things. "Why is that blinking?" I asked, stopping his rummage when I nodded the way the red light was barely blinking.

He stopped, looking over at what I gestured to and his eyes went wide, "She doesn't have enough time" he said, panicked clear in his voice as he rushed over to his bag, pulling out a phone and typing into the laptop.

"What does that mean?" I asked, panic pinching at my skin.

"It means that she is barely hanging on, she doesn't have much time left" he pointed to the dot. "That is her heart rate and if it's barely blinking then it means she is dying" he finished, looking into my wide eyes.

Fear filled my bones as my heart dropped to my stomach, my heart clenching. "She's d-dying?" I whispered, not wanting to hear it clearly myself.

**"We need to act fast, it's worse than I thought". He packed up his stuff and turned to me. " We leave tomorrow "**

# Chapter Fifteen

## Damon

"What?" I asked dumbfounded, my eyes wide with shock as I stared at Thomas.

"She's been moved and.." He trails off, his eyes reflecting a great amount of sadness as he looks away instead placing the iPad in my hands.

I looked down at the screen and felt my heart drop to my stomach, she was gone. The red light was no longer blinking, we lost her, I lost her. I stumbled back, my knees buckling underneath me as I dropped to the ground, staring blankly at the screen. "This can't be" I whispered repeatedly, clutching the sides of my face. "She can't be gone" my voice broke, pain overwhelming me as I felt my heart pang, my tesoro was gone.

I looked up, tears pricking my gaze as I stared at Thomas's teary eyes, "She can't be gone, she may be at her brick of death or they just found the tracker and removed it. Think positively please" he begged, sounding more like he was convincing himself than me

"We move out today, I'm going to kill whoever took the love of my life away from me, I'll avenge her, I'll torture them and show them what it's truly like to have fear mingle in you till you breathe your last breath. I'll enjoy every moment of hearing their ear cuddling screams and groans of agony, every sound would be like the blissful waterfall treading down shallow rocks. I'll make them regret targeting what was mine" I swore, determination dripping off my words as I stared at Thomas who nodded solemnly.

My heart felt numb, a darkness like no other consuming me whole as I sat here, staring blankly into my hands. The monotone ringing of my phone brought me out of my reverie. Absent-mindedly, I pulled it out of my pocket and held it to my ear.

"Speak" I commanded coldly, my voice harsh and gaze sharp, thick enough to cut through a piece of ice.

The voice came as a subtle shell of a whisper, coaxing me into my deepest warmth as tears threatened to slip through my welling eyes. "Damon. Come back please" The voice melted me from the inside out, my body tensed up, every muscle becoming rigid at the very sound, the commander of the voice still unknown yet the strange effect like a dark cloth on me covered me, invading my senses.

I let out a deep sigh, one I didn't even know I was holding in till now. "Richelle" I acknowledged, her name tasting ever so foreign on my tongue haven not uttered it for over a year now. I hadn't seen her for so long, I hadn't even been back in that house for so long...

I couldn't step foot into that house, it was too painful. Everything reminded me of her. Everywhere smelt like her, the intoxicating swirl of her feminine scent, her floral mist mixed with an underlining vanilla tinge, the scent so delicious it had my mouth watering.
The very aura that had me melting into her small embrace wanting to remain in her hands forever, to protect her from her mind, her demons, to keep her safe and with me... in my arms where she belonged and fuck I couldn't even keep her with me. Now I was here, a sulking mess not even worthy of her love. I was a fucking pussy, I couldn't even be the man she needed, the strong pillar she would fall back on whenever she became prisoner to her mind, whenever she crumbles, when she broke I would be there to put back all the little shards and pieces. I couldn't do such a simple thing.

I was so ashamed to look at myself in the mirror. I was raised better than this weak excuse of a man I was. She pulled me out of my ice barricades, the sea of numbness I had been drowning in. She swam through, gliding so elegantly against the tides that pulled back, she held onto my hands and pulled me out, despite the current that forced me back she availed, pulling me safely into the warmth of her love. Everything about her overwhelmed me, her essence stripped me of my walls, she saw me bare and took me all in. She showed me what it was like to live and now I let her go, she slipped through my hands like slippery grains of sand and I hated myself for it.

How did she love me?

Did she even still love me?

The thought of seeing her big brown eyes look at me with a blank expression, one void of all emotions, one empty and hollow, made my heart constrict in my chest. It made my body go rigid at the thought.

"I can't," I whispered, my eyes flickering to the necklace I had tied around my wrist, my tesoro's necklace as I put up a strong façade. I made a vow, I wouldn't step into that house, not unless I had her with me. That place wasn't a home without her. She was my home. Tesoro. Without her there felt empty, like me.

She sighed deeply, her resolve breaking ever so slightly before she sucked in a deep breath regaining herself, " There's someone her Damon" she said vaguely, pausing for a response but she continued after getting none, "It's Alisha"

Alisha?

As in Alisha Delvino?

"Alisha?" I questioned, confusion knotting my brows together. I sighed, running my hands through my dark midnight curls, pushing them past my forehead only to have them tumble back down. "I don't have time for her right now" I dismissed in my not-another-word tone and opted to cut the call but the next words Richelle uttered had me stuttering in my tracks, the mere sentence making my insides churn with a foreign feeling...

Hope

"She says she knows where Jasmine is and we don't have enough time"

I stopped, like actually came to a still. My hands stopped, my breathing seized and it was as if my heart stopped too and a breath of fresh air was breathed into my lungs, pumping every fracture of my dead cells back to life.

"S-she knows where my tesoro is..is she sure?" I stuttered, spluttering out my words like a fool but fuck I didn't care... I could find her now... I could save her... she would be back with me and I would beg for her forgiveness.

"Yes" she affirmed and I felt my heart stop, a thrill and excitement like no other overwhelming me. You know that feeling when you finally get on a rollercoaster you always wanted to, the gush of wind running through your hair, the cool breeze gliding across your skin and oh the content, the satisfaction washing over you as you arrive... that was how I felt. "But she says she would only talk once you get here so now?"

I gushed, spluttering orders out to my men who had sauntered into the room. "My men will come pick the two of you up and bring you here and no circumstances do you alert my mother, now hurry and get her here" I commanded and Richelle affirmed, cutting the call and I finally felt myself let out a breath of contentment.

"If she indeed has information on Jasmine then we still have hope but time would not be a factor we should consider as a friend" Thomas reasoned, making me purse my lips in thought. I hope she was alright; I'd hate myself if anything happened to her... if anything happened I'd die. I'd fucking die a million more times than I have the past year.


❋★◆★❋


I directed my dark gaze towards her, my eyes conveying the threatening message to her. I sat hunched in my seat, my hands interlaced with each other, my chin resting on them. I watched her

intently, the way she kept looking around like we were being watched, albeit she was paranoid.
I let out an impatient sigh, getting to my feet and strolling to the clear view of the whole city; standing in front of me, under my feet. "Where is she?"

"First you have to assure me you wouldn't rush in there" A disapproving grunt resonated from my chest as I turned to her, my fists balled, anger sipping through my veins to my fingertips.

"I will make those who have taken my love from me suffer, before I kill them I will mutilate their bodies and burn every last layer of their skin away" Darkness seeping through my words, venom dripping off each letter. "They will not be granted a peaceful death and that I will ensure"

Her face had turned pale, her eyes wide searching the wide expanse of my eyes for any sign of tall tales but there were none. I meant every word. She choked back a whimper, pushing herself onto her feet. "P-please Damon understand this. I know you want them to pay but the person we are dealing with is very powerful. I'm sorry, i-i was selfish. I wanted you to myself and I took on his offer, but now I regret it and I am willing to help you" she sobbed, shoulders shaking as tears pooled down her cheeks.

I stared at her dumbfounded, my dark gaze turning to slits, the algae hue in my eyes going dark. "What did you do?" I asked, my voice eerily calm but there was a certain deadly tone to it like the calm before a storm.

She wiped her tears, choking as she gasped for air"I-i helped him keep tabs on y-you. I was there when she was coaxed into entering a car and leaving your party. I-i helped him take her to him. I-i'm sorry" she croaked, crumbling into wrenching sobs and I stared down at her.

"Yo-you did this" I uttered accusingly taking steps towards her feeling the anger in me bottling over. "You're the reason my tesoro isn't with me anymore" I continued moving forward as she peaked at me through glassy eyes, fear filling her sapphire blue orbs.

In one swift motion a calloused hand gripped her neck, pulling her to her feet to meet my slits. My dark eyes bore holes into hers making her squirm in my hands. "P-please" she choked, more tears dribbling down her cheeks as she tried to pry my deadly grip away but failed miserably as I tightened it.

"Because of you my tesoro could be hurt!" I roared in her face making her flinch, more tears spilling. All I felt like doing was killing her right here and now. She was the reason Jasmine wasn't with Damon. She was the reason my tesoro was now in the hands of a monster.

"S-she isn't" she choked. "I-i saw her" she spluttered and I let her go, her small frame falling to the ground as she shuffled away from me holding onto her neck gasping.

"Talk"

"S-she is b-being k-kept in a cellar beneath this f-factory. It's at the borders of the c-city. H-he has people a-armed places everywhere..." she shut her eyes, tears pouring out as she gasped for more air. "I'm s-sorry p-please spare.. me" she begged, the red finger prints on her throat prominent enough to leave a lasting mark; a reminder of who she could never match up to.

I meant down to her level making her squirm away from me. A deadly look overtaking my features as I came only a few inches away from where she had hurdled up the wall "Do well to remember that you will never, ever be what Jasmine is to me. You will never be her. She is mine, I am hers and if I can't have her everyone will burn"

"If I find her dead" I continued, pulling myself to my feet as I rose. "You will not live to tell the tale of what happens when that is mine gets messed with" and with that I sauntered out of the office and straight for Thomas...

I'm coming tesoro

# Damon

A feeling of vengefulness and anger filled my veins as I watched the place where my tesoro was being held for the past one year. For a year I didn't have her in my arms, the only thing I had of her was the cruel memories etched in my mind.

I placed a kiss on the gold necklace I had wrapped around my wrist. It was hers, I whispered the silent promise I made to myself every single day I spent alone in my bed, every second I spent without her in my arms, every fibre of my being that itched to have her lips against mine, the ache to hear her melodious laugh, her big brown eyes that would fill with excitement whenever I'd agree to watch one of those her silly movies. Silly girl. My silly girl.

I missed her so much it hurts. It hurt whenever I'd walk into any room, my natural instincts searching for her only to have them crushed when reality would come smacking me in the face, she was gone. I let my tesoro go, I was such an idiot and I swore today I wouldn't leave without her in my arms, even if it meant I won't leave unscathed.

"I'll have you back with me, I swear" I whispered, placing another kiss to the gold heart dangling off my wrist. Come hell or high waters she will come back with me.

Unbeknownst to me it wouldn't be all that easy.

Walking back to the camp site I spot Thomas spitting orders to the men we had recruited. They were one of the finest a billionaire could get, the best money could buy. Anything for my tesoro. The men dispersed to their posts, as quiet as possible. "Tell me what we are dealing with here" I commanded in a serious tone, my brows creased with my lips in a tight line in no mood to joke. I lost my reason to smile at anyone, be it her uncle or not. I was respecting him all because he would be the key to getting my tesoro back but it didn't mean I wasn't mad he didn't come to me sooner with this. I made a mental note to enquire later on.

He looked away from his plans, eyes meeting my dark ones. "There are 30 guards littered outside the warehouse. They have shifts that they take at intervals which ensures efficiency at all times, but there is a loophole we could make our way through" he beckoned me forward to the table that had litters of papers spread across it. "They are split into three groups, each having 10 men heavily armed. Their breaks last for an hour and it takes each group 10 minutes to reach their designated posts so that's when we strike. Alisha did her research because thanks to her we know that the second group is currently residing as security and they are about to go on their break in the next 3,2,1" he smiled to himself and I turned to see all the guards disperse into different areas.

Our men met them halfway, pulling them aside and ending their miserable lives. I turned to see a malicious smile on Thomas's face and he shrugged it off going on to properly arm himself up. He looked ready for a war, we might as well be going straight into the battlefield. He wore all black, to be easily camouflaged with the darkness of the night. He had a strap around his torso, weapons like bombs, guns, dynamite and what I hoped was a pocket knife strapped precisely to his holster.

I padded up myself, pulling a little gun into my pants, simple, mobile and efficient just like I liked it. I had promised my mother never to be this person ever again but if bringing this part of me out meant I brought my tesoro back then I'd become the monster my uncle created. I slipped into my holster three pocket knives and one secretly into my combat boots. One lesson he taught me was to always come prepared for the worst case scenario and here we were like bait at the end of a fish line.

"We have 5 mins to get ourselves rooted to. Take out the next group. Let's move" he swiftly slipped past me, taking off towards the tall gates that were pried open.

I looked back to the gold necklace on my wrist and placed one last kiss on it before taking off after him.
We roped ourselves strategically behind the metal door and deposited half of our men to take care of the coming group. Thomas and I began our journey into the warehouse. From the entrance it looked like any normal shipment house. Big cargos ready to be shipped off but we knew better than to believe the carefully crafted facade.

Like Aisha told us there was a whole underground mansion under here. Tunnels that lead to different places would have had us confused but we had the map and we knew exactly where to go. Exactly where my tesoro was being kept.

"Go down there to the cellars and get my niece, my men and I will scale towards the living area for Bellamy"

"I want him alive, " I said, bringing him to a halt. A familiar look overcame his features but he gave me a curt nod before sauntering away with the rest of the men. I didn't need anyone following me to get my tesoro, I was going to take that risk all on my own. It was my redemption.

I made my way through the intricately woven hallways, my all black attire helping me blend well into the shadows. I crept through the hallways, stopping at a huge metal door, the smell sipping through the loose hinges almost making me gag. It made my heart squeeze thinking of the condition my tesoro had been in for the past year.

I was about advancing forward when I heard light footsteps approaching. I feigned ignorance and continued to push the metal door open, on hearing the footsteps closer I swiftly dodged, a bullet being fired, the noise bouncing off the walls.

"Shit!" I cursed under my breath knowing the sound must have alerted everyone underground. I moved to the side, dodging his punch and forcefully thrusting my gun into his side making him wrench and fall to the ground. I placed my gun to his knee and fired it, the sniper preventing any loud noises from attracting others to us. I watched with my dark slits as he screamed, gripping onto his bleeding limb in futile attempts to seize the bleeding

I turned down the walkway and continued down in the dark. A punch was thrown my way and I barely dodged before it scraped my jaw. My jaw ticket and I glared at the scrawny guard in front of me, he wasn't that little but compared to my immaculate Six foot 5 he was little. I smirked grimly, making him flinch as I threw an uppercut to his nose, the satisfying crunching noise of bones breaking like music in my ears. While the guard groaned housing onto his broken nose I kneed him in his mid section making him drop limp to the ground.

"Weak pussy's" I spat, swiping off the blood from my knuckles continuing down the walk path. The smell of blood and debris wafted up my nostrils making me scrunch my nose up as my lungs burnt for some fresh O2.

I continued down the role of empty cells whispering out to my tesoro as my heart clenched in my chest. I heard silent whimpering coming from further down and without hesitation I bolted to the cell.

Pulling off the keys from the ground I stopped dead in my tracks, the scene in front of me making my heart shatter into little shards that tore my soul to pieces. She was curled up in a ball, her shoulders heaving as she whispered coherent pleads not to be hurt

Tears whelmed in my eyes. Without removing my gaze from her I began opening the cell doors. The metal gliding across its hold made her body jerk as she began shaking furiously, sobs wracking her body.
"Tesoro". Her big brown eyes met mine and it felt like all the air was knocked out of my chest only for the pain to settle in when I saw the broken look in her tear filled eyes, the once vibrant pool of honey replaced with a hollow look of a broken child.

I came closer, a whimper resonating from her throat as her body kept shaking. I let the tears slip down my cheeks as I approached her cautiously, taking in her current state.

My heart broke seeing the open gashes spread across her naked form, her once beautiful sun kissed skin looked pale, the dark deep circles under her eyes told me she didn't have any luck sleeping either. Her hair was in disarray, her once healthy and bouncy curls were dirty, knot filled and dishevelled. She looked frail, like she was barely hanging on, it made my fists clench seeing her looking so malnourished. I lent down, holding out a hand for her, the look on her face telling me she didn't believe I was here, in front of her, after so long. I smiled, encouraging her I was real, I finally came for her. The way she looked at me with her empty eyes made my heart ache.

She extended her hand, gently slipping it into my outstretched one. She dropped it and I squeezed it in my hold, bringing it to my lips to frantically place soft kisses all over her hand. The feel of her skin on my lips was like air being breathed into my dead cells, I sighed, finally feeling whole.

She lunged towards me, wrapping her hands around my neck as her body wracked with sobs, tears dribbled down her cheeks. She gripped onto me with her life, not giving any room between her naked body and mine. I wrapped my hands around her waist, burying my head into the crook of her neck and deflating. She relaxed against my protective hold, sighing deeply as another sob resonated through her lips. I squeezed gently eliciting a whimper from her. I pulled away, examining the deep wounds that tainted her back, I winced, looking into her eyes to see the depths of hurt and torture clear in her hollow orbs. I shut my eyes tight, reigning back my anger. I needed to be there for her, I had found her and now wasn't the time to be angry and scare her, she was already shaken up.

I cupped her cheeks, rubbing my thumb along her cheeks, staring deeply into her eyes. I placed my forehead against hers, whispering calming words to her as tears burnt down her cheeks, a lone tear slipping down mine. My muscles finally relaxed, her skin against mine felt like heaven, pure bliss. Home. She was my home.

I placed a lingering kiss on her lips, conveying what I couldn't say at the moment. She kissed back, a little sigh leaving her lips as I pulled back. I pulled off my holster, slipping off my black shirt and pulling it down her form. She winced as the cloth came in contact with her open wounds. I strapped the holster back to my bare chest, picking my tesoro up, holding her protectively against my body. She had lost so much weight, I made a mental note to feed her all the Nutella and pancakes she wanted when we got home.

Pushing passed the metal door I carried her out to the open field, the darkness unnerving "Tom, where are you?" I asked into the talkies that were strapped to my holster. Wide brown eyes peered at me and I knew she wanted to ask me something but she was too busy basking in my warmth as she just shook it off and nestled her face into my neck. I stared adoringly at her, she was back with me. My tesoro.

"We have wiped out the whole floor but-" he stopped abruptly and my brows creased as I felt Jasmine tense in my arms, her eyes directed to someone beside me.

I turned and came face to face with Bellamy. He stared blankly at us, his jaw ticking as he exchanged glances from Jasmine to me. She started shaking in my arms, a whimper escaping her lips as she buried her head deeper into my neck. "P-please d-don't let him take.. Take me" she sobbed out and I clenched her tighter, never willing to let her go.

A wave of protectiveness came over me and I placed a lingering kiss on her forehead. "I will never let him have you, you belong with me, come hell or high waters you are leaving with me" I spoke confidently, my eyes gleaming with all the emotions that had gone dormant. Her eyes warmed, a tear slipping passed her cheeks as she nodded.

"Go back inside Cass" his dark authoritative voice commanded and felt Jasmine go rigid in my arms, squirming uncontrollably. I looked from her to the scarred hefty man in front of me.

"She goes nowhere. Do you think it makes you a man to abuse people smaller than you, hm?" I challenged, straightening out my stance as the man's eye twitched. "You're a pussy" I snarled but before I could get another word out a force hauled me to the ground, my back colliding with a nearby wall and Jasmine flying out of my hands and landing in a heap on the ground.

I groaned, clutching my rib tightly as I felt it crack. My eyes snapped open just in time for me to dodge the dagger that Bellamy was about to stab me with. I held his hands, twisting it awkwardly and the dagger fell to the ground. I kicked it away, going ahead to throw a punch to his face, satisfied when I heard his nose breaking, blood seeping down to taint his upper lip. He paid no mind to it, driving a leg into my side and I winced when it came in contact with my already bruised rib. The dull pain at the back of my head told me I was bleeding long before the blood had begun trickling down my forehead. I stumbled back, my eyes searching for Jasmine. I spotted her limp form on the ground unmoving. My eyes went wide and I went towards her only to be pushed against the wall, my back colliding with it and making a deafening cracking noise.

I grimaced, pulling out one of my knives and driving it into Bellamy's lap. He screamed but kept his hold on my neck firm.

He had a very high pain tolerance which would prove my victory difficult.
I elbowed his hand, getting myself out of his choke hold. I threw several punches to his abdomen, his face and his member. Luckily the last one did a number on him because he stumbled back and I lunged at him, proceeding to kick his sides, dodging as many punches as I could but he landed a big blow to my jaw making me see stars and I faltered. He used it to his advantage and punched my side, making me groan out in pain, my ribs throbbing as he continued to rain assaults. His fist collided with my nose, making me stumble back, my focus disoriented as I tried to see straight but it was futile

My head was pounding, my vision impaired, my ribs aching. I tried to shake myself out of the haze but to no avail. In my daze I saw him lunging at me with the dagger, but before I could react I heard the heart wrenching sound of the dagger being plunged into skin and the smell of iron filled my nostrils. I stared at Bellamy to see his face dim, his eyes void of emotion. I heard a whimper from below me and looked to see my tesoro. She fell back into my arms, her body going limp.

The deafening sound of a gunshot was heard, a grunt following as Bellamy fell to the ground, blood oozing out of his blood shot forehead, where I had put a bullet. I stared coldly at his lifeless body jerk till he breathed his last breath.

"See you in hell pussy"

I directed my gaze to Jasmine, she laid in my arms. I forced my hand to her open wound, trying my hardest to stop the bleeding but it just kept pulling out

"Fuck! No" I cursed, pushing a cloth to her wound. She choked, blood pouring out of her lips. No, no, no please.

I heard footsteps running our way and they came to a stop. I looked up with tears in my eyes to see Thomas staring at us, his face pale. "Don't just stand there!" I yelled. "Call the fucking ambulance she's loosing blood!"

I turned back to her to see her eyes slowly closing, her body running cold in my hands. "Please, please stay with me" I begged, tears pouring down my cheeks as the damn wound wouldn't stop bleeding. "Please" I whispered.
She brought a shaky hand to cup my cheeks and I leaned into her touch, sniffling as a sob broke through my walls. She was dying, her face was draining of blood, her lips were going blue. She was leaving me. No no no no

Please no

"Don't cry baby" she coughed out, using her thumb to wipe my tears but more dribbled down my cheeks.

"Why did you do that? You shouldn't have done that!" I scolded, my eyes burning with more tears. "Call the fucking doctor!" I yelled back at Thomas who just stood there rigid and unmoving. He shook his head, looking away and I knew what it meant. She wouldn't survive this.

"Damon, don't be mean" she stroked my arm, her voice coming out quiet and I sobbed the most. I was losing her, again, she can't leave me, she just couldn't.
"It'll be alright" she whispered, a traitorous tear slipping down her cheek.

"Please don't" I sobbed. "Please stay with me please. I can't lose you again please" I choked, holding her hand in mine like it was her life I was refusing to let slip through my fingers. "I need you to stay with me, stay with me please. The ambulance is on its way please; I'll call them"

"Shhh" she shushed me, smiling as she shook her head at me. "It's okay. Just hold onto me, I'm not going anywhere" she whispered, her cold hands coming up to soothe my cheeks.

I squeezed my eyes shut, letting the tears dribble past my cheeks and disappear into my stubble. "Please just fight for me, please". I crumbled, pulling her tightly to my chest as her body ran cold and stilled. " I love you" she smiled into my ear.

I pulled back enough to look at her as her eyes fell shut,"No please. Please" my heart clenched, my lungs screaming, every part of me was aching for her. I'd lost her again. I held her body tighter, crying into her shoulder as I relished in her scent. Please come back

"Please bring her back" I whispered, my eyes looking up to whatever higher power that was up there. "You can't just bring her into my life to take her away just when we found each other! You can't do that! Bring her back for me please!" I screamed, holding onto my life, my world, my woman. "Please just bring my tesoro back. You can't take what's mine from me, you can't do that! Please don't do that" my voice broke as I hugged her closer to me. Shutting my eyes tight as I whispered coherent words of plea.

# Jasmine

So this was how death felt. I felt the chill shoot through my hands, toes and limbs, dancing in my heart, making it slow down.
The only thing I could hear was my heart beat slowing down, I was hearing myself dying. For once, for once in my life I felt at peace, I felt calm. I was so tired of fighting, I could finally rest.

Finally, my heart stopped and I exhaled all the air in my lungs as they closed, unwilling any more air to enter. My eyes draped closed, succumbing to the darkness that pulled at my consciousness. I was done, finally done.

"mama”

# CHAPTER SIXTEEN

## Damon

Stumbling down the spiral stairs I inhaled a sharp breath, looking around. Shutting my eyes tight I strolled out of my house, slipping into my slick black Audi car and twisting the key, the mighty engine roaring to life.

I drove smoothly through the bustling streets of New York City, cautious of every road sign. I was in a good mood today so I hoped all the road users would appreciate it and stop honking like starved maniacs. Grumbling under my breath I parked, slipping out and coming face to face with the hospital building I had gotten so used to for the past 7 months.

I stumbled in, sending a curt nod to all the nurses who dared to give me sexy glances. My tesoro would have one or two things to say when I tell her. I could already hear her arguing with the staff I had hired especially for her.

She'd been here for 7 months now. She died, she'd left me, she'd left this world but she came back to me. I thought I'd lost her, after balling my eyes out we took her to the hospital expecting her to be pronounced dead but they found a pulse. I'd never been happier in my life. She was put into a medically induced coma to help her wounds heal. The first few months I'd visit I couldn't stand the sight; she looked so skinny and pale but  compared to now she had significantly improved. Her skin had gotten their rich chocolate glow back, her big brown eyes had turned warm once again but I could still see emptiness inside of them. She looked healthier and I couldn't be more grateful. Once the doctor informed me she would be waking up 5 months ago I decided to donate to as many charities as I could, I would give my wealth away just to prove my gratitude.

She had been walking for a month now but she still needed to be looked after. I made it my duty to be the first thing she laid eyes on when she woke up and I was glad to fulfil it. The joy I saw in her eyes as she cried into my chest, her little hands bunched my shirt into her fists, her tears staining my pristine shirt but I wouldn't have it any other way. Her hospital ward had become my second home. I'd come early in the morning before work to give her as many kisses as she wanted. After work I'd end up here to cuddle in the bed and watch her sappy romance movies. I hated it, but she was in my arms as long as she would be with me I'd sit through anything for her.

I pushed her ward door open and her big brown eyes full of anger and fire immediately softened when they landed on me. She pouted, gesturing me forward as the nurses just stood staring at the exchange. I walked in, dropping the treats I secretly stole from mother on the foot of the bed and kneeling in front of her to come to her eye level. She wrapped her hands around my neck and I wound mine around her waist, inhaling her sweet scent I sighed, satisfaction washing over me as my muscles finally relaxed. I held onto the nape of her neck, pulling her face away from my neck. I ran my hands through her curls, twirling the end of one strand around my long slender finger. I brought a hand to her chin, forcing her face to meet my gaze. I placed my lips against hers, sucking on her bottom lip sensually, pulling them between my teeth as I bit down, a moan leaving her lips. My baby, so responsive. It had been so long since I tasted her, she was like my salvation, my drug, all mine. I let my tongue glide across her lips, parting them with ease. I slipped my tongue into her mouth, letting it taste every crevice and inch of her. She tasted so fucking good it should be illegal. She slipped her hands into my hair and I tightened my possessive hands around her waist going to squeeze her hips. She arched her back into me, her round full twins pressing against my chest through the thin layer of her hospital gown. Fuck. Junior was getting harder by the second.

I stroked her tongue with mine, proceeding to scale my tongue across her bottom lip before pulling away. I watched her flushed cheeks turn beet red as she looked doe eyed at the nurses who for some reason were still in the ward. I sent a glare their way and they scurried out, leaving us alone. Just how I liked it. If they hadn't left I would have fired all of them. Respectfully.

Her cheeks blazed a bright pink as I brought a hand to tuck a stray strand of her dark bouncy curls behind her air. So fucking adorable. Her blush increased as I ran my thumb across her bottom lip. I lent down and placed a lingering kiss to the bridge of her nose making her giggle and I smiled, the melodious sound like a drop of water in the dessert that was me. I pushed myself to sit beside her, patting my lap. She blushed a little and came to straddle me. I rested against the headboard of the bed, letting my greedy hands hold her waist firmly. She wrapped her hands around my neck, struggling to pull herself up. Her barely covered sex rocked against my hardness in the process making me groan.

Shit

Not the time!

I opened my eyes to see her big brown eyes staring innocently at me, confusion clear as she looked at me.

"A-are you okay? Am I heavy? I should g-" before she could move to get up I held her hips firmly, squeezing them to prevent her from moving. She bit down on her lower lip, her nose a bright tinge.

"You're not heavy, baby and don't you dare get off" I said in a serious tone and she nodded giving a soft "okay" laying back on my chest, her face nestled into my body. I sighed, running my hands up and down her bare thighs "I missed you so fucking much tesoro you have no idea". I placed a kiss to the crown of her head, inhaling her sweet natural scent

She pulled her head back, peaking at me, her brown eyes held captive by her curly lashes that crushed against her cheeks as she blinked. " I missed you too" she whispered, dropping a soft kiss to my lips but didn't get the leisure of pulling away as I held her firm to that position, deepening the kiss. "Did the doctor's say I could leave yet?" She asked, her heart shaped lips swollen and red. Gosh I could kiss them all day.

Everything about her was addictive. Her taste, her scent, the way she kissed me. Everything.
"Yes, he said you can go home today. The nurse is getting your release papers ready" I answered after snapping out of my daze. She sighed resting her head back on my chest, her hands tightening around my waist. I ran my hand down the length of her velvet soft curls, my other hand drawing miniature circles on her exposed leg. "Tesoro?"

"Hm"

I bit down on my lip, hesitating. If Ray's idea ends up getting me in trouble, I'll kill him. "The contract is over", I began, feeling her intake of a sharp breath as she stilled in my arms. "I-"

The door was flung open and the doctor strolled in, only to regret it when his eyes landed on us. "S-sorry Mr. and Mrs. Black, i-ill come back later" he was about walking out when Jasmine stopped him, opting to slide off my lap but I held her firm by her hips.

"Hold on" my deep voice stopped both the doctor and Jasmine. I pushed myself to the edge of the bed, standing with her, making her wrap her legs around my torso. Her cheeks burned with embarrassment as I placed my hands on her derriere. She gasped as I squeezed them a little, smiling teasingly at her as she buried her face into the crook of my neck. I sat us down with her still straddling my torso "Check her" I ordered the doctor and he nodded frantically, his face blushed as he tried to ignore our position, doing what he was told

"Um.. She's fine y-you can take her home. Just make sure she rests and doesn't eat any spicy food for a w-while. Her medication will be given to you at the pharmacy." he stuttered, adjusting his big framed glasses on the bridge of his nose. "Just sign here" his trembling hands held the release papers and I took them, signing it with ease with my free hand. "H-have a nice day" he nodded, taking the papers and literally running out of the room.

Jasmine lifted her head from my neck, her eyes searching the room for the doctor. A deep chuckle left my lips, my body shaking as I laughed hysterically at her reaction. She pouted as I set her on my lap, smiling down at her.

"My pretty little baby" I cooed, nudging her nose with mine making her giggle, her finger going to flick my nose. I blinked a few times, taken aback.

I narrowed my gaze at her, going to squeeze her thick derriere. She moaned out, her face bleaching scarlet at the sounds she was making. The sexual tension between us was thick and sticky like caramel. It brought back all my thoughts of having her beneath me, in the living room, in the kitchen. Every fucking place. She tensed in my arms, her cheeks tinting as her eyes narrowed on my bulge. Fuck. It was getting harder the more she looked at it.

"Don't worry about it baby" I dismissed but she couldn't keep her eyes off junior

"I-is it okay?" She asked so innocently, biting down hard on her pink plum lips. My eyes followed her actions, junior moving a little and I could swear I already had cum dripping down my cock.

"It's fine baby, you could be reading, talking and I would still get hard for you. Only you" I grinned and she covered her blushed face with her hands.
"Come on let's get you out of this" I gestured to the pale blue hospital gown she had on and she nodded meekly. She slid off my lap, getting up with me.

I brought out the dress I had come with, gesturing to her to strip but her face went pale and she fiddled with her hands nervously. My brows furrowed in confusion but I decided not to push it. She nodded and scurried off, leaving me in the room to pack her stuff up. She alighted from the bathroom, my eyes meeting hers.

I stalked towards her, stopping before her to take hold of her waist, pulling her to me. I let my eyes soak her all in, my bulge getting worse. The little yellow sundress she wore was like a light kiss to her chocolate skin, the soft thin material hugged her hips, the inbuilt breast cups making her twins more prominent. I smiled at her, placing a kiss to the bridge of her nose. "You look so pretty baby, my gorgeous baby. Give me a twirl tesoro"

She giggled, holding onto my hand as I raised it, twirling her around, the little flair at the bottom of the dress sprawling out. It confirmed my thoughts, her derriere looked so good in the dress I was sure to hold onto her as we left, no wondering eyes would see what was mine.

"Such a pretty baby" I grinned and she blushed hard, tucking a stray lock of hair behind her ear. I smiled at her, raising a finger, signaling her to wait. I walked over to the bags, pulling out her beige colored scrunchy and walking back to her. I pulled her hair back, securing it in a tight bun, a few strands dropping to the nape of her neck. I twirled a strand of her hair with my finger, rubbing miniature circles on her hips. She played with my shirt buttons, biting down on her lower lip. "Something on your mind tesoro?"

She stops, staring at my forehead. She was definitely hiding something; she couldn't look me in the eye. I applied pressure to her hips, assuring her it was okay. She sucked in a deep breath, "Can…can we talk later?" She asked, fiddling furiously with my buttons, gnawing at her bottom lip.

My brows furrowed, confusion biting into my skin as I held onto her chin, raising her gaze to meet mine, "Speak to me tesoro" I urged, my thumb rubbing her jaw soothingly. She looked away, tears burning her eyes, a few drops spilling down her cheeks. Panic rose in me, the urge to protect her overwhelming me as I pulled her into my embrace, wrapping my arms around her, her little arms winding around my waist as she nestled her face into my chest, sobs breaking through her throat as she shook in my arms. "Shhh, it's okay baby" I cooed, running my hands in an up and down motion on her back, trying to soothe her.

I pulled away enough to meet her teary gaze, she sniffled, my slender fingers wiping at her tears. "I- I'm just tired" she sighs, an underlying meaning in her words but I chose to let her tell me at her own time. I nod in response, pulling her back into my embrace, kissing her face recklessly, making her erupt into a fit of giggles.

"My baby, don't worry we'll go shopping for your favorite" I promised, placing a kiss on her forehead.

"Really?" She asked, beaming like a little child. I nodded with a low hum and she placed a kiss on my jaw, giggling when I pouted down at her, demanding a proper kiss which she delivered whole heartedly. How did I ever live without this woman? The simple answer was I never did; I was surviving but never living

Yep, I was a simp, big one but fuck it.

# Damon

"She's still not fully recovered from the trauma, she's been distant" I whispered into the phone, my head falling into my hands.

"She'll come around, she's been through a lot, Damon" she sympathizes, her voice revealing her hidden stress and concerns. I sighed, my gaze travelling to Jasmine's sleeping form in bed.

We had spent the rest of the day cuddled in bed, she wearing my-her black oversized hoodie which she insisted on putting on by herself. If I didn't know better, I'd say she was conscious about me seeing her naked. Fuck. What if I made her feel body conscious? I'm so stupid.

"No! No please!" Her alarmed voice yelled, bringing my attention to her. My head snapped to her direction. I threw my phone aside, jumping to where she sat on the bed. She frantically tossed and kicked, screaming coherent words of plea as she pulled at her curls, tears dripping down her cheeks.

I grabbed a hold of her hands, detaching them from her bunched up curls. "Tesoro, baby calm down. What's wrong?" I asked, cupping her cheeks to force her attention to me. Her gaze met mine, the distant look in her eyes unnerved me, telling me she wasn't here with me. She was having a panic attack. Shit

"P-please don't let him hurt me" she begged, more tears flooding her cheeks as she pulled away from my touch. She scrambled to the floor, going to curl up into a ball. She pulled her knees to her chest, cradling back and forth as she whispered, "please please don't hurt me, I'll be a-good i swear" her voice broke, her eyes burning with more tears. She blocked her ears with her palms, begging to be saved and I just watched, my heart breaking every second.

I gently slid down the bed, careful not to startle her. I approached her carefully, my hands out to show I wasn't a threat. I leaned down, trying my best to look smaller, so I wouldn't look like a threat. She was shaking, her body trembling as she continued to cry. I pulled her into my body, wrapping my hands around her as I shut my eyes tight. She fought against my protective hold, sobbing furiously, her little fists going to bunch my shirt as she relaxed against my body, her silent sobs wetting my shirt.

I held onto her, my hand going to the nape of her neck to hold her face to my shirt. She broke, all the tears she'd been holding back burst like a dam. Her body shook violently as she cried harder, the sound of her sobs making my heart constrict in my chest. I ran my hand in an up and down motion on her back, whispering calming words to her, not letting her go. I felt her little hands release my shirt as she shoved at my chest, pulling away from me. "P-please leave me alone" she sobbed, shuffling away from me. I had never seen her like this. Fuck I had never seen her as anything less than the beautiful, playful tesoro I knew. Someone who loved cartoons at her age, someone who loved to move around the kitchen cooking, someone who absolutely adored the taste of cookie dough ice cream no matter how disgusting it truly was. Now I was seeing her as the person she had always tried to reign in. The broken, soft, hurt part of her and fuck did it make me hate myself for not encouraging her to bring this part of herself out for me. She looked so broken and fragile as more tears burnt her flushed cheeks

She didn't want me near her, she was breaking and I would be damned if I wouldn't be here to put her back together. My sweet baby was hurt. I pushed myself closer, for each movement I made forward she made one back in return. She brought out a hand to my chest, stopping me from advancing forward. "No, p-please leave me a-alone" she begged, her sorrow filled eyes gazing into mine and I swear it knocked out all the air from my lungs. The depth of despair and hurt I saw flash in her eyes had me faltering.

"Baby please don't push me away" I pleaded, my gaze softening as I looked at her. I stopped moving forward, giving her enough space to tell me what was happening, the last thing I wanted was to make her feel suffocated. "Please tell me what's wrong let me fix it, please" I nodded but she shook her head at me, more tears falling down her cheeks.

"You can't fix it" her voice broke as she gazed away from me. "You can't fix what he did to me" she trailed off, shutting her eyes tight as if remembering something before she snapped them open again, more tears falling down her cheeks. "H-he touched me" her voice broke, her hollow brown eyes met mine and I felt my throat go dry at the realisation. I pulled her into my arms, resisting her attempts to pull away. "I'm damaged goods, he hurt me, he whipped me. I'm injured, I'm bruised, I'm tainted" she cried out, the pain in her voice making tears flood my eyes. "O-once you see w-what he did you.. You're going to leave me for someone who is perfect, who isn't damaged"

My eyes widened and I finally understood what she was aiming at. My baby thought I'd leave her after everything, she thought I would hate her and wouldn't love her anymore. Idiot, my idiot.


"I can't stand you leaving me or hating me, so please if it would make you happy I-I'll leave" she whispered the last part and my hands tightened around her at the thought of her wanting to leave. "I-I'll just need some time t-to get another place-" I cut her short, smashing my lips against hers. I pulled her body closer to mine, winding my hands around her hips, squeezing them as I slid my tongue into her mouth, expressing all the feelings I had for her that I couldn't fit into words. After a while she responded, her hands going into my hair to play with my strands. I sucked on her tongue making her moan out. I slid my hands to her derrierè, lightly squeezing it as she moaned out again. Such a responsive baby.

I placed my hands under her thighs, gripping them firmly and standing making her wrap her legs around my torso. I walked us over to the bed, dropping her beneath me as I hovered over her, my body completely covering hers. Her face was flushed, her lips red and swollen. Her big brown eyes flickered from mine to my lips before they settled on my algae orbs. I brought my slender fingers to trail along her bottom lip, releasing it from her toothy grip "How could you ever think I'd want you gone?" I asked, my voice serious as I frowned deeply, letting her know how serious I was. She gazed away, avoiding my question but I grabbed her chin, forcing her gaze to meet mine. "No matter what happens baby, I don't care about your past or what that monster did to you. You are the sexiest, prettiest and most beautiful baby I have ever seen and no silly marks or wound would change that" I assured her, smiling in content as her eyes lit up, their gorgeous glow resurfacing. "You're an idiot for thinking that"

"Your idiot" she added, a blush running across her nose


"My idiot" I repeated, leaning down to peck her nose where her cute blush resided, my actions making her blush harder. Such an adorable baby. I captured her lips, sliding my tongue along her bottom lip, parting them with ease. I used her submissive response to my advantage, pushing my tongue into her mouth, letting it taste

every inch and crevice of her. She tasted like my salvation, a
blessing. She tasted so good I sucked on her tongue making her
moan, her hands coming up to slowly run down the wide expanse of
my chest, going down to caress my arms. She pulled at the collar of
my shirt and I smirked into the kiss knowing exactly what she
wanted. My baby wanted to see what was hers, who was I to deny
her that.

I pulled back, sitting on my folded legs. I pulled at the hem of my
shirt, taking it over my head, my gaze never leaving hers. Her big
brown eyes followed my every move and once my shirt was off she
inhaled a sharp breath, her eyes taking in all of me. Her cheeks
flushed beet red when her gaze finally met mine, embarrassed she
had been caught staring. I shook my head at her, leaning down to
pinch her jaw, raising her face up so her eyes could meet mine.
"Don't be embarrassed my love, I'm all yours, you can do whatever
you want" I released her jaw, certain her eyes were on me as I
proceeded to place her two palms against my chest. It felt like
fireworks burst through my body, burning my veins with pleasure as
she ran her hands down my chest, going down to slowly soothe my
tight abdominal muscles. I groaned, throwing my head back as her
hands arrived at the big bulge in my trouser. I watched her blush
deepen as she took in my arousal, her tongue coming out to wet her
lips, an action that made me harder than a hammer.

I took hold of her hand, forcing both of her wrists above her head,
my one hand going to hold onto her wrists, denying her any access to
touch me. It had been so long, I spent nights without her in my arms,
without touching her and now I was going to make the most of it. I
was going to show her just how much I worshipped her. My woman.

Connecting my lips with her jaw I trailed open mouthed kisses down
her throat, my tongue gliding across her soft spot behind her ear
making her shiver, a shaky breath escaping her parted lips as her
hands fought against their restraints. I let my other hand wander
down the hem of her hoodie, going under the fabric to caress her
bare skin. She whimpered in disapproval and I stopped, looking into
her eyes, fear and uncertainty swirling through them. "I promise, if I
do anything you don't approve of, just tell me and I'll stop baby".
She nodded, her eyes squeezing shut as I moved down to thug at the
hem of her shirt, swiftly pulling it above her head to reveal her

bright pink laced underwear. I froze, feeling my mouth go dry and my bulge grow harder.


Holy shit!


I stared wide eyed at her laced panties. Letting my eyes wander down her body I couldn't help but bite the corner of my lips. Damn she looked so fucking sexy. The sexiest, so fucking pretty.

My gaze flickered to her face, her cheeks a deep red tinge. Her hands tried to cover her twins as she gazed away, bringing her lower lip between her teeth to bite down hard as her blush increased. My gaze seemed to burn her skin as she let out a shaky breath, her eyes begging me to say something. I was too shocked. "Jesus fucking Christ. Gosh baby, you look so fucking sexy" I whispered underneath my breathe and her face blazed at my use of words. "So fucking sexy all for daddy, hm?" She nodded. I wet my lips, pulling her hands away from her twins to completely take in the gorgeous angel that laid underneath me. "Now let me show you just how beautiful you are"


I pinned her wrists above her head, leaning down. I trailed butterfly kisses all over her bare stomach, kissing over every scar, making her shiver, her breathing coming out laboured. She let out a breathy moan as I slid my slender finger to her already soaking core. "Fuck baby" I whispered, my gaze meeting her wide brown eyes, the excitement in them making me go crazy. "You're soaked and I haven't even gotten started" I teased, rubbing miniature circles on her thin underwear. " so fucking responsive".

I rubbed roughly against her panties, her hips jerk to meet my aggressive strokes, moans spilling out of her lips. Her mouth hung open, words wanting to come out but none coming out as anything more than moans. "Fuck" I cursed, increasing the circles as she arched her back off the bed, her toes curling with the surge of pleasure building in her lower region and surging through her body.

"P-please" she gasped, her hands threatening to slip through their restraints. "Please daddy" she moaned out and I smirked to myself.

"Use your words baby, what do you want?" I asked, shoving my fingers so close to her throbbing sex as she moaned out, her pleasured whimpers resonating from her throat.

"Please, please finger me" she burst out. "Slide your fingers into me!"

Smiling to myself I pulled my hand back and her eyes snapped open, a disapproving whimper leaving her lips. "Don't worry baby, I'll satisfy you" I grinned and her cheeks flushed at her carnal needs. "Now pull down your panties and show me what you're offering".

She meekly nodded, biting down on her lower lip as she sat up, gripping the waist of her panties and pulling them down to her feet. I crawled back on top of her, forcing her back down. I tugged her panties over her legs, throwing them across the room making her giggle. I held onto the back of her thighs, pulling them open. I stopped in my tracks to stare at her "You're so fucking beautiful baby. So damn sexy" I hissed, bringing my tongue to wet my lips as I stared at her.

Without hesitation I slipped my fingers into her soaked core. She moaned out, her body shaking as I began at a slow paste, pumping my fingers in and out mercilessly. Her hips jerked, meeting my sped up paste. Her thighs trembled, her release on the surface but I didn't stop. She cried out, begging to be let out but I refused "Hold it in" I commanded, adding another finger and she threw her head back, a cry resonating from her throat.

"Oh my god" she cried out, her legs shaking viciously. "Fuck, ohm"

"Scream my name baby" my deep gruff voice ordered.

"Damon!" She screamed, her thighs trembling as she came undone, squirting all over, her arousal dripping all over my hands and sipping into the sheets. I pulled out my fingers, making sure her eyes were on me the whole time as I drew my tongue along my soaked fingers, sucking on her juice. I brought my fingers to fondle her nipples, rubbing her remaining arousal all over them, moving my lips to capture them in the greedy strokes of my tongue.

# Jasmine

I moaned out, loving the way his erotic tongue teased and sucked on my nipples. My mind was going crazy, the burning flame of pleasure igniting throughout my body as he traced the curve of my breasts making me whimper, biting down on my lower lip.

He pulled away, excitement and mischief dancing in his hooded gaze. I watched him with ragged breaths, my need for oxygen becoming secondary to my carnal sexual desires. My desire for him.

He looked so sexy, his dark curls tussled, a few steady strands falling onto his forehead. His five o'clock stubble made his jawline look more prominent. His figure was so alluring, it oozed sex and dropped with dominant masculinity, one that I knew couldn't be matched by any man. For my Damon wasn't any ordinary man. The way the rays from the moon bounced off his muscles, giving them a sort of imaginary line. His big arms that always held me protectively but tenderly like I was some expensive very fragile piece of china. His tight torso that served as a hoop for my legs during cuddle time, his slender fingers that stirred me up so badly it had me gasping for more. There was no doubt this man was drool worthy, immaculately gorgeous. Respectfully.

With the blink of an eye he had flipped us, having me at the headboard, clutching it for balance while he laid beneath me, his face under my throbbing core. I looked down at him confused.

What was I supposed to be doing here?

His hands gripped my bare hips, rocking them back and forth, rubbing my bare sex against his greedy lips in the process. I got the idea. Reluctantly I clutched harder onto the headboard and began grinding my throbbing core against his mouth. I moaned out, my body shaking as his ravenous mouth devoured my clit; licking, sucking and nibbling on it. His stubble against my pussy was driving me crazy and I was certain it would leave marks. His marks on me. It sent a shock through my body, making my breasts jump with each raged and furious thrust. I screamed out, his hands gripping my derrierè hard as he increased the paste, rocking my hips back and forth against his face.

"Like your throne baby?" He asked, his voice deep and husky rumbling between my thighs, the vibration making me moan as pleasure wracked through my body

Oh my gosh
It felt so good, his mouth sucking on my cunt, teasing me with strokes of his moist hot tongue inside of me. It was like I was going to explode, I felt the immense pressure building up in my lower abdomen. I curled my toes, trying my best to reign in my climax, wanting more but at the same time wanting to release. His plum lips felt so good between my legs I wondered how I ever lived without this feeling.

Fuck! I was going to cum, everywhere, on his face.

"Damon!" I cried out, trying my best to warn him but he ignored my desperate cries and continued his pleasurable torture on me. I was on the edge, I felt like any moment I would pass out from the amount of pleasure I was feeling.

"Release baby, go on. Cum all over my face, cum for daddy". With that I released, letting everything flow out as my body jerked, one after the other waves of relief pooled out of me. I screamed, my body shaking as I squirted everywhere, holding tightly to the headboard, my eyes rolling to the back of my head.

••••••

"Morning baby" a velvet soft voice greeted, the tenderness in his tone making my eyes flutter open to meet a glistening pair of emerald green eyes. They looked like all the stars in the skies were stolen and woven beautifully into his captivating orbs. "You passed out on me" he whispered, making my face bleach beet red.

Did I really pass out?

I directed my gaze around the room to see the sunlight sipping through the thick curtains, their rays Illuminating the room, gently kissing my face. My eyes flickered to Damon's as he brought a hand to trail a stray lock of hair behind my ear, his long cold fingers feeling so good against my hot skin. He caressed my jaw, running his slender finger across the skin, making me lean further into his touch.

"Hi" I whispered, my face bleaching when his taut thumb traced my lips, his eyes following every movement

"Hey" he responds, leaning down to possess my lips in a gentle kiss. His cold possessive hands tightened around my bare hips. I gasped slightly as he pulled me on top of him, his hands sliding down to grab a fistful of my derriere making me moan into the kiss, my hands landing on the wide expanse of his chest. His erotic tongue parted my lips, sliding into my mouth to taste every inch of my sweetness, coming back to stroke my tongue. His teeth scaled my lower lip leaving me utterly breathless. Gosh this man could kiss.

Everything about Damon left me breathless, blushing like a high school girl all over again. His drool worthy features, his cold possessive hands, his dark curls that made me want to run my hands through them every second, his thick eye lashes that made me want to steal them right off the frame of his gorgeous captivating emerald green eyes. Everything about him was a masterpiece, a true work of art. He looked so beautiful but in a dangerous, risky kind of way, like a fallen angel, that was the best way to describe him. A name that once uttered made men reign their heads in submission to his power and dominant aura, made women burn with lust and desire. His cold hands that could destroy anyone he desired, he ruled the whole of New York. A business tycoon who was referred to as the devil in the underworld.

Yet he was all mine, mine and mine alone. His strong cold hands held me with such tenderness, his plum lips that uttered the worst of profanities claimed my lips with such ferocity and hunger it left me breathless. His tall elegant body cradled my body against his, claiming me in every way possible.

He pulled back, his luscious lips stretched in a smile as he stared at me. He looked at me like I was the most beautiful thing he had ever seen, the way his pupils dilated had me completely and utterly consumed. "I love you" he whispered, placing a lingering kiss on my forehead, making me giggle.

"I love you too" I replied, cradling his face in my hands as I ran my thumb along his stubble, gently running my nails down its length. "I love your beard" I smiled, my eyes meeting his adoring gaze.

"You mean you love it between your thighs" he teased, winking. A blush burnt my cheeks as I drew my bottom lip between my teeth. He was right. He pinches my jaw, bringing my face to meet his, his gaze sweeps over my face, settling on my lips. "Go on a date with me?" He asks, his eyes had that dreamy look as he strokes my bottom lip.

I cocked my head to the side, a smile settling on my lips "A date?" I question him and he nods. "Where to?"

"You don't need to worry about that, just be ready when I say, okay?" He winked and I giggled, bobbing my head. He leant down and captured my lips, running his tongue along my bottom lip, parting them with ease. He slid his tongue into my mouth, going to taste every inch and crevice of me. He sucked on my tongue, stroking it with his and I moaned, his hands going to caress my bare thighs. He pulled back, leaving me breathless as I stared at him with flushed cheeks. "Shower with me?" He asked and I blushed, looking around to see our clothes were already sprawled all over the room so we'd skip that step. I gazed away, nodding.

I didn't get the leisure of looking back at him before he was on his feet, carrying me in his hands like a fragile baby. I blinked a few times, trying to catch up with his swift movement.
He grinned down at me, walking us to the bathroom and kicking the door shut. He deposited me on my feet, his eyes never leaving mine. Without warning his hands gripped the nape of my neck, guiding my lips to his. The kiss was spectacular, a burst of excitement, an unquenchable desire and fiery passion. His hands slipped to my hips, squeezing softly as he pulled me closer till our naked bodies were completely flushed against each other. His hard abdominal muscles, his strong roped muscled chest against my bare twins made me whimper. He pulled my bottom lip between his teeth, biting down softly. I gasped, his tongue slid into my mouth, going to stroke mine sensually.

His possessive hands squeezed my hips, mine going to tangle in his dark curls. Squeezing my derriere, I moaned out, his hands slipped to grip my thighs and I jumped, straddling his torso. Never breaking the kiss, he walked us into the stand-in shower. He forced my back against the wall, his hands going to trace the curve of my breasts eliciting a breathy moan from me. Cold water started trickling down my skin, the sudden change in temperature making me gasp, pulling away from the kiss. I stared into his eyes, a sympathetic smile on his face. I let out a breathy laugh, my breathing erratic as I stared at the way his chest rose and fell, the water dropping down his taut tanned skin, making it glisten. His hair was drenched, their dark curls sticking to his forehead, giving him a boyish look. I couldn't stop myself from running my hands through his curls, pushing them back. His greedy face dipped to the crook of my neck, inhaling my scent he sighed, his hands tracing miniature circles on my derriere.

He let me down, his hands never leaving my ass. I reached for the body wash, squeezing a little too much into his back. I rubbed the body into his skin with my little fingers, my hands caressing his muscular back. I could feel his muscles relaxing underneath my touch, a groan escaping his lips. He pulled back, his hands going to hold my waist finally as if asserting his right to have his hands on me. He held my gaze as I slid my hands down his chest, letting my fingers work their way through his tight muscles, my hands relishing in the feeling of his powerful body.

I watched silently as the water droplets washed down all the body wash, leaving his skin glowing. My eyes landed on his very prominent member and my throat went dry. He was huge and… erect. I blinked a few times, realizing I would have to wash it next. I sucked in a deep breath, going to pull out the wash sponge. I lathered it and hesitantly held onto his length, stroking it in and up and down motion and I felt it harden eliciting a groan from Damon. He threw his head back, his husky voice groaning out profanities as I increased my paste, stroking it harder, letting my other hand join in on the action. I could see his arousal sipping down the head of his cock and I smiled, my eyes meeting his. I went on my knees, knowing his eyes were following my every movement as I took his length in my mouth, sucking on the little inches I was able to fit in. "Fuck!" He cursed, moaning soon after I began bobbing my head back and forth, my mouth tightening around his cock.

He held onto my head, guiding my mouth into a slow paste. He was so huge I couldn't fit it all in my mouth, instead I used my tongue to tease his head a little, gliding it across his length, slurping on his bulging veins. I circle my hands around it, moving both my head and hands in a hastened paste eliciting a husky moan from Damon. His body jerks forward, and he cums, the foreign salty thick liquid filling my mouth as he pulls away, his breathing erratic. A few drops had spilled down my throat, dripping to coat my twins. His eyes followed my every action as I swallowed his arousal, the foreign taste lingering in my throat.

"Fuck baby" he cursed, pulling me up, his possessive hands holding my hips firmly. His head dipped to the crook of my neck as he began trailing open mouthed kisses down my throat. My legs tremble underneath me, my core already soaked. I gripped onto his shoulders, my nails digging into his son and he moaned, biting into my skin making me arch my back against him. "You're turn" his husky voice whispered.

# CHAPTER SEVENTEEN

## Jasmine

"He's still such a baby" Darcy chuckled, shaking her head at her son's expense.

Richelle joined in, hurling over with laughter at the baby pictures of Damon that played on the screen "I never knew Damon had such a cute little bum" she choked, pointing at his cute round berries that were on full display through his very adorable soft lemon onesie.

"They're so full" I commented, staring wide eyed at them. That was definitely one thing that hadn't changed about him. He still had the cutest bum and I had to stop myself from slapping it any chance I got.

"Seriously mother" His deep annoyed voice cut me out of my reverie. My eyes flickered to his big frame strolling into the room. A playful pout on his face. "I thought we agreed to leave the baby pictures till after our marriage, at least then I'd know she wouldn't run away after you showed her" he stopped, gesturing to his adorable baby booty and I choked out a giggle, mouthing a sorry when he sent me a sulky glare. "That"

"You agreed, I never did" Darcy said in a matter of fact tone, crossing her arms over her chest with a wide grin on her face. Richelle and I literally burst like balloons, spilling with laughter.

Running a hand through his dark curls, a playful smile on his face. "Can I steal you for a second baby?" He asked, his gaze pointed straight at me, a boyish innocence in his eyes. My cheeks turned beet red at the use of that nickname in front of everyone. I couldn't help my mind from wandering to other situations where that nickname had turned me on.

"Um... S-sure" I replied awkwardly, pushing my thoughts away as I got to my feet and walked over to where he stood at the hallway entrance. Immediately I was within arm's length, his possessive hands snaked around my waist, pulling my body flushed against his. I couldn't help but let out a shaky breath at the feeling of his hard chest against my bare twins, covered by the thin layer of my pale yellow tank top. My cheeks flushed even more at the raw desire I could see in his eyes, their dark emeralds burning to life, each fragment that ravaged my body with their mere sight.

The look in his eyes made me feel bare, like he could see right through my denim shorts and tank top. Right through me. "H-hi" I spluttered, my voice coming out shaky. My cheeks were still as red as a tomato knowing full well that the two women still had their eyes on us. A gasp left my lips as I watched Damon dip, his hands going under my thighs, pulling them up and I jumped, rapping my legs around his torso. My eyes went wide as I met his gaze, our faces only inches away. "Damon" I breathed out, turning back to see mother and Richelle both pretending to be reading something that was obviously upside down. And for one it was a handbook, for the new blender Darcy got.

"Hey" he responded, leaning to place a lingering kiss on my lips, running his tongue along their plum heart shape. He pulls away, walking up the stairs and I could finally feel myself relax against him. We were finally away from their teasing eyes. I groaned, burying my face into the crook of his neck and wrapping my arms protectively around his shoulders. His hands fisted my derrierè as I stuffed my moan into his neck, my cheeks blazing as I heard his deep chuckle resonate through the quiet hallway. "My shy baby" he whispered, placing a kiss on my bare neck.

The smell of books, papers and old notes filled my nostrils and only when I was deposited on his desk did I realise he'd brought me to his study. He came between my legs, his calloused hands going to grip my waist firmly, holding me in place. He leaned down, capturing my lips in a slow, sensual kiss. His erotic tongue slipped through my lips, going to tangle with my tongue. His tongue strokes mine, going further into my mouth to taste me, every corner and every crevice.

There was just something about how he kissed me. Gosh it always left me breathless. His tongue was so skillful in my mouth it felt so good, but between my thighs...sugars. He scaled his teeth along my bottom lip, gently nipping on it and pulling it into his mouth, sucking on it hard, eliciting a moan from me. I pushed my hands into his hair, tugging on his curls, a deep moan of pleasure wracked through his body. "Fuck baby. You taste so damn good, my own slice of pure bliss and euphoric insanity"

He bunched up my top, fisting it in one hand he easily pulled it up, letting my full twins fall out, a shaky breath escaping my lips. He stared at them with such a raw ravenous look in his eyes. Like he could do this all day every day. Like he couldn't get enough of me. "So fucking beautiful" he whispered, eyes fixated on my pockured bud as he bit at the edge of his lips, eyes taking in all of me.

He looked at me like I was the most beautiful thing he had ever laid his eyes on. The way his emerald green eyes dilated, swirl of emotions polling into them. A look of adoration, desire, want, passion, all for me. It made me feel as beautiful as he always told me I was, despite all my scars.

A sharp gasp left my lips, followed by a moan. I couldn't focus on anything other than the way he took my buds into his mouth, sucking on it. His moist tongue glided over my bud as he fuddled with my berries. I arched my back into him, heavy breaths leaving my lips as they hung open, occasional moans slipping out.
He continued to suck on my twins, taking turns to worship each one of them properly. "So damn good" he hissed, nipping on it and I threw my head back, a pleasured sound escaping my lips. "I look forward to every day, my baby tastes so fucking good and no one will know how sinfully good you taste" he murmured, his thumb and index finger accompanying my other swollen bud, pulling and twisting it.

His greedy hand cupped my bare waist, pulling me into him the more, if that was even possible. I could feel my bud getting harder under his lips, the way his erotic tongue gilded its moist over it was making my core throb. It felt so good. I gasped as his teeth scraped my bud and he pulled away, the both of us panting for air as we stared at each other, our foreheads connected. He leant down to place a soft kiss to my bare stomach, his stubble against my skin making me shudder.

"I want to show you something" he whispered, trying his best not to sound out of breath, his thumb running over his tattooed name on my ring finger, his eyes never leaving the tattoo. I nodded, not sure I would be able to form coherent words after what just happened. I still couldn't even concentrate on anything other than my panting breaths and Damon's face only a few inches away, our breaths linked.

He pulled away, placing a kiss to his tatted name before standing to his full length.
My face flushed as he tugged at the hem of his shirt, pulling it over his head with ease, discarding it to the side. I let my eyes travel down his body, the way his shoulder muscles flexed as his hand came down, his abdominal muscles looked more prominent. He'd been working out. His bare torso plus his stubble made him look ever more powerful and sexy, if that was possible. Fuck I never wanted to look away.

How would his stubble feel between my thighs

My bashful thoughts were interrupted by Damon's cold thumb, running across my bottom lip, pulling it out of the captivity of my teeth. He cupped my jaw, raising my head up so our eyes could meet. "Jasmine, you are mine and mine alone and I am yours, only yours. You're my fucking salvation, you're my taste of heaven. You're my first real everything and I wouldn't have wanted it to be anyone else " he confessed, the depths of honesty and adoration in his eyes made my heart flutter. His thumbs drew circles on my face as his eyes held mine, wanting every single word of his to stick. "I want you in every way, mind, body, soul. You walked into my life like a breath of fresh air, reviving all the parts of me I didn't even know existed. I never thought I'd find myself completely and utterly consumed by any one until I found you. You took my hand and led me out of the tides and showed me what love is". He closed his eyes and inhaled a deep breath before opening his eyes, the next words he uttered went right through me. "I love you Jasmine" he finished, the way he said my name sounded like a song of praise, a name only worthy to be uttered with such elegance and passion.

It brought tears to my eyes as he smiled, turning around. A gasp left my lips, my hands flying to my mouth. I stared wide eyed at what Damon had drawn all over the wide expanse of his back and lower waist. I-it was my… my face. He had the most beautiful image of me tatted all over his back in black, intricate vines and gorgeous rose petals framed the edges, an infinity sign embedded along the lines. I didn't realize tears had started dribbling down my cheeks. I needed to make sure it was real. My heart was racing yet it was like everything slowed as I reached out my hand towards his back. I ran my hands along the smooth tatted frame, the tears now free falling down my cheeks as an overwhelming feeling of happiness overcame me.

"Oh my gosh, Damon" I exclaimed, covering my mouth in awe. He turned around with a wide grin on his face.

He captured my lips, running his tongue along the tender skin of my bottom lip. "It's you baby, I will always wear you proudly no matter where I go. Everyone would know you are mine, all mine. You're big brown eyes, your wild bouncy curls, my sexy vixen. All mine"

I stared at him in awe, tears dripping down my cheeks. I didn't deserve this, I hadn't even told him about my past yet. I can't move on from it without telling him first. Softly I placed my hands against his chest, his possessive hands going to hold my waist firm. I gazed into his dark eyes, so much raw unfiltered emotions pooled through them.

"I'm ready to tell you" I whispered, my eyes searching for any reaction.

He looked confused but after a minute before his face fell and concern washed over his features "Are you sure baby? I don't want you remembering anything that would hurt you" he reasoned, his rough thumb drawing miniature circles on my cheek.

"I-i'm sure" I spluttered, shutting my eyes tight I inhaled a deep breath. "If I want to move on I have to completely let it go, that means coming to terms with everything that happened to me" I repeated the words that had been ringing through my head. Damon nodded, his hand trailing down my cheek bone to tuck a stray lock of hair behind my ear. He leaned down and placed a lingering kiss to the crown of my head, his thumbs rubbing circles on my little hands he held in his. "Mother and Thomas weren't from rich families, if anything their family suffered a lot and it didn't help that they had narcissistic parents. Uncle had enough and decided to leave. He wasn't granted any freedom and he was made to feel guilty for everything he felt. He left mother with her parents promising to come back after he'd made something of himself" I inhaled a sharp breath, my eyes landing on Damon's softened gaze. Shutting my eyes tight I continued, "When he came back after so many years he was late" my voice wavered, tears began burning my vision and I could feel the lump forming in my throat but I swallowed it, the heat Damon's body was emitting and his loving touches calmed me. "S-she had been sold to-"

"Bellamy" he finished for me and I nodded, struggling not to burst into tears.

"W-when I was 6 I started noticing the heart wrenching bruises that covered my mother's body" I croaked out, my tears free falling down my cheeks. Damon pulled me into his chest wrapping his hands around my shoulders. I buried my face into his shirt, my little hands wrapping around his waist. "Whenever I asked her about it she said she'd fallen and it was okay, she would be fine, but she was never fine" I cried shaking my head into his body, more tears dripping down my cheeks. "It all got worse when I turned 7, it had become a routine for me to come back every day from school and find my mother's brutally beaten body, laying half dead on the living room couch" my sobs broke through, shaking my entire body. "I tried my best to treat her, every time she told me she'd be fine. But I knew she wouldn't be, something came over me that night and I hugged her, I just let her squeeze my small body into her arms. I didn't even know that would be the last time I'd see her" I sniffled, taking deep breaths to calm myself but it was futile, my tears continued pouring down my cheeks. "I woke up very late, I don't know what woke me up. I walked down to see the kitchen lights on. I-i thought mom was m-making cookics so I rushed there. But I met her lifeless body " a heart wrenching sob tore through my lips before I could finish, my entire body shaking as I cried into Damon. His hands tightened around me and he just held me there, he let me break, his possessive hold promising to fix me no matter how much I broke. "I tried to wake her u-up. She wasn't answering, her c-cold brown eyes were all I was met with". I shut my eyes tight, flashes of her lifeless corpse flooded my vision and I shivered. " i-i stayed by her side till morning but when I woke up I was in a cellar. That was when the abuses started, he called it my fair share. He said it was only fair because I was the reason my mother died. I took it all if it meant she would forgive me for being the reason she died. At that little age I d-didn't understand what he meant, but my mother's forgiveness was so important I didn't mind. It went on for 3 years. I had gotten used to the beatings, the occasional starving, the whipping" I shuddered, a calloused hand rubbing up and down my back soothingly, the known feeling making my tense muscles relax. "One day Thomas came to visit. I wasn't allowed out of my cellar so I wasn't aware he had come. He walked into my cellar and carried my nearly lifeless form out. I could barely see anything but when we came out the house was burning. I remember yelling out for him to stop and save my mother's things. As a child I couldn't understand anything, I didn't know anything"

"He took me in and changed my name. He gave me my mother's maiden name, he gave me a new identity, he transformed my life but he could never heal the mental scars that had been inflicted on me, no therapist he took me to could. My sperm donor still haunted my dreams, the dark mists of my mind. To everyone else Cassandra Dominic was dead, buried and no more and that day Jasmine Scott was born from her ashes. From that day I promised never to be that vulnerable little girl and I tried everything in my power to get as far away from my past as possible. I never knew being vulnerable was actually not bad, love was vulnerable, beautiful and scary, very very scary" I whispered, tears burning my eyes. I gazed into Damon's eyes, tears also building up in them. I rushed to cup his face, my thumb catching a drop of his tear before it fell. I shook my head at him, silently scolding him for crying for me. "Don't cry, you're my knight. You saved me. You showed me that love can be such a beautiful feeling, even if it meant being vulnerable to the person you loved. It was all worth it. You ignited my dark skies" I turned his hand, bringing it up to my lips I placed a soft kiss against his knuckles. "You are my salvation Mr businessman" I giggled, tears falling down my cheeks, happy tears. "I don't know what is going to happen after now and for once I don't care, as long as I'm with you, I'm ready for the unknown"

"I love you"

# Chapter Eighteen

## Jasmine

"Such a pretty baby" Deep dulcet voice rang in my ear. I sighed, turning round in the mirror to see my open back, my back dips clearly on full display. Pulling at the hems again I tried in vain to bring it down.

At least my derriere looked cute.

He trailed open mouthed kisses from my neck to my bare shoulder, his long slender fingers going to tuck my hair to the side, granting him full access to my exposed shoulders. "So fucking pretty baby" he whispered against my skin, his hot breath flushing across my neck.

"It's a little too much don't you think?" I asked, looking at him through the full framed mirror we stood in front of. His calloused comforting hands wrapped around my stomach, his big frame leaning behind me as his head was tucked in the crook of my neck, momentarily dipping to inhale my scent. He pulled back, turning me around in his arms to face him. My hand instinctively went for his shirt, my little fingers playing with his buttons, knowing all too well his adoring eyes were on me, taking in what was his.

"It's beautiful baby, only worthy of you" he assured, cupping my cheeks with his hand he nudged my face up, my gaze meeting gorgeous emerald green orbs swirling with love, adoration and lust."So fucking gorgeous. You look like mine"

The dress wasn't a typical one you would wear on a dinner date.

No

It was those kind of dresses you would admire and walk past because you know you would never be able to pull it off. It was a gorgeous beige colour, backless satin dress. The fabric felt so devilishly good against my skin but the thin hands didn't do much in hiding my collar bones. The beige of the dress made it look classy, and by classy I meant expensive. Diamond stud earrings adorned my ears, a little teardrop necklace dangling from my neck. I looked like a million bucks. My chestnut hair cascaded down my shoulders in waves, their light highlights prominent in its tides. A few strands sweep across my shoulder in little effort to hide their exposed skin.

"Yours" I whispered slowly, like a silent promise. Reaching on my tippy toes to plant a soft kiss on his cheek, pulling back with a cheeky smile curved at my lips.

He tucked a few strands behind my shoulder, leaving some exposed skin out, "Honestly tesoro you look like a piece of art, my own personal dose of madness and heaven. My salvation, all mine" he placed a lingering kiss to the tip of my nose, making me scrunch it up, giggling. His greedy hands trail down to grab a fist full of my derriere making me gasp. "Gosh baby you look so damn sexy in this dress, don't worry" He nudged my head up, pinching my chin. "I don't care if you don't think you're pretty, but for me you're the epitome of beauty"

My heart skipped, as in skipped; jumped two steps and jumped again. The depth of truth and endearment in his eyes almost made my knees buckle underneath me. He really felt that way, gosh. I gazed away, in a failed attempt to hide my colored cheeks. He leaned down, placing kisses all over my face, making it blaze brighter.
"I so want to kiss you right now" he breathed out, desire and want echoing in his voice as his eyes travelled from mine to my plum lips "But I'm afraid if I do you won't be able to walk after" he smiled.

I cupped his face, letting my fingers trail down his prominent jaw line, running over his stubble. He looked down at me, eyes burning holes into mine. "What if I don't want to?" I asked, looking up at him with a seductive gaze, my hands running down the wide expanse of his chest.

He honestly looked immaculate in his all black attire. His black t-shirt that flushed shamelessly against his build, his fitted suit trousers and his expensive Italian dress shoes. His shirt had their first three buttons open, revealing the swell of perfectly sculpted chests amidst clear tan tatted skin. His suit jacket was sprawled lazily on his bed. He looked more physically powerful and domineering without it. Delicious.

"Fuck baby" he breathed out, staring down at me with his darkened gaze. "You're making me lose control, tesoro. You won't like the sinful things I would do if you keep looking at me like that" he warned, his hand trailing the open curve of my back.

I let out a shaky breath, fisting his shirt "Sinful things?" I asked, feigning innocence. Running my fingers down to his buttons I started fiddling with them, momentarily looking up at him to see his gaze transfixed on my fingers. "Like what?" I enquire, letting my eyes run slowly down his form.

"Let me show you" he whispered huskily into my ear, sending shivers down my spine.

Shit

"Wh-" a pleasured sound left my lips, cutting me short, his hands tightly gripping my derriere. His head dipped to the crook of my neck as he trailed open mouthed kisses from the nape of my neck to my shoulder.

I threw my head back, granting him more access. My breathing heavy as I stifled my moans, biting down on my lip. The way his plum lips danced along my skin, branding me made my heart race in excitement at his possessive actions, claiming me in every stroke of his tongue. Every inch of my skin burning with passion. My core was sipping with my arousal as I gripped onto Damon's broad shoulders, my nails digging into his shirt.

"Fuck baby" he cursed under his breath, running his tongue along my collar bone making me shudder. "So fucking sweet"

He brought his face close to mine, my heavy breaths hitting his face. He connected our lips, running his tongue along my bottom lip, gently pulling it into his mouth to fully suck on it. I gasped, his tongue using the chance to slip into my mouth, going to taste my sweetness. His hands held steady the nape of my neck, deepening the kiss. His tongue glided against mine, stroking it in sensual movements making him groan in satisfaction.

He pulled back, sucking on my lips "Such a sweet baby girl" he cooed, tracing the curve of my breasts I squirmed, humming in approval. Before I could blink my back was against the wall, Damon's huge form completely overshadowed mine, his calloused hands securing my two wrists in his fists, above my head, leaving me completely under his control.

The dark look in his eyes made my heart race, my chest rising and falling with my heavy breathing. "Fuck the dinner" he dismissed, desire filled eyes taking in my whole form. "Fuck, I want to rip this dress right off your sexy body and devour you" he drew his bottom lip between his teeth, his eyes burning holes into my skin. "I want to run my tongue deep into your mouth watering pussy, sucking on it till you cum all over my face, over and over again"

My core was throbbing with each maliciously sinful word that left his lips. My skin itches with want, want for him to destroy my innocence fulfilling every word he had uttered.
My hands itched wanting to touch him, to feel his tight muscles against my palms, to have his stubble deep between my thighs.

"To thrust my dick so hard in you I fertilize your eggs. And I will, but not now" he inhaled a sharp breath, pulling his head from the crook of my neck. "The best things take time and I intend to take as much time I please. When I fuck you baby, you will beg me to go on and on and I will all night"

"But tonight I will treat you like the queen you are. My queen" he smiled, leaning down to place a lingering kiss to my lips, conveying all his unspoken feelings. "Come my lady" he pulled back, taking my hand in his he placed soft kisses to my knuckles. Flashbacks of our first encounters playing in my mind making a smile take over my lips. Then if I was told I would end up falling for Damon I would have laughed so hard I'd pass out.

He led me out of the room, hand in hand. We got to the bottom of the stairs, and a large bouquet of roses sitted on the couch. I gazed from the beautiful bouquet to Damon, a wide grin on his face. I giggled, walking over and taking the flowers in my hands bringing them to my nose. I inhale deeply. A bright smile covered my lips at the sweet scent they had. My heart instantly melted at the lovely gesture. "Don't use all your smiles here, we still have a long way to go" he called out, bringing out his arm for me to loop mine into, the gorgeous bouquet hanging in my other arm as we walked to the elevator. As the doors closed I noticed a pink floating heart shaped balloon at the corner, something metal attached to the end.

I gazed at Damon to see all his attention on me as he smiled, encouraging me to go forward. I cocked my head to the side, studying his features, trying to unveil the rest of his plans but none of his expressions told me anything other than he was a love struck puppy who loved me to bits. I turned towards the balloon, walking cautiously to it I took the long string in my free hand, not wanting my huge bouquet to fall. Pulling it closer I spotted cat keys at the end of its pink string. Untying it from its confinement I admired it. If my guess is correct then...

The doors to the elevator dinged open, the garage coming into view. Damon took my hand and led me inside, passing so many cars. I wasn't aware people lived in the building

As if reading my mind "They are all mine baby" he answered looking down at me and winking.

There was no way. I looked around dumbfounded, all these different models of cars were his?
I swore I saw three different models of Mercedes, Audi and... like 2 Range Rovers

What the fudge!
I just remained quiet.

We walked for a few more steps before we stopped. In front of us stood a gorgeous white Rolls Royce. It was like the exterior was completely drenched in white colour but the insides were a gorgeous carbon fibre red. My eyes went wide with realisation and I gazed up at Damon. He held my hand, pushing the car keys and the car beeped to life. I stared at him in bewilderment, still not wanting to hear what I knew was true.

"It's yours baby" he smiled, leaning down to kiss the bridge of my nose. I froze, my gaze going from him to the clearly lavish car in front of me. I shook my head, years building in my eyes. He nodded, a smile stretching his lips. I turned, carefully placing my bouquet on the trunk of the car before lunging at Damon, throwing my hands around his neck. He chucked, his chest vibrating with the deep echoes of his laughter. His hands wrapped securely around my waist, keeping my feet off the ground. "You like it?" He asked, staring lovingly into my eyes. I nodded frantically, too shocked and ecstatic to form coherent words. He leaned in, placing kisses all over my lips, smiling against them when I erupted into giggles. Cupping his cheeks, I kiss him, running my hands along his stubble.

God I loved it

"Wanna get in baby?" He asked, placing me on my feet. I nodded, scurrying over to the car door he had softly pulled open for me. My gentleman. I slipped inside the driver's seat, my derriere appreciating the comforting carbon fiber. I ran my hands along the steering wheel, smiling cheekily to myself. It was red. "Do you like it?" His voice came, drawing me out of my state of amazement.

"Of course!" I exclaimed, smiling from ear to ear, a joy like no other consuming me. "Whose driving?" I asked, staring sulkily at him.

He smirked, a sinister look in his eyes, "Who says anything about you driving?"

My brows creased in confusion, "What?"

I didn't know it then, but I would regret asking that.

# Jasmine

My hands gripped the steering wheel tight, my head falling back in absolute bliss as soft moans spilled from my lips. Shit

My eyes threatened to flutter close but a light squeeze of my hips had them hovering. "Don't close your eyes, baby. Keep them open, eyes on the road" His deep voice commanded and I willed my eyes to remain open but the feel of his pleasured assault on my shoulders made me unable to obey the command.

My derriere deposited on his lap, his possessive hands gripping my waist firmly as he planted open mouthed kisses all over my neck, shoulders and throat. His erotic tongue danced along my skin, igniting the fire of passion all over my body. My core throbbed, sipping with my arousal as I felt his very prominent member poking my arse. "Feel that tesoro?" He grumbled into my neck, his hot breath tickling my skin.

I nodded, not registering his words. Fuck, the only thing I could concentrate on was the way his tongue glided across my skin, branding me with slow sensual . His head lowered to my open back, his plum lips trailing wet open mouthed kisses down the curve of my back, pleasures sound leaving my lips as I maneuvered the next U turn.

"D-damon" I panted harshly, my inner thighs wet like he had touched me but he hadn't. The way he kissed my bare skin felt like he was touching all over me. His skilled lips wicked on my skin making me grip tighter onto the steering.

"Fuck you look so sexy baby, " he spoke, depositing kisses all over my throat, tasting my sweet scent. "You are a walking sin, you could make any saint fall to his knees for you baby, do you know that?" He asked, sucking on the tender skin of my neck. "Just the way your walk seduces me"

I brought the car to a stop, letting go off the steering to grip the dashboard as he continued his assault on my body. He pulled back his tongue, inhaling deeply, "You did so well tesoro" he hummed in amusement and pride. He flipped me, turning me around to straddle his waist. A slender finger coming to tuck a loose curl behind my ear, his finger caressing the side of my cheek as his eyes wandered around my face, taking in my appearance. "So fucking gorgeous. I want to fuck you right here and right now. I want to destroy your pussy" he drew his lips between his teeth, sliding his hand between my thighs to cup my core. A shaky breath escaped my lips, my forehead met his as he slipped his fingers into my panties, ripping them off with ease.

I gasped, watching him discard them in his suit pocket, a mischievous smile on his face. "Tonight baby I will fuck you so hard you will beg me to go harder" His finger circled my core, tracing my lips. I whimpered, breathing heavily. My body burned with excitement -sinful, malicious and carnal."That sound drives me crazy and I will make you scream tonight. But now I will show you just how much I worship you. I will spoil you baby" he promised, pulling the hem of my dress down, helping me out of his lap and out the car.


✧.°. : *✧.°.:*

In awe I looked around, absolutely at the beauty of this place. It wasn't like any other place Damon and I had gone to. This place was huge, it was gorgeously adorned with white and gold interiors, and gold velvet curtains draped the walls. White table clothes covered the chairs and tables, to watch the white flower like designs of the floors. Everywhere looked absolutely breathtaking. Fairy lights hung from the roofs, creating a kind of dreamy glow. But one thing confused me, the place was empty, not a single soul could be seen.

I turned to Damon who stood smiling proudly beside me. "Where is everyone else?"

"Not here" he simply said, leading me to one of the tables he pulled out a chair, holding it out for me to sit. I propped down, keeping my confused gaze on his as he walked over to the other chair and sat down. "I booked the place for us, it would just be the two of us". I stared at him confused, blinking a few times to make sure I wasn't dreaming.

"Baby" he called out, holding onto my hands across the table. "I know you get anxious around crowds and the last thing I want is to make you uncomfortable tonight so I arranged to have only us here. The only thing I want to look at is you" his rough thumb caressed the back of my hands, his eyes soft and warm.

I smiled, my cheeks coloring at the look of pure love and utter adoration for the woman that was in front of him. He took my hands to his lips, placing soft kisses at my knuckles before depositing them back on the table.

The next second a waiter came in, serving different dishes of my favorite foods. I didn't hesitate before grabbing my fork and diving into it. Amidst my chewing and satisfied moaning I noticed a pair of eyes on me. I gazed away from my food to find Damon staring at me with the most heartwarming smile on his face. "Stop staring" I whined, pouting at him. Rumbling chuckles erupted through the pin drop silence, filling the room and warming my heart. I stared at him, the way his lips stretched to his ears, his pearl white teeth on full display.

"Sorry baby" he apologized, amusement filling his eyes. His gaze flickered to my lips, an unmissable spark of desire and want flashing in his eyes. "You just look so beautiful, a masterpiece"

My cheeks colored and I gazed away, feeling like a baked potato. Mostly because I had stuffed myself and I doubt I'd be able to walk on my own.

Nice going Jasmine

"Dance with me tesoro?" Damon's soft dulcet voice came like a spell, pulling me into their depths. As if in a trance I nodded, wordlessly slipping my hands into his. I was completely and utterly consumed by him, emerald green eyes that glinted with love and endearment gazed at me like I was the most beautiful thing he had ever laid eyes on.
He gently pulled me to my feet. Hand in hand he led us to the center of the restaurant where he pulled me in, his possessive hands going to grip firmly to my hips, mine going to wrap round his neck. He smiled down at me, his eyes shimmering with want, hunger and an unquenchable desire. For me.

Out of nowhere our song started playing. I couldn't help the smile that took over my lips as I looked back at Damon. He had a wide grin on his face, his eyes shimmering with love and amusement. The first time we heard this song was in his room; I was listening to it on my phone when he walked in, smiling from ear to ear. He walked over to where I lay on the bed and picked me up, pulling me into a hug. I hugged him back with a blissful sigh leaving his lips as his head dipped to the crook of my neck, inhaling my scent.

He had another bad day at work. I smiled to myself, running my hands through his curls. My big baby. I pulled back enough to cup his cheeks, a sulky pout on his lips. I opted to cheer him up, "Wanna dance?" I asked, a smile on my face.

He cocked his head to the side, a crease between his brows. I giggled, wrapping my arms around his neck and pushing play for the song to start. He got on board really quickly, pulling me across the room, my feet following him in sync as we danced along to the song. His grin surfaced, a knowing look in his eyes.

"This song is just perfect for us" I beamed, smiling from ear to ear. He chuckled slowly, shaking his head at me.

"Our song" he leaned down and captured my lips.

I giggled as his forehead met mine, snapping out of my reverie- a look of pure bliss and serenity filling his eyes. We started moving slowly to the beat, our steps in sync with a slow rhythm in our movements. His hand caressed my hips, lighting my insides on fire. We danced silently, our eyes conveying all the words we couldn't begin to utter. The raw look of love and want in his eyes had my insides fluttering with nerve wrenching butterflies.

"Everything is so beautiful, Damon. I love it" I whispered, not looking away from his eyes once.

"Anything for you my love" he smiled. Taking hold of my hand he pulled back, a hand at his back he twirled me around, my frame gliding across the room. He pulled me back into his arms, claiming my lips. His hot tongue delved into my mouth, finding mine and stroking me with a passionate filled rush.

He kissed me with such urgency and underlining craving. The way he claimed me- sucking on my tongue, pulling my bottom lip into his mouth and devouring me whole made my insides throb with want. I needed him, every inch of him.

He pulled away, pressing a soft kiss to my forehead, his calloused hands cupping my cheeks. He stepped back, leaving me breathless, a protesting pout on my lips.

He got on one knee, holding my hand in his and at that moment my breathing stopped. It felt like everything slowed and he reached into his blazer and pulled out a small box. "Jasmine, my love, my woman, my world. You're the only one for me, my salvation, you're my personal dose of pure euphoric bliss and I don't mind getting drunk. From the moment I saw you I knew I was fucked" he chuckled, shaking his head to himself. "I knew I'd do absolutely anything for you. I was absolutely love struck. You had me under your control and you didn't even know it, maybe you did but it never stopped you from claiming my heart, my soul and my very being in every way possible. Those big brown eyes of yours put me under an everlasting spell. I fell for you so fucking hard it hurt. Whenever those sweet lips of yours curved up to smile at me, Jesus fucking Christ I almost melted. The way you touched me, branding me forever with your skin"

"Every day I dreamt of you. And whenever I was up you would be lying peacefully in my arms and I thought I was dreaming. Fuck I never wanted to wake up. You are like a dream to me. I pray for you every single day, wishing on whatever higher power that you would remain with me as long as I breath" his eyes softened and I thought he would cry. "When you were stabbed. I died every single day, I lived but I wasn't alive. God knows I was a shell of a man. The moment you were pronounced alive I felt like I was saved. When I saw you after a year, god that was pure torture. It was like life had finally been breathed into me, reviving every dead cell"

"You are the love of my life, tesoro. I would die and come back if it meant I'd meet you all over again. From the moment I saw you I knew I wanted to spend the rest of my life with you and I don't care if that sounds so cliché but it's true" I shook my head at him, sniffling as tears pricked my vision. I couldn't help the smile that settled on my lips as I watched the man I'd fallen hopelessly in love with say the words I always wanted to hear.

"I don't know a lot about love. But someone told me if you love someone you would do everything in your power to see them happy even if it meant that wasn't with you. To me that's bullshit because without you I'd die. I would never let you go tesoro. Fuck any therapist that tells me otherwise but I absolutely adore you baby. The mere taste of you drives me crazy. I'm mad over you baby and I don't give a fuck. I'm completely and utterly yours. I want to spend the rest of my life waking up to your beautiful face every morning. I want to spend the rest of my life making you pancakes in the mornings because you'd be too grumpy to do it. I want to spend the rest of my life listening to you complain about every character in every movie. I want to spend the rest of my life showing you just how much you mean to me because words could never do them justice"

"I want to rub your swollen belly and massage your feet when it hurts from carrying our babies. I want to hold our children in my hands and kiss them all day and love them so much because they are a piece of you. I would forever thank whatever brought you to me because you are my salvation. Jasmine Scott would you marry me" he finished, pulling open the box to reveal a stunning diamond ring.

Everything came tumbling down on me at once. I stared at the man I would give my life for, the very reason for my existence. The love for my life. Tears dribbled down my cheeks as I nodded frantically. Yes!

"Words baby" he instructed, grinning up at me.

"Yes! " I gushed, an overwhelming feeling of happiness and love filling my chest, warming my insides. "But you have to get me a puppy"

He chuckled, nodding "Deal" he stood, sliding the stone onto my finger. I stared at it with teary eyes, the way it perfectly fit my finger like it was made for me. I lunged at him, wrapping my arms around his neck while his rippled arms wound around my waist holding me firm against his body.

I pulled back enough to stare into his eyes. He claimed my lips, sucking, nibbling and devouring my mouth. His hand cupped the nape of my neck, guiding my lips closer to his, deepening the kiss. The way his erotic tongue invaded my mouth, tasting my sweetness had my body burning to life. The kiss conveyed everything we couldn't put into words- how much we loved, needed and craved one another. The way his tongue branded mine had my core throbbing and my body itching with want. The kiss was passionate, deep and hunger filled. He kissed me like there was no tomorrow, like he could taste me for the rest of his life. Because we did have the rest of our lives. I moaned softly as he bit into my lower lip, drawing it between his teeth.

I pulled away just in time to witness hundreds of balloons cascading down, rose petals following soon after. I giggled as they dropped to my feet. "Fuck baby" he cursed breathlessly, bringing his tongue to slowly run along his lips as he stared at me. My cheeks flushed with the look of his raw carnage desires. "I want to do so many sinful things to my fiancé tonight so no drinking, is that clear baby?" He asked in an authoritative voice and I nodded. "I want you to be fully in your senses when I take you, when I fuck you I want you to remember every thrust of my cock inside you. I want you to remember how I feel inside your sweet pussy"

My body shuddered with want, anticipating his crude words. That was Damon, he was deliciously passionate, meaning every crude word he uttered. My core throbbed with excitement at his words.

"I will fuck you into oblivion and when you are about to pass out I'll fuck you some more. I want to have you under me begging for release while I drive my cock inside your sweet cunt, thrusting so deep inside you" he spoke so sinfully into my ear as his hands grabbed my derriere, squeezing strongly and I moaned softly, my soaked core throbbing harder.

# Jasmine

I stared into a pair of large dark orbs, plum cupid half bowed lips coated with a layer of dark red lipstick. Full cheeks were covered with blush, a bright pink color overtaking their skin.

"You look absolutely gorgeous Jasmine" Penelope gushed, smiling at me through my reflection. I sighed, rubbing my clammy palms together, looking myself over in the mirror. She walked forward, placing her head comfortingly on my shoulder. "You okay?" She asked, worry lacing her features.

"Yeah" I answered, playing with my freshly pedicured nails. "I just-" I started, letting out a heavy sigh. "I'm scared" I finished, gazing at her beautiful face.

Penelope smiled, turning my chair around so I could face her, "They're just pre wedding jitters honey" she assured.

Penelope was the sweetest person I had ever met. I was the most excited person in the world when Uncle Tom introduced me to his long time girlfriend. Few weeks ago Damon and I had gone on a double date with them and when I say they were the sweetest couple I meant every word. She was sweet, considerate, understanding and the best person I could ever imagine for my uncle. I honestly think I loved her more than my uncle did. She didn't mind uncle's line of work nor the fact he was hardly ever around, she didn't mind, all she wanted was to be with him and I admired her for her commitment.

"Are you worried?" She inquired, her words meaning more than they let on.

I shook my head without hesitation, "No of course not, I know Damon is the one and I love him and I want to marry him"

"But?"

"But I'm scared," I whispered. "What if he doesn't like my dress o-or I trip on my way down the alter-"

"That's not happening" a voice interjected. I turned my head to the doorway as uncle Tom walked in, dropping a kiss on Penelope's cheek. They looked so adorable wearing the same colour. "Hey champ" he cooed, squatting down to my level as much as his maroon three piece suit would allow him"

He took my hand in his, bringing them to his lips to place affectionate kisses on my knuckles. "I won't let you fall okay?" He assured, his eyes boring into mine with a look of certainty. "You look so beautiful my dear. Just like a princess" he smiled, tears welled up in his eyes as he caressed my cheek with his thumb. "I always wanted to see your mom in a wedding dress but I was never able to," he sniffled. Penelope took that as a sign to leave, not before placing a kiss on his cheek. "At least I could walk you down the aisle and fulfill my responsibility" he smiled, blinking away his tears

I willed myself not to cry. I didn't want to spoil Penelope's hard work.

"I promise I won't let you fall, okay?" I nodded frantically, sniffling as I giggled. "Now there's a certain groom waiting anxiously at the alter. He looks like he's about to pee his pants if you ask me" I scrunched up my nose, shaking my head at the thought of my Damon being as nervous as I was about this.

I sucked it up, taking Uncle's hands I let him pull me to my feet. Hand in hand we walked down the hallway to the grand double doors. The only things that stood between me and the next chapter of my life. I looked over at my uncle, a reassuring smile plastered across his face. He gently squeezed my hand and the doors were pulled open.

Anxiously I walked down the long path, the hundreds of eyes boring holes into my dress, making me feel exposed. The soft music started playing, tears Welling in my eyes at the memories behind it. My gaze flickered to meet the pair of mesmerizing emerald green eyes I had fallen in love with. His eyes softened, their dark orbs taking in my form. I could see a mix of love,pride, satisfaction and an unquenchable desire in his eyes. Everywhere looked absolutely breathtaking, the white flowers and soft curtains that hung from the walls matched with my white Floral print gown. Their long entrails flowed behind me as I walked.

His eyes raked me from head to toe and suddenly I felt my cheeks go red as we finally reached the end of the aisle. Uncle Tom placed a kiss on my cheeks before giving my hand to Raymond. He smiled at me, winking as he helped me to my position in front of Damon.

My veil was lifted, bright light hitting my eyes. My eyes fluttered open, a tender look on Damon's face. I let my eyes travel down his form and that act alone made my throat go dry. He looked ever so dashing, dripping with domineering masculinity I knew only he could pull off. He had the sweetest heartwarming smile on his face as he looked at me.

At that moment I knew he was all I ever wanted and all I would ever need, I knew I would love him till I breathed my last breath. I knew I would want to carry his babies in me and deal with all the pain as long as it would make our family complete. I knew he was mine, only mine. He was made for me. I had to admit I wasn't the same person two years ago but I wouldn't change it for anything. I met Damon, the love of my life. He drove me to the brink of madness, he pushed my limits yet I wouldn't change it for anything.

The priest started the vows, Damon and I answering with our gazes never leaving each other's.
His eyes swirled with love, love he had for the one woman in front of him. Deep emotions that made my heart melt into puddles. He grabbed my hands, holding them in his, slowly stroking my hands.

"Do you Mr. Damon Blackwood take Mrs. Jasmine Scott to be your lawfully wedded wife? To be by her side in sickness and in health, in riches and in wealth, till death do you part?"

"Yes"

I gazed back at Damon, his lips curling into a smile. "To spend the rest of my life smuggling cookie dough ice cream with you late in the night" he added, making me blush scarlet. "To be by your side while you ramble on and on about your favorite characters and how stupid they are" he smiled. "To hold you in my arms every night and wake up to your beautiful face every morning. Gosh I'm so fucking obsessed with you it hurts. You're my taste of heaven, my personal dose of pure euphoric bliss. I'd go to hell and back if it meant I would always have you with me. You're mine and no one else's, only mine. I fucking do. I love you tesoro" with that he pulled me closer, his possessive hands gripping my waist he leaned down and captured my lips in a sweet sensual kiss. I wrapped my hands around his neck as the crowd erupted into cheers, the priest pronouncing us husband and wife.

This was it, everything I ever wanted and didn't know I needed. Him, it was always him. It started and ended with him and fuck I couldn't get enough. I would never be able to et enough.


# Damon


She looked so fucking gorgeous. Mine, all mine. My wife, my soulmate, my one and only. Mine.

Her gorgeous floral print dress flowed behind her as she gracefully mounted the alter, her head bowed, her beauty and splendor shielded by the thin fabric of her veil. She was absolutely breathtaking. She looked so graceful like an angel, my angel. I pulled at her veil, depositing it behind her. The moment her big brown eyes met mine it was like all the air in my lungs had escaped. I couldn't utter a word. All my dreams of this day were coming true. I had to resist the urge to capture her lips right here and now. Fuck she looked so mesmerizing, it should be illegal to look this good.

She was finally and rightfully mine. I had dreamt and prayed for this moment ever since the day I laid eyes on her. Her big doe eyes, framed with thick long lashes. Her full cupid bow shaped lips, her small button nose that always darkened with colour whenever she was embarrassed or startled. Like the pussy whipped idiot I was, I smiled, letting my eyes run down her form. I couldn't stop the desire from reflecting as clear as day in my gaze.

The past two years have been my happiest. I never knew I wasn't living until she arrived. She came like a breath of fresh air, pulling me out of the dark tides that I had been trapped in. Nothing else mattered when she was with me, I didn't care about anything else.

She was fucking mine
All mine

"Yes" her soft voice rang out, warming my heart into puddles, leaving me hopelessly falling more and more in love.

"To spend the rest of my life smuggling cookie dough ice cream with you late in the night" I added, making her cheeks blush scarlet. "To be by your side while you ramble on and on about your favourite characters and how stupid they are" I smiled. "To hold you in my arms every night and wake up to your beautiful face every morning. Gosh I'm so fucking obsessed with you it hurts. You're my taste of heaven, my personal dose of pure euphoric bliss. I'd go to hell and back if it meant I would always have you with me. You're mine and no one else's, only mine. I fucking do. I love you tesoro"

I gripped her hips, pulling her flushed against my hard chest. I captured her lips with mine, sealing her forever to me, branding my lips to her forever, in a promise of forever.

**THE END!**

# ABOUT THE AUTHOR

Nuella Ogwu is a Nigerian teen with the dream of having her books read by many young people like her. She is a fellow book lover and has had this dream since she found out what books were and the magic they held. She started her journey on Wattpad.